W9-BFO-780

First World Problems

Rea Keech

Copyright © 2017 Joseph Rea Keech
All rights reserved.

No part of this publication may be reproduced, stored in, or introduced into a retrieval system, or transmitted, in any form or by any means (electronic, mechanical, photocopying, recording, or otherwise), without the proper written permission of the copyright owner, except that a reviewer may quote brief passages in a review.

ISBN 978-0-9983805-5-1   Paperback
Library of Congress Control Number:
2017939997

PS3611 .E332 F57 2017

Published by
Real
Nice Books
11 Dutton Court
Baltimore, Maryland 21228

Publisher's note: This is a work of fiction. Names, characters, places, institutions, and incidents are entirely the product of the author's imagination or are used fictitiously, and any resemblance to actual persons, living or dead, or to events, incidents, institutions, or places is entirely coincidental.

Illustrations by Barbara Munjal.
Set in Sabon.

Also by Rea Keech:

A Hundred Veils

Publishers Weekly BookLife Prize: General Fiction Finalist 2017

"Set in the lead-up to the Iranian revolution, *A Hundred Veils* is a rich portrait of cultural and personal discovery and forbidden love. Keech uses both humor and drama, as well as finely chosen details and rich description, to bring the characters and their world to life."

— **Eleanor Brown**, best-selling author of *The Weird Sisters*

BookLife assessment of *A Hundred Veils*:

Prose: The writing is as economical and succinct as a film script. The narrative moves along swiftly, and yet it's studded with evocative detail.

Originality: This gripping book is a romance with humor and cultural insights that readers will find original and intriguing.

Character Development: The characters here are well developed and fully formed. Marco in particular feels vivid and real.

Also awarded
**Best literary/mainstream novel 2017
by the Maryland Writers' Association**

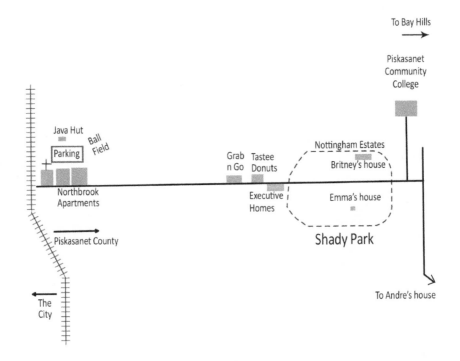

To Bay Hills

Piskasanet
Community
College

Java Hut

Ball
Field

Parking

Nottingham Estates

Grab
n Go

Tastee
Donuts

Britney's house

Northbrook
Apartments

Executive
Homes

Emma's house

Piskasanet County

Shady Park

The
City

To Andre's house

Shady Park and vicinity

Riverside Village

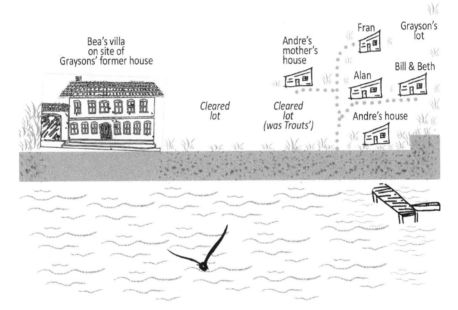

Bea's villa
on site of
Graysons' former house

*Cleared
lot*

Andre's
mother's
house

*Cleared
lot
(was Trouts')*

Fran

Grayson's
lot

Alan

Bill & Beth

Andre's house

Piskasanet River

I

1

Proper perspective

Charles sat with a blank look, leafing through documents he'd brought to the breakfast table, one hand on his treasured Employee of the Month mug.

"Intake-documents or psych-profiles, Charles?" Emma liked to tease him about his social services lingo.

"Mmm." This was his answer to any question when his mind was elsewhere.

Emma shrugged, stirring her steaming coffee. As she reached for the Half 'n Half, a stamp-sized flake of yellowed paint fluttered down from the ceiling and settled into her cup.

"Whoa," Todd said.

"Mmm," Charles answered.

Emma lifted the paint out with her spoon and flicked it into the trash basket. "Charles, we have to do something about the cracked ceiling."

"Mmm."

"Are you going to apply for that promotion at work? We need the money."

"Mmm."

As she reached to pick up her coffee, there was a dull, ripping sound and a thick hunk of plasterboard crashed onto Emma's hand.

"Whoa," Todd said.

"Oww!" Emma held her hand to her lips.

"You OK, Mommy?"

Charles sprang up. "Emma, Emma. What's wrong?" He put his arm around her, gaping down at the sheet of plaster as if wondering how it got there. "Where does it hurt? Show me, Emma."

"I'm all right, I guess. The coffee was hot."

"Cold water. Here, let me take you to the sink."

"Yeah, Mommy," Todd put in. "That's what our teacher told us to do."

The pain was almost gone, but Charles insisted on holding her hand under the water anyway. She kissed him on the cheek. "Don't frown like that, Charles. I'm fine." She wiggled her fingers to show him.

Charles didn't seem convinced. After Todd had left for school, he declared, "I'll stay home with you today."

Emma chuckled. "That's silly. My hand's not hurting. Look, it's not even red any more."

There was a glimmer in his hazel eyes. "Still, I want to." He pulled her close.

"Oh. Oh, OK." She felt her face flushing. "My hand's fine, though. So—"

"Emma!"

He was stroking her beneath her T-shirt.

She lifted her arms to let him pull it off. His fingers flitted across her bra. She clasped them to her, closing her eyes.

As they started to kiss, a chime sounded. Charles blinked.

"It's your phone, Charles."

"Mmm."

"You'd better answer. Might be important."

Unfortunately, it was. "Domestic abuse," he told her. "Ongoing. I think I need to go."

Emma watched Charles hurry out, then managed to pull herself together. Coitus interruptus? She slipped her shirt back on and held her hands to her cheeks, turning to survey the mess on the table, then raised her eyes towards the gaping hole in the ceiling.

She poked the ceiling with a broomstick. There was a hole the size of a dinner plate, but the area around it didn't seem in danger of falling. Cleaning up would give her something to do when Todd was at school and Charles at work. She knew the crumbling ceiling didn't bother Charles. When she'd mentioned it before, he told her to keep things in perspective. At least they had a ceiling. One of his "clients" had been living in a car for the past couple of weeks.

She couldn't blame Charles for letting things go. He really put himself into his work—probably too much. He would come home emotionally drained from counseling heroin addicts and children who were taken away from violent parents and put into foster homes. He got to know the families he worked with, fretted over them, and made follow-up visits on his own time. Sometimes when he told Emma about them, there were tears in his eyes.

Emma missed going to work herself. She missed talking about autoclaves and purity levels and acidic concentrations and mostly the feeling that she was doing at least something small to keep the earth safe for people to live on. She missed watching Charles smile when she told him about a project to remove carcinogens from wastewater or find a way to keep birds out of vineyards without poisoning them. It had been devastating when government funds were cut and Envirotech had to lay her off. Suddenly, the family income was cut in half.

Without a job, she felt obliged to do most of the mopping, dusting, and washing clothes. She kidded Charles about having to pick up the dirty underwear left all over the floor by her "two boys," the third grader and the thirty-four-year-old.

With more time at home to notice dripping faucets, running toilets, cracked windows, and overgrown bushes, she'd started to feel overwhelmed. As long as she'd been working, none of this seemed important. Now, with time to hang around with PTA friends like Chip's mom Britney who lived in million-dollar homes over in Nottingham Estates, she was embarrassed by her house's run-down condition.

Emma finished cleaning up the plaster and went out to get the newspaper. A high school boy was supposed to deliver it on his bike. That sounded good when Emma subscribed. But after about a week, the boy quit and his mother had to take over the route, driving along in her car and throwing the papers out the window. Emma eventually realized that kids didn't deliver papers any more. Their mothers did it for them.

Sometimes the paper was in the road in front of the house, sometimes on the sidewalk. Sometimes she found it in the forsythia along their driveway, and once it was high in a juniper near the front porch. Now it was out in the street again, black tire tracks running across it.

Employment

She always read that section of the *Shady Park Ledger* first. Of course, nothing. She only checked the newspaper for jobs out of habit, anyway. Newspapers were dying out. People hardly read them nowadays, at least the paper version. Any job she'd want would be listed in LinkedIn or Indeed.com.

She'd majored in Bioenvironmental Science. There were never any jobs in that field nowadays. The country was still recovering from a big recession, the news reports said. A lot of jobs with "enviro-" in their titles had been eliminated.

The only jobs Todd's classmates' moms talked about were things like making stained glass angels for patients in hospitals—volunteer jobs that didn't pay anything because they didn't need the money. Chip's mom made angels. Or at least she'd tried to make one.

Police blotter

Sometimes she found Charles's "clients" in this section.

Sports

Little League registration for eight- to ten-year-olds this

Saturday. She couldn't wait to tell Todd. He'd wanted to play last spring but was too young.

There was plenty of time to kill before Todd and Charles got home. Emma made herself a second cup of coffee. She'd gotten into the habit of reading articles in the Features section of the paper.

"Getting the Promotion You Deserve"
"Ten Steps to Financial Independence"
"Current Trends in Haute Couture"
"Exotic Vacation Getaways to Enrich Your Life"
"Designing the Perfect Second Home"
"Finding a Contractor to Turn Your House
 into the Home You've Always Wanted"

Charles kissed Emma on the forehead. His early morning ardor had cooled. "Hand OK?"

"It's fine. Spouse abuse case taken care of?"

"Yeah. Found a shelter for the mother and her kid." He dropped into the cracked leather chair his mother had given them ten years ago. Feet up on the hassock, he paged through the newspaper. Emma lingered beside him gazing at his gold-flecked eyes. In their first days in the house, before Todd was born, they sometimes went straight upstairs as soon as Charles got home. These days he headed straight for his chair.

When they'd met at State fifteen years ago, she'd been swept away by his striking confidence that his mission in life was to go out into the world and help people in need. While most of her classmates chattered about devising "startups" they could sell off for millions to DuPont or Exxon or Somebody Big, Charles introduced her to the university's Social Action Force. After one date with this sincere man who seemed totally unaware of his good looks, Emma switched her major from chemistry to environmental science. It wasn't just his handsome face. He was polite, kind to others. A gentleman—

that was her mother's comment when she met him.

Charles turned to the national and world news, which the local paper crammed onto page two. "Listen to this, Emma. Heroin use nationwide is up 60 percent in the past two years—people looking for a cheaper replacement for the pain medicine they're addicted to."

Emma put her hand on his shoulder.

"Hmm. Another school shooting in the Midwest. The parents are saying the teachers should carry guns."

As soon as he'd skimmed the world news summary, Charles would switch to the Health section.

"Gluten: The Danger Lurking in Your Favorite Foods"
"Preservatives: Are They Destroying Your Body?"
"Health Benefits of Sea Salt"

After putting the paper down and nodding to himself as if to verify he already knew about the food dangers of the day, Charles usually dropped contentedly to sleep in his chair until dinner. But this evening she noticed he was staring at a Zales ad for a diamond necklace. "What do you want for your birthday, Emma?" He gave her a childlike grin.

"A diamond necklace."

Charles's face turned scarlet and he folded the paper. "I wish I could get you one."

"Just kidding. How about a gallon of ceiling paint and some patching plaster?"

"Heh-heh. Yeah. Sorry. Some day I'll get you that necklace." He really seemed to believe it.

"Great. Does that mean you applied for the supervisor's position?"

"No. I couldn't."

"Couldn't," Emma repeated. "Uh-huh."

Charles went through the mail while she got dinner ready. She usually had everything prepared and ready to cook before

Todd and Charles got home. It wasn't easy. Charles insisted she buy only organic food. He didn't seem to notice that food labeled organic costs more. He even insisted on organic eggs, for cripes sake. Organic eggs. What did that even mean? Charles was a good social worker, a good Psycho-Social Interventionalist, as the county called him, but Emma doubted if he had ever passed a chemistry course.

The food thing was all his friend Andre's fault. He had preached to Charles about what should be eaten and what should not be eaten, and Charles believed it all with the zeal of a convert. Andre himself constantly jumped from one theory of life to another. Now he lived mostly on donuts and pizza and declared the most harmful thing for the body to be stress.

"Emma, look. Our real estate taxes went up." Charles handed her the notice. "Almost doubled."

"Doubled! Now how are we going to get my car fixed and replace that junker of yours?"

"Guess the cars'll have to wait."

Charles didn't care what kind of car he drove. Food additives. Pesticides. These things concerned him. He left Emma to worry about paying the bills, keeping the house in shape, sending Todd to school in decent-looking clothes. She waited until Todd was in bed before bringing the supervisor position up again.

Charles stood naked in front of the dresser, solemnly raising his precious "Eat Green" shirt from the drawer like a partisan flag. She couldn't help looking him over. The organic food certainly hadn't done his body any harm. And being home alone all day made her . . . whatever. She wanted to put her hands on him. But she forced herself to turn aside. "You promised you were going to think about applying for that position."

"Emma. I just can't do it."

"But why? The position's vacant now. It could be years

before there's another chance to move up."

"Because supervisors sit in the office all day shuffling papers. It's not the kind of work I want to do. They're out of touch with the people we're trying to help."

She shook him by the shoulders. "Oh, Charles. You act like you worry more about drug addicts than you do about your own family."

"Emma, that's not fair."

"People do what they have to do to take care of their families, even if the job doesn't meet their idealistic criteria."

"When we got married, you said you liked my idealism."

"I did. I do. But, Charles, the kitchen ceiling's falling down."

"Come here." He pulled her close. "I love you, Emma. Don't worry about the ceiling right now. I'll fix it somehow. Those deep brown eyes still excite me. Can you tell?"

"You always end the discussion this way. It's not going to work this time."

It did, though. And she had to admit: maybe it did put things temporarily into a different perspective.

2

Dwelling maintenance and other compulsions

Just as Emma was about to turn on the vacuum cleaner, their friend Andre knocked on the door. Typical Andre. Three o'clock in the afternoon, everybody else working, and he had just gotten out of bed and wanted to talk. Emma suspected he got away with it partly because of his pale blue eyes, year-round tan, and—maybe she was the only one who noticed this—the curve of his lips when he smiled.

Emma kept her hand on the doorknob. "I'm vacuuming. Charles doesn't get home till six."

"I don't mind waiting." Andre slipped in and leaned back in Charles's leather chair. "I guess Charles likes his job. You mean he works this late every day?"

"Yes. Most people do." Emma was too polite to switch on the vacuum while he was talking to her, and he seemed to know it. He kept talking. "It's a shame. You have to admit it. Nine to six, day after day. I guess it's hard to get out of that rut."

You seem to have managed, Emma wanted to say.

Andre asked if Todd, her third-grader, was around. It was clear he didn't know what time of day it was or what time kids got home from school. "I hope they're teaching them some of the important things they skipped over when we were in school."

Meaning how to survive on nothing but donuts, pizza, and tea, Emma presumed. That and how to use an occasional dull lower-back pain to get disability benefits.

"They should teach them about the government in Sweden. Don't you think? They know more about what's important in life there. Here you're expected to devote yourself to making some corporation rich."

"No big corporations in Sweden?"

Andre never answered questions that might interrupt his train of thought. When you asked Andre a question or said something to him, it was like a black fly landing on his face that he didn't notice. He went on talking. Then, later, the fly would bite and he reacted to your question. And so Andre was bringing an end to his disquisition on the advantages of a socialistic society when he stopped short and said, "What? Oh, those Swedish corporations aren't run the same way. Do you have any tea?" With a spoon of honey if she didn't mind, rather than sugar.

Emma hinted that she needed to do some housecleaning. Andre said go ahead. It wouldn't bother him. He would just drink his tea. It was interesting the way people felt the compulsion to improve their dwellings, wasn't it? The amount of time spent on this had to be phenomenal. And, really, how did something like that matter? It was absurd when you thought about it.

Emma had been to Andre's dwelling only a few times. He lived in the former fishing village of Riverside beyond the south end of the long, straight highway that led from what her friends, with a vague sense of dread, called "the City" at the north end down to Shady Park and on towards the Piskasanet River at the south. Andre lived alone in a three-room house by the river that he inherited from his aunt. There he ate donuts, drank tea, and read about "important ideas." Now and then, when his head was full, he paid visits to Charles and Emma without warning and poured out his observations onto them. One February, he atypically called ahead to say he was coming to visit. But when he poked his head outside, he immediately went back in. He called back and said he couldn't come: the winter was lasting longer than he'd expected. Piskasany Andre, Charles called him.

Andre finally paused, and Emma saw her chance to switch the vacuum back on. It felt rude, but this was the only time she had to improve her dwelling. As she cleaned, she thought about Andre's house. If you weren't careful when you walked in, you might stumble over his dumbbells. One of his three rooms was devoted to trash, meaning pizza and donut boxes, moldy crusts, and dried-up tea bags. Andre's mother bagged it all up once a week, according to Charles, and put it out with her own trash. His mother lived on the dirt road behind his house. She was the only woman in his life.

Emma had had a crush on Andre in her first semester at State. Compared to the rest of the straggly guys in freshman English, he looked like a movie star—clean-shaven, neatly dressed. He observed her with his head slightly cocked whenever she asked the professor questions, and he started following her into the hallway after class to talk.

She found it flattering that the most intelligent and well-read student in class was interested in her. Yet talk was all it amounted to. Talk at lunch, talk over a few dinners together. He walked her to her dorm every evening for maybe a week, talking all the way. One night she took his hand as they stood outside the entrance to her dorm—a signal for him to stop talking and kiss her. He didn't.

"Don't you realize that guy isn't into women?" her roommate laughed.

Emma—naïve college Emma—was stunned. "That can't be. He's so, well, so manly. He sounds like James Earl Jones when he talks."

"Talks. Right."

It all made sense. Emma felt foolish.

But it wasn't long before Andre introduced her to his

friend Charles. Charles was handsome, too. Dark hair, sea-green eyes. Emma at first feared the worst. But it didn't take Charles long to show where his interests lay. After the English class was over, she hardly saw Andre any more. Charles and Emma were inseparable.

Todd rushed through the door. "Want to play some catch, Mr. Andre?"

The fly of Todd's question landed but didn't bite. Andre asked him how old he was—he did this every time he saw him—and what his friends at school were like. Then the fly bit. "Oh. You're really that interested in baseball? You don't feel like it drains your time?"

Todd's mouth formed a perfect O, but nothing came out.

Emma picked up his baseball. "We're going out back for a while, Andre. Come out if you want. Charles will be home in three hours or so."

Andre brought his tea out to the back porch to watch. He sat on the step with the pouty lips he got when ideas were swarming in his head and nobody would sit and listen. He was frowning, too. Emma wondered if something else was wrong.

"Throw it harder, Mommy," Todd yelled.

"OK. Here goes." She wound up and threw as hard as she could.

"Gosh, Mommy. Way over my head." He stepped through the daffodils at the edge of the yard to get it, then threw a long shot straight into Emma's glove.

"Ouch." She took her hand out of her glove and shook it. "Good one, though. Let me try again." She threw him another one that smacked into his glove.

Andre clapped his hands, the pouty look gone from his face. "Looking good, Emma. Really good." His blue eyes beamed in the sunlight. His head was slightly cocked the way she remembered it from her freshman English class years ago.

"Andre was here."

"Oh?"

"He stayed more than three hours. He didn't leave until I said I had to get dinner ready."

"Sorry." Charles put his hands on his hips. "I know he makes bad choices sometimes."

Emma was upset. "Choices? I'm sick of hearing people talk about choices. Deciding between vanilla and strawberry—that's a choice. Dropping in and taking up half my day is an inconsiderate act."

Charles pulled her to him and kissed her. A grin spread over his face.

"What?"

"Face it. What man wouldn't want to spend three hours alone with you?"

Emma knew she was blushing.

Charles's phone pinged. Message from Andre Smyth.

"What does he want?"

"It's about that friend of his, the student teacher he met at the charter school."

Andre had made several ventures into the world of work over the years. None lasted longer than about a week. The last was a job teaching social studies at the City Charter School, which didn't require a degree in education. That "didn't work out," he told Charles and Emma. "Fixed curriculum. Too regimented."

"He texted you about his friend Johan? What about him?"

"Says Johan broke up with him." Charles stared at the phone. "Funny way to put it."

"You think?

Charles had known Andre even longer than Emma but had never come to the conclusion that he was gay. Emma had used the word now and then over the years, and Charles always objected. "The human sexuality spectrum is too complicated to assign labels like that," he informed her.

"Anyway, I wish you'd tell Andre not to come by when you're not here."

"I will. I did."

Of course, that wasn't the solution. Andre scoffed at "scheduled living," as he called it—meaning other people's schedules.

3

The Fontainbleau

Todd came in with his friend from school. "Can Chip stay and play, Mommy?"

Chip's mother Britney wasn't the kind of person Emma felt comfortable being friends with, but for Todd's sake she tolerated her. Emma texted: *Todd and Chip playing catch in yard. Will bring Chip home by dinner time.*

Britney: *Chip does not have glove. Will drive it over.*

Emma: *No need. Couple of old gloves here.*

Britney: *Chip has custom fitted glove. Bringing it over.*

Britney pushed a strand of amber-dyed hair behind her ear and handed the glove to Chip. She looked askance at Charles's leather chair.

"Go ahead and sit down, Britney. Can I get you anything?"

"Glass of Perrier?"

Britney was a pain, but Emma felt a little sorry for her. She'd met her two years ago when Todd came home crying because the teacher said his friend Chip might not come back to school. Emma found Chip's home number, called Britney, and found out Chip was in the hospital with difficulty breathing that puzzled the doctors.

"It can't be from vaccinations," Britney had told her. "I wouldn't let them give him any."

Britney had joined a national anti-vaccination movement she found on Reddit and was working to get the county to drop the requirement that children be vaccinated. When the doctors finally realized Chip had whooping cough, Britney wouldn't believe it. "The internet said there are almost no cases of whooping cough nowadays."

The lack of logic astounded Emma, but Britney's grief was real. She was a wreck. For a week, Emma spent her evenings telling Britney her boy was going to recover. When he did, Britney cried on Emma's shoulder, thanking her again and again as if it had been Emma who cured her son.

If Britney wanted Perrier, fine. Emma kept a two-liter bottle of Valu Brand soda water—close enough—in the refrigerator for Britney's visits. She splashed some into a glass and brought it out to her.

Britney ran a finger over a crack in the leather chair. "I'm going to give my whole family room a redesign, Emma. You know that gold and cream Queen Anne chair? I could give it to you and you could get rid of this delightful item."

"That's Charles's favorite chair. He'd never part with it."

The phone Britney kept jammed into the pocket of her Capri pants burst into the chorus of *Animal Instinct*, by the Cranberries, a favorite from her high school days. She dug it out and tapped. Britney always raised her voice when she talked on the phone. "No, Esmeralda. Chip won't eat peas. No, Derek doesn't like tomatoes because of the seeds. Well, I don't know. Just look at those lists on the pantry door. That's what they're there for. Cook something that's not on anybody's Won't-Eat list." She shut off her phone. "Honestly. It's hard enough getting through the day without having to deal with her."

Britney's maid Esmeralda was lucky, Emma thought. Charles's list of interdicted foods wasn't as simple as a bunch of things he didn't like. Charles wouldn't eat anything nourished with synthetic fertilizer, preserved with chemicals, or sprayed with pesticides. You had to be a scientist to shop for him. As for herself and Todd, they would eat anything if allowed to.

Britney said, "Emma, you say you're looking for a job. Our friend Bea is in real estate. I could set something up. There's a real estate reception coming up. I'll get you an invitation."

"Oh, I don't think so."

"Really? You need to learn how things work, Emma. Derek's always telling me. It's all about connections."

Britney's husband Derek talked about nothing but subprime loans, deeds of trust, collateralizing, and equity cash-outs, and he drove a red Jaguar. As for Britney, her clothes were all Ralph Lauren, Prada, Calvin Klein or other designer brands that Emma didn't even know. Her makeup was perfect—Sephora her favorite—and she wore bracelets and necklaces that even drew the attention of men. Maybe not Charles, but most men. Charles said she was dumpy looking. But he was only talking about her body.

They were still talking when Charles came home, early for a change. "Guess what. I have a new student to tutor in English, Ngoc Dung Tran."

When he went to get an organic beer from the kitchen, Britney turned to Emma and lowered her voice. "The right kind of connections, of course."

Charles peeped out from the kitchen with three green bottles of beer between the fingers of one hand, one opened and two not. "Beer, Britney? Emma?" He had to know from experience they didn't like beer. Yet he always asked. When his clients kept making the same mistake, he would call it a learning disorder. Emma preferred to see this as just Charles's way of being polite.

"What do you think, Charles? You and Emma coming to the realtors' reception with me."

"Oh, I don't—"

"I want Emma to meet Beatrice, my friend in real estate."

Emma was nervous. She asked Britney, "What do you wear at these affairs?"

"Oh, kind of formal, I guess."

"Then, no, I don't think so."

"Good excuse to buy a new dress." Britney lifted one eyebrow.

Excited by talk of Emma in a new dress, Charles trapped a mouthful of beer, nodded, swallowed. "Use the money I've earned from tutoring."

"That's for swimming lessons."

"Oh, you *have* to start Todd in the eight-year-old beginners," Britney insisted. "You don't want to be the kind of parent who lets her child grow up dog-paddling his whole life."

Emma and Charles had had this discussion before. Charles believed overt instruction in physical activities could interfere with one's innate kinesthetic awareness, possibly delaying the desired outcome. Sometimes Emma wondered if psychological jargon had dulled Charles's brain.

Emma shifted back to the realtors' reception. "I really don't know if I want to sell real estate. So . . . ." She looked at Charles for support. He took in a breath but no words came out. She wondered how he would characterize this loss of words in one of his clients. Selective mutism? Aphonia?

The Fontainbleau was a huge new "Event Palace" located towards the north end of the highway but a few miles safely south of the railroad tracks that marked the city line. It sparkled with colossal electric chandeliers, gilt trimmed mirrors along the walls, and massive glass fountains flowing over artificial spikes of ice. Emma glanced at herself in one of the mirrors, combed her fingers through the lush bobbed hair that curled in just short of her chin. Not bad. But she wished she'd been able to buy a new dress. Her high-necked gray PTA outfit was obviously too severe for the occasion.

For an event that Britney described as formal, there was an almost deafening high-pitched chatter from the realtors and Chamber of Commerce people sipping from their plastic Champagne glasses. Charles clung to her hand.

"There she is." Britney led Emma and Charles to a blond woman in a low-cut red dress who seemed to be flirting with a tall man with a bulbous chin.

The blond woman took Emma's hand. "Call me Bea," she said in a throaty voice. "And this is Pastor Mitchell Rainey. It was five years ago that the pastor brought Jesus into my heart. And I have been rewarded." She crossed her hands on her breast. "The pastor and I work on some projects together."

"Just call me 'Pastor Mitch.'" With his bushy eyebrows and tuxedo, he reminded Emma of one of the Muppets—she couldn't quite place which one—except, un-Muppet-like, his mouth was filled with huge teeth when he grinned.

Bea held her hand out to Charles. "And this must be your husband." She put her other hand over her bosom and took in a huge, swelling breath. "Excuse me. Your eyes. I've never seen such beautiful hazel eyes. Praise the Lord."

Charles blinked but, of course, said nothing. Emma gritted her teeth. After an uncomfortable moment, Britney told Bea that Emma might be interested in a job in real estate.

"We always need agents." From a tiny red bag strapped to her waist by a thin red belt Bea pulled out a business card with a large gold seal. "So, what have you done?"

"I worked as an environmental chemist until I was laid off."

"That's nice," Bea said, eyes glazing over. She raised her head and looked around. "Excuse me. There's somebody I have to talk to."

Emma watched her rush away, silky dress swishing with each step. "Oh, my," she said.

Britney whispered, "Did you see those earrings? Three karats, at least." Then, "Refill, anyone?" She slid away to get one herself.

Pastor Mitch winked at Emma. "Bea's always busy at these affairs and rushing off. But you won't find a better mentor. She's Gold Tier, you know."

Charles's phone pinged. He turned it so Emma could read: *Message from Andre Smyth.* "I'll text him back later." Andre had seemed needy since losing his friend Johan.

Pastor Mitch's eyes widened. "That's an unusual name. Would you believe it, I came across that name recently. Andre Smyth. Spelled with a *y* like that."

Charles asked where he'd seen it.

Pastor Mitch waved his hand in front of his face, flashing a heavy gold ring in the chandelier light. "Ah, not important. Another champagne? Emma? Charles? I'm going to put in a good word for you with Bea, Emma, when she doesn't have so much on her plate."

A waiter came by with a tray of hors d'oeuvres. Emma took a mushroom polenta, Pastor Mitch took a shrimp wrapped in bacon, but Charles just looked at the platter and shook his head. Emma knew why. The items might contain MSG. Instead, when another waiter came by with a tray of champagne, he took one of those—ethyl alcohol apparently not being harmful to the body. As he lifted it to his mouth, he spilled a little.

Emma grinned. "Got to work on that kinesthetic aware- ness, Charles." She squeezed his hand in hers. He was cling- ing to her the way Todd did in a crowded place.

A gray haired black woman overflowing her ebony sat- in dress stopped and gave Pastor Mitch a bear hug. "Pastor Mitch. So nice to see you with the real estate crowd. You know, I can't tell if being a pastor is your main thing and in- vestment is your sideline or vice-versa."

"Maybe it's politics." Pastor Mitch chuckled. "Emma, Charles, you know Amanda Winwright? Chair of the GOP Central Committee."

Charles shook her hand and glanced sideways at Emma. She knew what he was thinking. Republican? The party that just eliminated breakfasts for poor kids in the county schools? She hoped he wouldn't say anything.

Amanda Winwright smiled. "We'll have to get you on the donors' list."

Emma nodded, squeezing Charles's hand harder. It didn't do any good. "I'm sort of a Green Party guy," Charles blurted out.

Amanda Winwright looked him over, then eyed Emma's dress. "I see."

"We're trying to get Ms. Winwright on board with gun rights," Pastor Mitch interposed. "It's what the Republican faithful want, you have to admit, Amanda."

Ms. Winwright's glad-handing smile turned to a pained expression. "I'm from the City, you have to remember. We have one-point-two murders a day there. For us, guns are a major problem." She placed a hand on Pastor Mitch's back. "Don't get me wrong. I'm not totally against a citizen's right to bear arms, but it just seems reasonable that—"

Ms. Amanda Winwright and Pastor Mitchell Rainey were called up to the stage.

After they'd left, Emma pursed her lips. "I guess my dress is a little plain for this event."

Charles touched her arm. "Emma, all night I've been thinking how beautiful you look in it. You're the loveliest woman at this reception."

4

Life coach

Britney had invited them to dinner to get to know her realtor friend Bea better. Charles didn't want to go. Emma didn't either. But she felt it would be rude not to.

Charles complained, "Britney's not my type. Know what I mean, Emma? She's kind of controlling."

"Who's your type?"

"You are."

"Not Praise-the-Lord Bea?" Emma batted her eyelashes at him. "I guess you noticed she wasn't at all interested in me at the reception."

"Aw, it's not the kind of job I see you doing, anyway, Baby. Taking people to look into other people's closets."

"You have to understand, Charles. We need the money. Our income was cut in half when I was laid off. And you won't even apply for a position that would pay more."

Charles put his arms around her. "We can't keep up with Britney and Derek, if that's what you want, Emma. We never could, even when you were working."

Emma turned her face. She felt tears coming and didn't want to ruin his collar. "I don't want a life like Britney's. I just want us to be able to pay our bills. We both have master's degrees, and here we are struggling to get by. It doesn't seem fair."

"I'll get more tutoring jobs, Emma."

It was hard to get Charles worried about things like bills. As long as he was Doing Good for Others, he was content. But, then, that's why she'd married him. She hadn't realized back then that doing good for others would pay so little.

"I might have some good news," Charles told her. "You know I've been pushing for the department to start funding life coaches. Guess what. They approved it."

"Oh. Great. I guess." She tried to show a little enthusiasm, but it was hard to believe Charles could take something called "life coaching" seriously. Was his mind going soft? If so, it wasn't from an overdose of MSG or tripolyphosphate or thiamine mononitrate. That much she knew.

"So, listen to this. I already started this online life coach license program. It's actually kind of easy. Like some of the work I do with my clients. In another week, I'll have the license."

"A license to coach people how to live?"

He ignored the cynicism. "How to set goals, develop plans to meet those goals, that sort of thing. And I'll be able to do private sessions after work. Do you realize what they pay? Ten, twenty, thirty times what English tutoring pays. Maybe more."

That was good, Emma guessed. Britney had implied Ngoc Dung Tran wasn't a useful business connection. But, face it, she liked picturing Charles tutoring Ngoc Dung Tran more than picturing him "life coaching" some rich person with enough time and money to hire a guy to do her thinking for her. Somehow she assumed the life coaching "clients" would mainly be women.

Charles and Todd were underhanding a baseball back and forth in the living room—which Britney always called their family room, as if they had a separate room somewhere else that was their living room.

"How about taking that ball outside? And remember, we're leaving at seven."

Father and son turned back.

"We're going to dinner at Britney and Derek's tonight, remember? To get to know that realtor woman."

"Oh yeah. I almost forgot. Guess I did forget." Sometimes

31

Charles's confused half-grin made him look like a kid.

Todd lowered his glove. "Chip's house? Can I go, too, Mommy? I want to go."

"Grandma's coming. I told you. You'll have fun with her."

"Oh. OK. Cool."

Charles predictably went on the alert. "Just don't let Grandma give you anything with sugar or salt in it. And no computer games. Play with the legos."

"I know, Daddy. Develop my motor skills."

Nottingham Estates had been carved out of the woods near the old village of Shady Park. You couldn't see any of the houses from the highway. You had to drive through the entrance gate and along a winding road through trees interspersed with azaleas, and then here and there you saw a driveway that led up through more trees to what looked like a mansion, but a brand new one. The entrance gate to Britney's driveway had newly-cast concrete lions on each side.

Esmeralda opened the door. The foyer and family room ceilings in Britney's house were two stories high. Emma wondered how you'd ever fix those ceilings if the paint started to flake.

Britney's lips were purple from wine. It could have been the way she sipped it. The realtor Bea came up to them. She'd clearly already had a few glasses of wine, too. She hugged Emma, then stroked Charles's shoulder. Her soft, clingy blouse highlighted breasts held up on display by a pushup bra. "And Charles!" she crooned. "Those hazel eyes have been literally haunting me since the reception. You don't mind if I say that, do you, Emma? Come sit next to me, Charles." She led him by the hand to a white Victorian sofa. "Pastor Mitch tells me you have some interesting friends."

Esmeralda brought around mushrooms stuffed with lobster, salmon canapés, and prosciutto-topped cucumbers. "My personal trainer will kill me," Britney quipped, taking a mushroom. "Please, folks. Don't make me eat all of this by myself."

Britney's husband Derek was a sharp-featured man, with a crooked nose. He wore a blinking bluetooth headset in his ear and kept getting up and going out to the glass-walled patio to sit on the edge of the sauna and talk, holding the earpiece in with one extended finger. He looked silly, but Emma assumed he was doing some developer business.

When they sat down to dinner, Derek shot a glance towards his wife. "That was my golf partner on the phone."

"Pastor Mitch?" Britney took a quick sip. "What does he want?"

"Something new about Riverside Paradise. He said Beatrice might have told you about it."

Bea interrupted, "No, I haven't mentioned it yet. It's still supposed to be a secret."

"Anyway." Derek looked over his half eyeglasses at Emma. "Bea's a good choice for a mentor. She's a Gold Tier agent. I work with her a lot."

Britney finished another glass of wine. Emma passed a plate of salmon to Charles, whispering, "Omega-3s. Good for you, Charles."

Charles tilted his head. "Maybe." He spoke softly to Esmeralda. "Sorry to ask. Is it wild? There are PCBs in the farmed salmon."

"Is fish."

Charles took a glass of wine instead. He passed on the asparagus, too, since he believed that "organic" fertilizer made with nitrogen extracted from pig poop was better for you than "chemical" fertilizer made with nitrogen extracted from air.

Emma gobbled up everything with gusto. As Esmeralda put a kale salad in front of her, Emma said, "Everything you're serving is organic. Right, Esmeralda?"

"*Si?*"

"There you go, Charles. Dig in." He was having his fourth glass of chardonnay and needed to eat.

Derek tapped his glass for a refill. "Charles, you still doing that social worker thing or whatever?" Charles swallowed some kale and nodded. Derek's nose wrinkled. "You're a smart guy—college and all. You think you might be wasting your talent there? It can't pay much."

Charles said he liked the work. He glanced sideways at Emma.

Emma ignored his uneasy little frown. "A supervisor's position opened up. I'm trying to get Charles to apply for it."

Derek stopped his fork half way to his mouth, a large piece of salmon skewered on it. "Uh-huh. But there's got to be something better than working for the county, don't you think?"

When Charles looked down at the table, Emma gave him a pat on the knee, sorry she'd put him on the spot in front of everybody. It wasn't like her. Maybe she'd had a little too much wine, too. "Charles helps people, and I like that," she said.

It was time to change the subject. Other than yoga—and nobody else at the table did yoga—Britney had only one thing she was interested in. Her children. Chip had a sister four years older, in the seventh grade. Apparently there was some problem with the test grades the teacher gave her. "I mean, I've got to focus on Chelsea's future. Do you know how hard it is to get into the right colleges these days?" Britney sighed.

Bea didn't have any children and wasn't any more interested in that topic than in yoga. "Mm, mm," she said, sipping her wine. "Tell me, Charles. Andre Smyth, how do you know him?" She touched her fingers to his arm. "If you don't mind me asking."

"We were in college together."

"College," she pronounced as if it were a sacred word. "So

you've known him a long time."

"Yes." Charles sipped some more wine. He wasn't good at dinner conversation.

"Boooring!" Britney interrupted. But Bea went on. "I think your Mr. Smyth might live quite near my new place. I insist on meeting this long-time friend of yours." She pointed to Charles's glass, and Esmeralda filled it. "Now tell me about you. What is it exactly you do?"

"Social worker, like Derek said," Charles muttered. Emma knew he needed to stop drinking the wine. He wasn't used to it. Charles added, "I'm going to be a life coach."

"Glory be. Thank you, Jesus, for leading me to this man. A life coach is just what I've been looking for."

They'd finished eating, and Britney wasn't interested in the conversation. "Emma, come with me. I want to show you what I've done with Chip's room. Why don't you all go into the living room for coffee?"

Emma tried to give Bea a warning glare before following Britney upstairs, but Bea seemed not to notice.

Chip's room had blue walls. Britney had picked out the color in consultation with her home decorator. "The room has a space motif," she explained unnecessarily. She pointed out the constellations she'd had painted on the ceiling, the cloud-like curtains she'd ordered for the windows, the lamp that looked like Saturn with its rings, the pictures of NASA rockets hanging on the walls. "I'm kind of proud of it," Britney said.

"Obviously Chip likes astronomy."

"He should. He will. I'm doing what I can. They say it's a fabulous career choice." A slight shadow of worry, perhaps doubt, clouded Britney's face. "As for Chelsea, it's so hard to know what I should do in there. I mean, at first I did her room up in a medical motif. I found a wonderful catalog that had wallpaper with stethoscopes and sphyg-mo-ma-no-meters and otoscopes. Proud of myself for learning those words. And I made Chelsea learn how to say them, too. Then, would you believe it? When she was about eight, she declared the wallpaper was 'gross.' Now I don't know what to do with her room. The walls are all white until I decide on a theme."

A female voice rang out from the first floor. The only word Emma could distinguish was "Jesus." Britney rolled her eyes and led Emma back downstairs.

Derek had disappeared onto the patio with his cell phone. In the living room, Charles was leaning back on the couch, eyes closed, and Bea was kneeling in front of him, her hands folded on his lap.

"Charles?"

His eyes opened at Emma's voice. He seemed confused. Probably drunk. Emma reached to shake him out of it, nudging Bea aside.

"Goin' be 'er life coach," Charles slurred.

Emma had to help Charles take off his shoes and clothes and roll him into bed that night. Somehow he didn't realize that the alcohol he'd drunk at Britney's was more harmful to his body than any traces of whatever might have been in the food he refused. Charles led a life based on theory rather than empirical observation. He fell asleep on his back in his underwear and emitted a deep, gurgling snore.

He woke up in the morning looking confused, holding his head. Emma couldn't tell what he remembered of the evening before. He didn't say anything, just dropped his underwear on the floor and went into the shower.

When Emma got back from waking Todd up, Charles was sitting on a towel in a shirt but no pants, staring at his shoes on the floor.

"Coach?" she called. "You all right, Coach?"

He winced.

She knelt down in front of him, putting her hands on his knees. "Oh, Charles. Will you be my life coach? Please. Please, I pray you." She slid her hands up his thighs.

"Heh-heh." The embarrassed grin showed he did remember something, at least.

"My life is in disarray. Coach me. Coach me, please. I need more properties. And maybe love, too. I need your hazel eyes to guide me."

Charles rubbed his eyes. It was coming back to him. "Emma, that woman Bea. She told me she'd pay me $150 an hour. So I said sure."

"Charles, you agreed? What would you teach her, Hon? Not financial advice, I'm guessing."

"See, the way coaching works, I won't know until we've had a few sessions. It takes a while before a coaching plan can be drawn up."

"The woman was kneeling there with her hands in your lap, Charles. I have to say that looked funny."

"I think I fell asleep."

"Uh-huh."

"It was all about Jesus wanting me to be her life coach." He scratched his head. "And something about Andre, too. She has some kind of fixation."

"Uh-huh. I noticed. Keep away from her."

"A hundred fifty dollars an hour, Emma."

He left for work. Todd left for school. As usual, Emma cleaned up after both of them. Todd's room was a mess. Books and papers hid half the carpet. The other half was covered with dirty clothes from yesterday and the day before. Charles left a trail of clothes between the bed and the bathroom. She picked up his trousers, took out the belt, and emptied the pockets so she could take them downstairs to wash. In one pocket was a folded-up piece of newspaper. She opened it up. It was the Zales ad for the diamond necklace.

5

The executive class

Emma kept Charles's tutoring money in a red Valu Food coffee can on top of the refrigerator. It wasn't even enough to pay for swimming lessons, not to mention the increase in real estate tax. Politicians were always talking about helping the middle class. Like almost everybody, she assumed she was in the middle class. At least she was in the middle between having to take the bus like Esmeralda and driving a luxury SUV like Britney. But Emma's Ford Focus had a hole in the muffler, and the brakes squealed, and there wasn't enough left this month to get it fixed. She felt like her family was slipping out of the middle class. That's what she was trying to tell Charles when she urged him to try for the supervisor's position. Now it looked like maybe she had pressed him too hard.

Rather than have Charles start that life coaching thing with Bea, maybe she could bring in some extra money as a real estate agent—even if she had to work for Bea. And it wouldn't hurt to keep an eye on that woman.

She wore the charcoal skirt suit she'd worn to the Envirotech interview nine years ago. It still fit. The wide collar was out of fashion, but it would have to do. She wore pumps. Bea was a little shorter than she was, and the *startanewcareer.com* article said to dress business-formal but avoid anything an interviewer might interpret as threatening. Like being taller? Emma wondered. The idea was to impress the employer without making her worry that some day you might be a competitor for her job. Some chance of Bea ever worrying about that. *Realestatebasics.com*, she hoped, had given her enough to talk about without sounding completely ignorant. She had even started in on *mortgage and brokerage essentials.com*. Charles had stood behind her, a disparaging look on his face.

"What's equity skimming, Charles?"

"I wouldn't know."

"Not interested?"

"In my opinion, Emma, real estate agents are like dogs peeing on telephone poles to mark their territory. They put up For Sale signs to stake their claim of a percentage of the sales price, no matter who sells it."

This wasn't the way *realestatebasics.com* described realtors, but she tended to agree with Charles. And here she was trying to become one of them.

She knew where Bea's office was. Last winter she'd taken Todd to the Olde Tyme Bowling Alley and was surprised to find it was gone. A huge red, white, and blue "Executive Homes" sign hung above the doorway. She'd taken Todd to play with Chip instead. Britney said her husband had helped finance the Executive Homes remodeling. "Bowling's more a pastime for people up in the city than for people we know," she informed Emma.

Now the building sported a lofty fake roof peak over the entrance. She parked in one of the newly-painted "Visitor Only" spaces in front of Executive Homes. Executive getaways, executive hotel suites, executive dining—she guessed you couldn't say "upper class" in our democratic country. Besides, "executive" implied they worked for their money, they deserved to be rich. This is what Derek always said, usually quoting Mitt Romney or Donald Trump. Hiding behind the half-opened Focus door, Emma straightened her skirt, then locked her car. You had to lock it with a key. No remote. They only came with the executive models.

Bea came out from her office in a rush of white ruffles. "Emma, dear. What a blessing you came. I was just talking about you with Pastor Mitch. Mitchell Rainey, you remember? Kind of a partner of mine. Come in so we can talk."

The carpeting was so thick Emma wondered how Bea could walk on it in high heels. The phone beside Bea's computer rang. "No calls now," she called out to her secretary. "Important meeting." She closed the faux walnut door and pointed Emma to a chair upholstered in a dark floral chenille. "So. Pastor Mitch says he was impressed with you at the reception."

"I hardly talked to him."

"It was through Pastor Mitch that I came to know Jesus. I gave up Catholicism and became a True Christian. I hope you, too, will let Jesus into your heart."

Emma felt herself starting to squirm. It was all she could do to keep from saying she hadn't had an imaginary friend since she was three.

"And Jesus has poured out his love upon me." Bea ran her eyes across the richly paneled walls and Hepplewhite tables and chairs. "Emma, I don't believe it's a coincidence that you came to see me today. I believe you were sent here by the Lord."

Emma muttered that she'd actually come looking for a job. Her voice cracked as she tried to explain that, although she didn't have any direct experience in real estate, she'd always been interested in it—a lie that made her cheeks feel hot—and had studied up on it. She did her best to throw in some of the internet real estate jargon she'd found.

"Of course, of course. I'm certain we'll be able to set you up." Bea stretched her arms out towards Emma. "But let's get to know each other first." She wasn't dressed in what Emma assumed *startanewcareer* meant by "business-formal." Rather, as she leaned towards Emma, her buxom décolletage transmitted more a calculated sexuality.

"Sure." Emma straightened up.

Bea pulled her chair directly in front of her so they were sitting knee to knee. "So tell me about you and Charles."

Bea's questions made Emma wring her hands. Did she and Charles ever think about moving to a bigger house? Did they have lots of friends? Who was this Andre Smyth who texted Charles at the reception? Where did he live, exactly?

These weren't the kind of interview questions Emma was prepared for. She found herself answering them mechanically, without the "enthusiasm for the job" that *startanewcareer* urged. No way she was going to be hired. But Bea seemed thrilled at every answer, especially the last.

"Andre lives on the Piskasanet River! Praise the Lord. We thought so. I've just built a vacation house there myself. Does your friend know what he could do with that land? I'll tell you, Emma. Pastor Mitch and I know what those old fishing shacks are like. Your friend doesn't have to live that way."

"Andre's house?" Emma fidgeted again, afraid of the new aggressive tone in Bea's voice. She said Andre seemed content to live there just as things were. He wasn't much for home improvement or whatever. Now and then he fished in the river.

"Of course, of course. He sounds very interesting. I'd like to meet him."

"Meet Andre?"

"Since he's my neighbor. If you could arrange it. Maybe at your place."

Emma's chest tightened at the thought of Bea seeing her house. "Oh, I don't . . . ."

Bea squeezed her pearl-pink lips together in disappointment. She stood and walked behind her desk, shuffling some large sheets of stiff paper that lay on top of the polished surface. She looked up at Emma, then stared back down at what Emma now recognized as blueprints.

"I'll be ready to take the realtor's exam next month," Emma assured her.

"Realtor's exam?" Bea seemed to be coming out of some kind of fog. "Yes, yes. That's what you should do."

"I promise I'll pass it."

"I'm sure you will. And even if you don't, there are ways you can profit from association with us." She walked back to Emma's chair. "Emma, will you pray with me?"

"I don't really—"

"Lord Jesus, help Emma to see the path that leads to a rewarding life guided by your loving hand. Help her to welcome the abundance of your grace."

Emma stood up. But Bea went on, holding her palms up and raising her eyes to the ceiling. "Help Emma to lead her friend Andre to the life he deserves, a life graced by your endless bounty."

Emma moved towards the door.

"And help us all to share in your eternal munificence." Just as Emma was reaching for the doorknob, Bea said, "Amen."

Emma turned. Bea's breasts heaved as she inhaled to catch her breath. The two women stared at each other. Bea looked like she might be in what Charles would call a manic state. This wasn't somebody Emma could work for. She thanked Bea for her time.

"Emma, dear. I know the Lord is calling me to meet Andre. Please. Will you see what you can do?"

Emma tilted her head noncommittally as she slipped out of the office.

She threw her wide-collared jacket over a chair in her bedroom and pulled on jeans just in time to go down and let Britney in.

"So? How did it go? I know you went to see Bea. She called me."

Emma never liked to say negative things about people. Her mother often said, "You're seldom going to be sorry you kept your mouth shut."

"Come on. She told me everything. She said you walked out on her."

"Yeah, I don't know. I don't know if real estate's for me."

"It's Bea, isn't it? I know. You don't have to tell me. Derek calls listening to Jesus-talk an occupational hazard of working with her."

"It's not just that."

"The life coaching thing with Charles? She told me about that, too."

Emma felt her face get warm. She pursed her lips and said nothing.

"And she wants to meet Andre, doesn't she?"

Emma nodded. She said, "See, I don't really think Andre is the kind of person Bea would like." She thought of her mother's injunction but went ahead. "Andre's a little strange."

6

Crazy Mommy

She called Charles at work, but he didn't answer his phone. He had a preset text response on it that he could press: *Busy with a client. Call you later.* But he didn't send that, either. The phone just went to voicemail. Emma held her head in her hands, running her fingers up through her hair. Todd called her "Crazy Mommy" when she did this. He thought it was funny. Sometimes, if he refused to pick his dirty clothes up off the floor, she used both hands to push her hair up and glared at him with her eyes popping open. Even though he laughed, it worried him a little. He always picked up the clothes.

Chicken casserole for dinner. This was supposed to be a "Quick 'n E-Z" meal, and it *was* if you used Campbell's mushroom soup, but not so E-Z if you had to mince organic mushrooms, make sauce out of organic milk, and cut up free-range chicken.

Todd burst in from the back yard dropping his glove and ball by the back door.

"Crazy Mommy!"

"Oh." She smoothed her hair down.

"I'm hungry, Mommy."

She'd already wasted too much time trying to get a job she really didn't want—from a woman who was halfway insane and probably had designs on her husband. She reached into the cabinet behind the bags of organic whole wheat flour and sea salt and pulled out a can of Campbell's.

Charles kissed her when he got home. "What's wrong, Emma? Something wrong?"

"You smell like perfume."

"I do?" Charles the Simple. If he were a king, that's what he would be called. He said, "Guess what. I passed the online life coach test. They're mailing out my certificate."

"Good for you. Did you have to pay anything?"

"$219. But Bea paid for it on her credit card."

Emma tried to "process" this, as Charles liked to say instead of "think about." She said, "Bea came to your office?"

"No, I went to hers."

"That's where you took the test?"

Charles nodded.

"Why did she do that? I mean, pay."

Charles shrugged as if this hadn't occurred to him. "She needed me to be a qualified life coach, I guess."

"Still . . . ."

Her concern didn't register. "Emma, I saw online there's a life coach conference coming up in New York. Four days. Kind of expensive, though." He stole a look at her. "I guess maybe I can go next year. It'd be a good chance to meet people in the profession, learn how to get new clients."

Emma couldn't believe he was talking about life coaching as a profession, but she left it at that for now. When they sat down to dinner, Charles and Todd gobbled up the casserole. "You've outdone yourself, Emma." Charles shot her a broad grin. "Best casserole you've ever made."

Emma held her suspicions about Bea in check until they went to bed. Charles began touching her. "I like you in this red nightgown. I like the way you feel."

"Hold on, Charles. Tell me more about your day at work." She turned aside so his hand slipped from her breast. She knew it was going to be difficult for him to shift gears now.

"Um. Work?"

"Were there any interesting interventions today? I called your cell. No answer."

"Interventions? Oh, no. As soon as I passed the test, we

had our first session. And guess what? I already made $200 for the initial interview." He beamed at her for a reaction. "Life coaching is like doing an intervention, sort of. That's how I caught on so fast."

"Except life coaching interventions are more aromatic, I take it."

"What do you—? Oh, I get it. Bea's perfume." He reached for her hand, but she pulled it away. "Emma, you don't think—? Bea's my life coaching client. That's all."

"This coaching took place in her office?"

"No. We went to her villa, where we could work in a stress-free environment."

"What!" She'd always found Charles's ingenuousness charming. But this verged on simplemindedness. Assuming it wasn't deceit.

"It's near Andre's house, it turns out."

"I know. Bea told me. When I went to her office, all that woman talked to me about was how she wants to meet Andre. It was clear she wasn't really interested in hiring me." She gave Charles her eye-popping glare. "And I don't think she's really interested in having a life coach."

Charles stared away in a frown—his hurt look. "You think she's interested in Andre, not me?"

She clutched her hair in her hands. "I can't believe this. That's not the point. You sound jealous, Charles."

He was moping. "You *used* to think I was interesting."

"We're not discussing whether you're interesting or not."

"I have to say, Bea seems to find me interesting."

"Charles. Listen to yourself." She grabbed a pillow, pounded him on the head. She was breathing hard, tears clouding her vision.

He gripped her arms, turned her to meet his eyes. "Hey, 'Crazy Mommy.' Come here." He pulled her head to his chest, smoothed her hair with his palm. "You know you're the only woman I care about, don't you?"

They eased down on the bed, Emma sobbing on his chest until she fell asleep.

7

Self-improvement

There was an early afternoon knock at the door—Britney, in matching black tank top and tight leather-trimmed Replay Joggers. "You need to get a doorbell."

Emma ignored this. Britney said it every time she came to the house. "Nice outfit. Yoga?"

Britney ran her hands over her hips. "Derek swears these don't make me look fat. I don't know."

They did, but Emma said they didn't. Emma had no fat on her, but she would never walk around outside in clothes as tight as Britney was wearing.

"Ugh," Britney breathed out, sliding her hips across the brown leather of Charles's chair. "I feel my chakras are *so* out of alignment." She held her hand on her stomach, her Manipura chakra, which Emma could identify from previous conversations.

When Emma first told Charles she was having a hard time paying the bills, she joked that she was going to rent an office near Nottingham Estates, the gated community where Britney lived, and hang a sign on the door: CHAKRAS ALIGNED WHILE U WAIT. Charles smiled and hugged her—and that's when he started tutoring to bring in a little extra money. Which he'd now given up for life coaching, apparently. "Britney, can I ask you something about Bea?"

"Her Svadhishthana chakra is too open, if that's what you want to know."

It was, actually. "Because, you know, she's hired Charles as her life coach."

Britney assured her Charles was safe with Bea, if that's

48

what she was worried about. After all, Derek was with Bea constantly, working up business deals, and there was nothing going on between *them*. "It's Bea and the pastor I sometimes wonder about."

Emma took a breath through her teeth. "The life coaching thing doesn't make sense. On the internet I see life coaching is a lot about becoming a financial success. She's got plenty of money already, I presume."

"You can never get enough, Emma."

"Does she really think Charles is the kind of person who could help her get more?"

"You might be surprised." Britney put her hand over her Vishuddha chakra. "Punchy says my communication drive could be brought more into balance with my thought center." Punchy was what the Nottingham Estates wives called Punchatantra Ramadhithma, their tantric yoga instructor.

When Emma nevertheless encouraged more outflowing of Britney's communication chakra, Britney said she'd just say one thing. It would be a bad idea to discourage this partnership between Charles and Bea.

Partnership. That sounded very different from a coach-trainee relationship. Emma was embarrassed to ask Britney any more questions. She'd rather look into this for herself.

Britney's phone sang out *Animal Instincts*. "Ah. It's Chip. I have to pick him up at school and take him to his golf lesson. Derek's pro says it's never too early to start them. You ought to think about giving Todd lessons."

Instead, when Todd came home, she played catch with him in the back yard.

"You're getting better, Mommy."

Throwing a baseball wasn't anything she'd ever tried to be good at, but his praise gave her an unexpected jolt of pleasure. She concentrated, threw straighter and straighter. "Baseball

Mommy!" Todd called out. "Put it right here in my glove."
A drop of sweat rolled down to the tip of her nose, and she
shook it off. Her mind was clear. She thought of nothing but
smacking the ball right there into his glove. Her chakras,
Punchy might say, were in perfect balance.

Charles texted her: *Be home late. Don't wait dinner. $$$.*

A lump formed in Emma's throat. In the first few years
after they were married, he used to end his texts with *XXX*.

"I'm hungry, Mommy. What's for dinner?"

"Grilled cheese sandwiches."

"Oh, boy!"

Todd was already in bed, and it was close to 9:00 by the
time Charles got home. When he kissed her cheek, Emma
noticed that same perfume again.

"Look, Emma. For four hours' work." He opened his wal-
let and showed her a stack of bills. Emma glanced at the mon-
ey, then looked him in his hazel eyes. "Praise the Lord," she
said.

Charles blushed.

"Have you been with Bea all this time?"

"Yeah. Life coaching. This pays way more than tutoring.
I'm going to have the money to buy you something nice."

"I don't need anything nice. I just need to get the car muf-
fler fixed."

He said he wasn't hungry and was ready for bed.

"Go up and take a shower. Wash off that perfume smell. I
can't stand it."

She tidied up downstairs, stopping beside the table next to
Charles's chair. Sometimes he brought work home, and there
was a folder lying there. She listened. The water was running
in the shower. She picked up the folder, smelled it. The same
perfume. She opened it.

♥ Beatrice Doggit ♥

LONGTERM GOALS

Lose 5 lbs — from stomach only
Glorify the Lord in all I do
Earn Golden Tier award for 5th straight year
Riverside Paradise
Get to know more of the right people
. . . maybe some other things !!!

Emma couldn't help thinking of Benjamin Franklin's autobiography. Her favorite of his self-improvement resolutions was *Be humble. Imitate Jesus and Socrates.*

This couldn't be hundreds of dollars' worth of long term goals. She flipped the page. Nothing on the back. Apparently this life coaching proceeded at a very deliberate pace—a lucrative pace for the coach, she had to admit. After the list there was a stack of printouts from a computer. Names, addresses, and phone numbers followed by county property descriptions and survey drawings. Most of the names had pink check marks next to them. The remaining few had pink frowny faces. One of the names with a frowny face was underlined in pink: Andre Smyth. As she looked to see what else was in the folder, she heard Charles coming down the stairs and quickly closed it back on the table.

"What're you doing?"

"Straightening up."

Charles put his arms around her from behind, cupping her breasts. The perfume smell was gone. Now he smelled like soap. She could feel him against her.

"This Bea thing, Charles."

His fingers slid lower. She trapped them with hers as they moved below her waist.

"Do we have to talk about her now, Emma?"

"Stop. Yes, we have to talk about you staying out till late at night with another woman."

Charles turned to face her. "Life coaching. I hope you don't think I'm having an affair or something?"

"I want to make sure you don't." She'd been determined to give him an ultimatum: stop seeing Bea or . . . . She didn't know what. Before she could get it out, he pulled her close.

"You're the only one I love, Emma. Come upstairs. Let me show you."

She felt his warm hands sliding up her back beneath her blouse, and a stream of pleasure shot through her, different, more piquant than any she remembered. It was desire now mixed with a thrill of possession. She pulled him tight against her. "You're mine, Charles. Nobody else's. Am I right?"

He managed a throaty "yes."

"It's me you want? Just me?"

"Emma. Yes."

She closed her eyes and let him sweep her away.

8

Detective work

Charles dried his face and dropped the towel on the vanity. As he got dressed, Emma picked it up and hung it on the towel rack. She picked up his pajamas from the rug and put them under his pillow. She always had to check on the cluttered dresser to make sure he had taken his wallet and keys. The online advice columns Britney quoted to her frowned on this "enabling behavior" that women often found themselves providing for their adult children and husbands. Emma didn't mind, though. Or she hadn't until Charles turned into a sexy woman's life coach.

"Don't forget the folder you left on the table."

Charles kissed her and drove off in his rusty but beloved VW Beetle with its "Antique" license plate. A classic, he called it. He ignored the hole in the driver's side floorboard.

She scanned the *Shady Park Ledger* on the off chance there'd be a job. Housecleaners, companions for the elderly, telemarketers. The same ads every week. Here was a new one: Bargain Mart greeter. No. At least, not yet.

A ping sounded. Coming from upstairs. She went up. Sure enough, Charles had forgotten his phone on the dresser. She picked it up. *Message from Andre Smyth.* Her hand was shaking. She'd never opened one of Charles's messages. He would know she'd opened it. She opened it.

Beatrice Doggit really a friend of yours? You gave her my number? She won't stop texting me.

She looked at Charles's other recent texts. Yes, he had texted Andre's phone number to Bea. And before that, Bea had texted her villa address to Charles: Riverside Road, the winding gravel road on a low bank along the Piskasanet River that Andre lived on. Emma Googled the villa address and saw it was only a few houses from Andre's.

She called Charles's office to say she could bring him his phone if he needed it. The office administrator said he wasn't due in until late in the afternoon.

Her car crunched over the rough white stones and oyster shells of Riverside Road. This was different country from the manicured suburbs where she lived. The catalpa trees had burst into bloom, their orchid-like white flowers lit by shafts of sunlight filtering through the huge leaves. Wild locust and mulberry trees sprang up haphazardly along the inland side of the road.

Unpainted shacks and one-story cottages sagged and tilted in the brush, nearly obscured by pampas grass. Rusty abandoned cars, some on cinder blocks with their wheels missing, littered the yards, along with the rotting remains of small wooden fishing dories. The houses had all once belonged to fishermen when there were still fish to be caught in the brackish water of the Piskasanet River, actually a long inlet of the bay.

On the other side of the road, the land sloped down creating a wide vista of the river. Instead of fishing boats, Emma saw motor yachts and sailboats, white against the glistening, slate-colored water. She was driving slowly to take in the view when a horn blast and the airbrake hiss of a huge cement truck behind her scared her nearly to death. She pulled over onto the dirt shoulder on the river side to let it thunder by, wondering where it was going in such a hurry. Pickup trucks and flatbed trucks loaded with huge pipes followed, and she let them all pass before she pulled back onto the road.

She was getting close to Andre's house. Driving past one, two, three large lots cleared of any sheds or cabins and stripped of all vegetation, she slowed down, saddened at the total obliteration of evidence that the fishermen Andre knew had ever lived here. The cement truck that had passed her was already pouring a level pad on one of these lots, and the pipe truck was pulling onto the lot next to it.

She didn't remember any houses on this road that could be called villas, but suddenly in the middle of a huge clearing rose an incongruous mansion that looked like it might have been picked up and dropped there from the Italian Riviera. The pale colors were new, clean, and bright, giving it a sort of Disneyland appearance. Bulldozers were parked alongside piles of rubbish and trees that had been knocked down to build it. Emma stopped. There was a red and white mailbox shaped like a lighthouse next to the driveway. She read the number. This was it.

She pulled onto the shoulder again—paved in front of the villa—leaving her motor running. She put on sunglasses and tilted her sun hat lower across her face. No cars were parked in the driveway. But there was an attached four-car garage bigger than Emma's house where Charles and Bea could have parked.

She still had Charles's phone. There might be messages from Bea on it. She'd never imagined herself spying on him before and felt like she was going to cry. It was all his fault.

Before she could check the phone, a lime green delivery truck rumbled down the road and pulled into the villa driveway. The huge yellow logo on its side read *Organic Chef* and *We deliver only the best*. The villa door opened, and there was Bea in the chilly spring air spilling out of a skimpy black bikini, a beach towel draped around her shoulders and a gold cross the size of a stiletto dangling from her neck. She glanced briefly at Emma's car before taking a tray of food from the Organic Chef, who had put on a tall chef's hat to deliver it to the door. Emma eased her car forward and drove on down the road, pretty sure Bea hadn't recognized her.

She knew the road came to a dead end just beyond where Andre lived. There was a turnaround at the end, but she didn't want to go past his house. She turned around in the dirt driveway of a cottage that had been torn down, then headed back the other way. This time she was going to go as fast as she could past Bea's villa, hat very low on her head.

Just as she approached it, she saw a rusty VW Beetle pull into the driveway. The villa door opened, and Bea came out to meet Charles wearing the same black bikini.

Emma jammed on the brakes before they could see her. They squealed, and her heart jumped into her throat. Luckily, Charles and Bea didn't notice. Bea was giving him a hug, and then they both went inside. Should she go knock on the door—a jealous wife tracking her husband down? She couldn't do it. She needed to go home and think this over.

As she turned off the highway onto Forest Road towards her house, there was a scraping noise under her car. Not a loud one. Just *skritch . . . skritch*. In the mirror she saw she was leaving a dark line on the street. The noise got louder when she turned onto her own street, Shady Park Lane, which was older and rougher. It was more like a *skrunch . . . skrunch*. "Why don't you get them to repave your road?" Britney griped almost every time she drove to Emma's house. Emma thought of pulling over, but the old Focus was still going. She made it into her driveway.

She knelt and looked under the car. As she suspected, the tailpipe had broken off from the rusty muffler and was dragging on the ground. Replacing the muffler and pipe wouldn't be cheap. "Why do you keep dumping money into that old thing?" Britney always said. "You could buy a new car with all the money you spend on repairs." Not really, Emma knew.

She brought out a coat hanger, licked her finger, and touched the tailpipe. Ouch. She put on her gardening gloves and wired the pipe back up off the ground. The pipe and the back half of the muffler had completely rusted through.

Scrubbing her hands, she looked in the mirror over the sink. Black smudges from the underside of the car dirtied her cheek and forehead. Her hair was dusty and tangled. As she stared at herself, a picture of Bea's face popped up before her. Flowing blond hair, obviously bleached. Long eyelashes, fake. And Bea's body. Puffy breasts, rounded hips, and—Emma now knew—a silky smooth stomach with a deep navel. Bea looked like the woman you see in magazines posing next to a new car or a boat. Charles had always laughed at those ads.

She washed the dirt off her face and brushed it out of her hair—short and dark, with glossy highlights. Charles always said he loved it. She brushed it to one side the way Bea wore hers—and laughed. The glamor magazine look, something else Charles always made fun of. Her hair immediately fell back into its natural bobbed position. She put her hands on her breasts. Just last night Charles had kissed them and said how beautiful they were. He'd never seemed the kind of person who thought more was better.

It was hard to imagine Charles being attracted to a woman who strode brazenly out of the house in a bikini to meet a delivery man. Or a life coach, for that matter. But maybe she was wrong. Maybe he found Bea's lack of shame erotic. Maybe there was a hidden side to Charles that she or even Charles himself had never been aware of.

Women were attracted to Charles. She'd seen that. LaKisha from work. And that Nicaraguan woman he used to tutor. It had sometimes pleased her to see them fawning over him, especially since Charles never seemed to notice it himself. Bea's fawning, however, did not please her.

She sat in the kitchen and added another item to her spiral notebook: "Muffler and pipe — $300?" She took the coffee can from the top of the refrigerator and dumped it out onto the table—money Charles got from tutoring. There was a little less than $300. It might cover the muffler, but there would be nothing left to pay for swimming lessons.

Charles got home before Todd. He didn't smell of perfume, but there was alcohol on his breath. He was carrying something wet in a red, white, and blue beach towel that wasn't theirs.

"What's that?"

"Oh, I went swimming in Bea's pool."

"She has a pool? What, in the back?"

Charles gave her a funny look.

She didn't wait for an answer. "What did you wear?"

Charles grinned, his face reddening. "My underwear."

"How could you go swimming, Charles? It's not even 70 degrees outside."

"The pool is heated. Low 90s, Bea said. You can see the steam rising above it."

Emma followed him into the laundry room where he held up the towel, letting it unroll to plop his wet jockey shorts into the washing machine.

"Charles, this is outrageous. What were you doing swimming in Bea Doggit's pool? Instead of going to work."

"I took the day off. Couldn't pass up the life coaching money." He had an infuriating twinkle in his eyes. Charles the Simple. Or was it Charles the Stonewall?

"I mean, Charles, life coaching in a swimming pool?"

"Heh-heh. Bea's idea. She's paying, you know." Still the twinkle.

She followed him up to the bedroom. He wasn't going to get away with this. "So. I guess you made a longer list of goals? While you were in the pool?"

"Longer?"

Emma felt her own face get hot. She watched him take off his khakis—naked underneath. He dropped them on the floor and started to pull on dry underwear. Emma kept her eyes on his. She wasn't going to be distracted this time. "Pick up your own clothes from the floor, Charles."

Grinning, he picked up the pants and took out his wallet. "Look, Emma. Another $450. Three hours." He held it out to her, but she wouldn't take it. Instead she grasped him by the shirt. "I want to know everything. Everything you did. Everything that woman said to you."

He looked like he was drawing a blank. "She talked mainly about the development she and Pastor Mitch are planning."

"Riverside Paradise. Right. And she needed your advice on that?"

"Not directly. I just helped her set goals. Set up reasonable expectations. Devise means of achieving her objectives."

"Come on, Charles." There was a catch in her throat. "You know she can't be paying you all this money for something called life coaching."

He dropped the khakis back on the floor and pulled her against his half-naked body.

"I'm serious, Charles." She twisted out of his arms. "Besides the life coaching, you and Bea must have talked about other things. When you were swimming around in the pool in your underwear, I mean."

"I guess that sounds bad, huh?"

"I want to know."

"It was mostly about Riverside Paradise, how great it's going to be. The two lots down from her are cleared and ready for construction. And then there's Andre's old cottage, the last one on Riverside Road. That's pretty much it. Oh, and she wants to invite Andre and us for a barbecue and cocktails at her villa."

Emma stomped out of the room. That evening in bed, Charles wanted to make love, but Emma turned away from him and pulled the pillow over her head.

9

The owl has landed

Todd was off to school, and Charles was off to—wherever. Emma had said almost nothing to him in the morning. When he came to kiss her good-bye, she pretended she heard the microwave beeping and ran into the kitchen.

She called her mother. "I don't know what to do, Mom. I can't ignore it any longer. I think Charles might be having an affair."

Her mother listened while Emma told her about Bea "hiring" Charles. At the phrase "life coach," her mother couldn't suppress a snicker.

"It's not funny, Mom. You know Charles. Once he gets an idea in his head, he holds onto it."

"Yes," her mother said. "This does seem to be worse than the organic food thing."

"Mom, seriously, what should I do? Should I confront Bea? Tell her I'm going to report her for stalking or something?"

Her mother paused for a moment before she answered. "I'd confront Charles first, Hon. Just be careful not to say anything you'll be sorry for later."

"When I try to talk to him, he acts like I'm being unreasonable, Mom."

"Then just keep your eyes open. But let me say Charles doesn't seem like the type who'd be interested in another woman."

"Maybe not, Mom, but he is a man." Emma started crying.

"Why don't you come over for lunch, Hon? I'll fix you some nice chicken—fried in bacon fat, the way you love it."

Emma ate her mother's chicken with defiant delight. Unlike Britney, she never needed to worry about putting on weight. Britney did yoga. Emma did housework and yard work. It seemed work used up more calories than yoga.

"How can I get dandelions out of my lawn, Mom?"

He mother chuckled. "To tell you the truth, they don't bother me. I guess you could say I've made my peace with them. They're pretty yellow flowers, after all."

"Britney mentions them every time she comes to my house."

"Yes, your daddy used to worry about what the neighbors would think. I'll see if I can find that special tool he used for digging them up." Her mother held her in a hug. "Don't worry, Hon. I'm sure things will work out just fine."

When Emma got back to her house, a white box was sitting on her doorstep. Inside was a bouquet of black-eyed Susans and bluebells in a white ceramic vase shaped like an owl. There was a Nottingham Flowers tag addressed to Charles: *Thanks for your help. Bea.*

Why would she send a vase that looked like an owl? Not really a romantic choice. Maybe Bea had phoned in her order and let the florist choose the arrangement. Whatever. She picked up the box and was heading for the trash can around back when Todd came home.

"What's that, Mommy? You get a present?" He saw it was flowers. "Ah."

Emma couldn't let him see her throw it away. That would be hard to explain.

"Hey, look, Mommy. They're in an owl." He wanted to hold it. "Cool."

Todd was helping her set the table when they heard Charles's car in the driveway. Emma didn't go to the door as she usually did.

"Busy day," Charles said. He was in great spirits. "Tell you what, Todd. Maybe we can go to King's Dominion when school's out." He went to kiss Emma, but she turned away to get olive oil for his arugula and cucumber salad. During dinner, she didn't speak to him except to answer his questions with a "yes" or "no."

The days were getting longer, and there was still plenty of light for Todd and Charles to go out and play catch after they ate. Emma stayed inside and busied herself washing the dishes. Her hands were shaky, and she broke a glass putting it onto the drain board.

That night, she closed the bedroom door behind them. Charles was still ebullient. "Emma, you wouldn't believe how much money I'm getting for life coaching."

"Uh-huh. And apparently you get flowers, too." She pointed to the owl vase she'd put on the dresser.

Charles picked up the card and read it. "Mmm."

"That's all you have to say, Charles?"

"Don't you have to put water in the vase?"

Emma took off an instruction card that was hooked around one of the flowers. "Let me see. It says, 'Discard flowers immediately and use vase to hold all gigolo pay.'"

She pulled out the flowers and threw them into the waste basket. Charles's mouth gaped open. "Emma! What's gotten into you these past few days?"

"I'm the only one who's allowed to send you flowers, Charles."

He was still hung up on "gigolo pay," apparently. He said, "Life coaching is a legitimate field, Emma." He took out his wallet. "Look. Another three hours, another $450." He pulled out a wad of bills. "There's, let me see, three times $450 right there." He tried to give it to her, but she wouldn't touch it.

"Stick it in that owl there," she told him. "Or, better yet, give it back."

"You want me to stop life coaching and go back to tutoring English?" As he said this, his mood changed. His eyes dulled to a flat gray.

"Go back? You mean you've quit tutoring? What about that guy you were so pleased to be helping? N-gok or something."

Charles sat down on the bed. "Tran. He goes by his last name. Americans have a hard time with the first. And the middle name . . . . Yeah, it's a shame. Tran works nights and weekends now. The only time he has off is during the day, when I'm at work."

"Or life coaching."

Charles, as she might have expected, missed the sarcasm. "So we had to give it up. It takes him an hour and a half to get to the tutoring center and back on the bus. Poor thing. It only takes ten minutes each way by car." His brow lifted in a frown. "I went to his house on my lunch break a couple of times, but that was stretching out the break too long. Maybe I can find somebody else to tutor him."

They sat silently for a time. Emma felt her respect slowly reviving for the man who wanted to help parents struggling to feed their families and help immigrants like Tran working to make a new life for themselves. He put his arm around her, and she closed her eyes.

Emma knew Charles wanted to make love to her. But as they lay there, even when she closed her eyes, she imagined the owl vase was watching them.

10

Crabgrass

The houses on Shady Park Lane were all slight variations of popular post-war designs. Cedar shingle or clapboard Cape Cods or arts-and-crafts Sears bungalows. Most had a garage in the back yard, but not Emma's. There was just a driveway. That needed resurfacing, too. At least, that's what Britney told her.

Britney also said Emma needed to work on her lawn. The neighbors on both sides already had lush green grass. Soon they would begin watering their lawns, and you'd hear the thrashing of sprinklers all along the street.

Maybe she could at least work on her front yard, the part that could be seen from the road. She tramped down some mole tunnels, then got the special tool her mother had given her for digging up dandelions. You had to jam the digger deep into the ground. It took some effort to lever the plants up by the roots. She dug up one after another, then gave up. There seemed to be no end to them.

And the digger didn't work on crabgrass. The roots were too spread out in the dry ground. Apparently, crabgrass didn't need a lot of water. She punched the dirt around the stiff, yellowish grass and pulled on it with her hands. Only the loose blades on the top came up. This was the strongest, most persistent plant life she'd ever seen. She almost had to admire it. She dug at it some more and then stopped. Not because she was tired but because it felt pointless. First-world problems— that's what Andre called dandelions and crabgrass. Maybe he was right to be amused at people who worried about them.

She took the digger back inside and washed her hands,

elbows, and knees. Was digging up dandelions and crabgrass really how she'd imagined spending her prime years? This wasn't what she pictured herself doing back when she was in the college Social Action Force.

Todd wouldn't be home from school for hours. She put on a skirt and blouse and found Tran's telephone number, which Charles had written on the kitchen calendar. She called. Tran couldn't understand her well, but she got across the idea that she was coming to tutor him in place of Charles. In his apartment, not in the community college center.

She ignored the roar and rattle underneath her car as she drove up North-South Highway towards the city. The farther north she got, the more congested the highway was, and the more it was lined with auto body shops, tire and battery stores, and liquor stores.

Ngoc Dung Tran's apartment was in the basement of the gray brick Northbrook complex just on the county side of the tracks marking the city line. There was a large lot behind the buildings but nothing Emma could identify as a brook unless it was the dry ditch that ran along the entry road.

Tran's wife opened the door. She was slender with straight black hair and skin as shining and white as the face of the baby she was holding. She didn't speak English and bowed instead, guiding Emma in with her free hand.

The baby smelled like he needed his diaper changed. It was all he was wearing, probably because of the heat. There was no air conditioning in the apartment, and there was only a single half-window high on the back wall at sidewalk level.

It immediately struck Emma that there was no furniture at all. This was the living room-dining room, she supposed. There were piles of clothes in different places on the floor. A huge cloth sack of rice lay next to a large rice cooker, also on the floor, beside an old-fashioned black telephone plugged into the wall. Cup Noodles and Ramen packages were piled up next to a single electric burner with a pan on it. Rows of unrecognizable seasonings in red and green bottles sat on the floor next to the burner. And a stack of teacups, one inside the other, leaned against the wall. Emma didn't see a single toy.

The door to one of the two other rooms was open, and Emma could see there was no furniture in there either. She saw piles of sheets, pillows, and blankets. Also what looked like a very old television with rabbit ears, not plugged in. She wondered if they'd retrieved it from the dumpster outside that she'd parked next to.

Mrs. Tran smiled, putting a folded blanket down for Emma to sit on while she boiled water in the pan. She mimed putting on a tie as she pointed to the closed door. It opened, and Tran came out, wearing black trousers, a white shirt, and a black tie. Apparently, he considered being tutored a formal activity. He knelt and bowed in front of Emma. With two hands and bowed head he held out a well-worn booklet. *Practice for American Citizenship*.

Emma said, "Can you read this, Mr. Tran?"

"I read," he answered.

His wife, still carrying her baby, put a cup of tea on the floor next to Emma.

"I present you my wife," Tran said. "Hue Tran Thieu." Emma paused a moment. At first, she thought he'd said "Hue Tran, too."

"*Enchantée*," Thieu said, bowing again.

Tran showed Emma into the bedroom and pointed out a higher stack of folded blankets where she could sit. His wife carried the tea into the room. Emma looked at the book while Tran sat cross-legged opposite her in perfect silence.

"All right. Here," Emma said. "Questions You May Be Asked in the Naturalization Interview." This section was filled with light pencil marks in Vietnamese over almost every word. "Maybe I'll ask you these questions and you see if you can answer them." She cleared her throat. Tran sat as motionless as a statue of Buddha.

"Who was the first president of the United States?"

Tran smiled. "Jo-ji Uaseeto."

"Very good," Emma said. "Let's see if you can say it more like I do."

They had gone over five or six questions when a dark haired little boy burst into the room carrying a whiffle ball.

"Papa. Play catch baseball with me."

Tran's wife called out something in Vietnamese, and the boy noticed Emma sitting there. He bowed. "I am sorry, teacher." He backed out of the room.

Tran worked five days a week from 7 p.m. till 3 a.m. and 8 a.m. to 8 p.m. on Saturday and Sunday.

"I can be your tutor," Emma told him. "Here, in your house."

As Emma left the apartment, Tran's wife handed her an envelope, bowing low.

"No." Emma shook her head. "You don't have to pay me. It's all right."

She walked outside with Tran and his son.

"My name is Henry," the boy told her. "I am five."

The pale green lot behind the building was empty except for mothers carrying their babies and watching their toddlers chase each other. The older kids were in school.

Tran and his son played catch with the whiffle ball. Henry dropped a throw from his father, and the ball rolled towards Emma. She picked it up and lobbed it straight into Henry's glove. Tran's mouth gaped. Emma tried not to smile.

There were so many apartments in the complex, and obviously so many children living there, Emma wondered how the grass on the lot survived the heavy use it must get. Maybe it was something special, something her neighborhood Little

League could use. She looked at it more closely. Crabgrass.

Emma's home phone rang when she opened the door.

"Mrs. Bovant? This is LaKisha. From Social Services? Just calling to see if Charles is all right. He doesn't take sick leave very often, so—"

"Sick?" She thought a moment, then lied, "Oh, right. Thanks. He's—he's sleeping now." Emma felt her face flush.

"That's probably the best thing for him. We hope he's better soon."

It wasn't like Charles to lie. OK, he might have said he was sick so he could save his vacation time to work on the house. But she'd never known him to lie about anything. His problem was more the other way around. Like when they applied for their mortgage and Charles volunteered that Emma might be in danger of losing her job. Which was true, but they didn't get the loan, and they had to go to another bank with Charles promising this time to let Emma do the talking.

He didn't lie, and he didn't suspect other people would, either. The realtor who sold them the house said they could certainly refinance at a much lower rate within a year. Emma's mother's comment: "And he believed it? The dear boy." Charles's naiveté was something Emma always loved about him. But she had learned it could cause problems.

Todd dropped his backpack next to the door. "Want to play catch, Mommy?"

She offered to take him to the Nottingham Estates field since Little League was starting on Saturday.

"They're working on the grass there. Besides, kids aren't supposed to play there by themselves."

Emma must have looked confused.

"You know. Without a coach. Chip's mom made the rule. They don't want the kids to get hurt or anything when their parents aren't there." He shrugged his shoulders. "That's what Chip's mom says."

Emma grabbed Todd's baseball hat from the knob on the wall. "Come on, Todd. I know a place you can play."

The sprawling Northbrook lot was packed with kids now that school had let out. Emma heard as much Spanish being shouted as English. The younger kids were playing catch with a whiffle ball behind Tran's building. Todd ran over and joined them. He played with Henry for a while, but Emma could tell he was getting bored. Too big for this group. He kept glancing farther out onto the field.

A hardball game was going on out there, using a blue dumpster at the other end of the lot for a backstop and tires for bases. The kids ranged from a little older than Todd to teenagers. They had one bat and one ball. There were gloves, but not one for everybody. When one side came up to bat, they tossed their gloves to boys going out to take the field.

Emma went to take Todd's place in whiffle ball. "Go ahead out on the field, Todd. I bet they ask you to play."

Todd jogged out towards the log marking the pitcher's mound. He said something to the pitcher, who pointed to the outfield. Todd grinned back at Emma as he took up his position as the second outfielder on the team—sort of center-right.

Henry tossed Emma the ball, smiling. "Infield practice."

She bounced one over the ground towards a girl younger than Henry.

"Fly ball," Henry called, and Emma tossed one into the air. They kept her busy. Finally she said she was getting tired.

Somebody tapped her on the arm.

"Missy Bovan." Tran's wife, baby in one arm, beamed at Emma. She indicated a concrete slab of a bench. "Shit here."

Thieu was picking up English fast by mouthing the answers to the citizenship test questions along with Tran. Emma thought it best to correct her pronunciation of *sit*.

69

Thieu bowed her appreciation. She looked out onto the field, eyes lifted as if trying to recall something. Finally, she exclaimed, "We the people!"

11

Universal knee pads

"Take the field, Sharks. Batter up, Bears." It was the first game of the season for the eights and nines, and the teenage umpire was trying to hurry things up and get the game started. The two parent coaches were shouting and in some cases taking the boys by the shoulders and moving them to the correct positions.

Andre had come to their house unannounced, and when he saw they were leaving for the game, he followed along. Charles, Emma, Andre, Britney, and twenty or so Little League parents sat on a low metal grandstand behind the backstop. Esmeralda put down a cooler beside the stands and sat on it. She wore a black and orange baseball cap, and her face was glowing. "Love baseball very much," she sang out to Emma.

"Go, Bears! Go, Bears! Go, Bears!" Britney shouted.

The coaches were pitching. Todd was up next. He swung the bat more confidently than some of the others. The open play at Tran's Northbrook lot might have done him some good.

"Does that helmet fit him?" Britney stood up. "Would that really protect him if he got hit? Who approves these things?"

Emma tapped the bench beside her. "Come on. Sit down, Brit. It's an old helmet, but it's fine. Let's watch the game. They're so cute."

Emma didn't yell *eye on the ball* or *wait for a good one* or *swing if it looks good* like lots of the other mothers did. She didn't want to imply she knew how to bat better than the kids themselves. Swing if it looks good—*like I do*? Give me a break.

Todd popped up into the infield. "Drop it," Britney yelled. One of the other mothers gave her a dirty look. By the time the third baseman did drop it, Todd was already closing in on second. The throw to second was wild, and the outfielders weren't ready to back it up. Todd rounded third, and the coach waved him in for an in-the-park home run. "Yay! Yay! Yay!" Britney shouted. "Woo-hoo!" She nudged Emma. "You better go hydrate him."

"What? Oh, you mean water? They have bottles under their bench."

"And where did that water come from? I brought my own for Chip. You want Esmeralda to take him some?"

"No. Look, Britney." Chip was stepping up to the plate—in a shiny new helmet with matching batting gloves.

"Chip! Chip! Chip! Go, Chip!" Britney stamped her feet on the metal stands.

Ball one.

Ball two.

"Come on, Chip. Swing! Get a hit."

Ball three.

"Hit the ball, Chip!" Britney was holding her hands at her mouth. The coach who was pitching could usually throw a strike. Britney's shouting might have been distracting him. He glared at her but said nothing.

Chip hunched over, presenting a tiny strike zone. Ball four. Chip was on base.

"Oh, gosh. Hit the ball, Chip," Britney groused.

Charles spoke up for the first time. "He played it right, Britney. Just watch. Bet you anything he scores a run before the inning is over."

He did. Todd gave him a high five, and Britney sent Esmeralda over to the bench with Evian water to hydrate him. Andre, in unbelievably short shorts, followed her, possibly thinking the game was over, then noticed and came back.

Charles introduced him to Britney, but she was too involved in Chip's game to pay much attention. "Come on, Chip!" she shouted. "Catch it if it comes to you."

Andre commented, "I'm surprised to see how all these boys like to play baseball."

"It's our national sport," Emma noted.

A ball dribbled through the shortstop's legs into shallow left field.

"Get it, Chip! That's yours. Get that ball. Move!" Britney was on her feet again.

When the ball dribbled through Chip's legs, too, Andre remarked, "He looks more like fishing would be his sport."

Britney shot him a warning look. They heard one of the other mothers say, "Those giant knee pads might be slowing him down." Britney turned in her direction. "They can't be," she called out. "Top safety rating, suitable for any sport."

Andre was pursuing his own train of thought. "I always liked fishing as a child. I still do."

Strike three! The first inning was finally over, and the Bears came back in to the bench. Britney and some of the other mothers rushed over with orange sections. "Quick energy," Britney said. "Vitamin C."

The kids didn't really look tired to Emma. She wondered if Charles would ask if the oranges were organic. He did.

Andre put his finger to his temple. "Charles, Emma, how about bringing Todd down to the river to go fishing tomorrow?"

"Maybe," Emma said. "But Todd can't swim. I worry about him going out in a boat."

"We can fish from the pier." Andre grinned, his eyes gleaming. "If you want to be extra sure he's safe, we can get him some of those universal knee pads. I hear they're suitable for any sport."

12

Surf and turf

They couldn't go fishing because Charles had accepted an invitation from Bea to a barbecue at her villa. Andre was invited, too. Emma agreed to go only because Todd begged her to let him practice swimming in Bea's pool. It was warm for spring. He was bouncing up and down in his seat as their VW beetle pulled into the villa driveway. Britney's SUV was there, along with a black Mercedes. A column of smoke rose from the back yard. They could hear men's loud laughter and Britney's unmistakable chatter. Bea minced barefooted along the flagstone pathway to greet them, bulging out of a chartreuse bikini, two Martinis in her hand. She touched her cheek on Emma's and gave her one glass, then did the same with Charles, touching his back with her free hand. Old friends.

Charles put the six-pack of beer he'd brought down on a table already spread with elaborate hors d'oeuvres. The beer looked out of place, but Charles didn't seem to notice. Britney's Esmeralda whisked it into the house, and another woman who spoke only Spanish brought smoked salmon cornets and shrimp bruschetta to the table.

"Todd!" Chip swallowed a mouthful of potato chips and ran to the pool. "Watch how I can swim."

Britney shouted out, "No running. Chip, I said no running. Come here. Put on your life jacket. Look at you. You need more sunblock. It's practically all washed off." She set her drink down on the patio to root through a Celebrity Cruise bag she kept beside her chair, retrieving flippers, goggles, and nose clips but no sunblock.

"I've got some in the car he can spray on, Brit," Emma

offered.

"Oh, hi. No the sprays are bad for you. Cancer. Ah, here it is."

While Britney lathered Chip up, her husband Derek, in white Bermuda shorts and high black socks, approached Emma and Charles, smoking a cigar. He was with a man in a silky long-sleeved white shirt and long black pants. Pastor Mitchell Rainey.

"We met at the Fontainbleau," the pastor reminded them. He handed Charles and Emma each a card identifying himself as Pastor of the Church of the Invokers of Jesus. "So," he said to Charles. "Bea tells me your friend Andre will be coming today." He checked his Rolex. "You told him we're starting at two o'clock, didn't you, Bea? Oh, well. I guess he might be running into traffic. Huh-huh."

"Andre's not too exact about time," Charles explained.

"Interesting. Interesting. I'm dying to meet him." He held an olive on its toothpick and licked off the last of the Martini. "He's our neighbor, after all. Bea's neighbor, I should say." He gave Bea a wink.

Emma saw Todd running for the pool with Chip and went over. She dipped her foot in. Sure enough, the water was very warm. She'd brought her bathing suit, but the air was still too cool for her to go swimming. She glanced over at Bea. Definitely too cool for a bikini, for cripes sake.

Todd could float a little, holding his breath and kicking, but he couldn't really swim. "Watch, guys. I can float." He kicked away from the side of the pool.

Chip adjusted his goggles. He'd had a lot of lessons and was wearing a life jacket, but he looked a little scared of the water. He stood on tiptoes even though it was only up to his chest in the shallow end.

Britney came to the poolside to check on her son. "You're watching the kids, right?" She raised her brows at Emma and went to get another drink.

Emma looked across the lawn to see what Charles was doing. He was talking to Esmeralda. Probably about the food. Bea was sitting in a deck chair, and Pastor Mitch stood looking down at her, taking in the view of Bea's half-naked bosom. Better him than Charles.

When Bea got up and went into the house, Pastor Mitch came to the pool and looked down at Emma. He smiled, revealing big white teeth—veneers?

"Nice place, don't you think, Emma? Look at that view of the river across the road. Beautiful."

"It is."

"Bea tells me you're interested in real estate."

"Oh, I don't know." His stare caused a chill to run through her body. "Excuse me, Mr., uh Pastor. I'm going to find Charles."

"He's in the library. Come, let me get you a drink."

"Later, if you don't mind."

Emma stood barefoot and shivering on the icy cold tile floor as her eyes grew accustomed to the darker interior of the house. She took a few steps and looked into a room with built-in shelves, all empty except for a few rows of real estate brochures. There was Charles standing with his back to her, his phone up to his ear. Bea stood behind him, her hand on one shoulder and her breast squished against his arm. She was bending her head towards his as if to listen in on the conversation. Neither noticed Emma standing just inside the doorway.

Charles ended the call and told Bea, "He went to the river first. He's on his way now."

Bea took his head in her hands and kissed him on the cheek. "Praise the Lord. Charles, I know Jesus sent you to me. I'm never going to let you go."

From outside, Derek's booming voice rang out. "Steak's

ready. Come and get it."

Emma's heart jumped into her throat as Charles and Bea turned and saw her standing there. They all froze. Emma glowered at Bea, gripping her hands into fists, forcing the woman she'd caught kissing her husband to speak first.

"Ah, Emma. I was just thanking Charles for helping me with something. I don't know what I'd do without him."

Emma waved her finger at her. "I'll see that you find out." She met Charles's dazed look. "And, Charles. This ridiculous woman? You're stupider than I thought." She turned and ran out, Charles and Bea following her.

The grill was smoking. Derek, in a red apron reading "Man in Charge," seemed to be ignoring his wife, focusing instead on forking pieces of filet mignon onto a tray.

"Emma, come over here," Britney called out. "I'm trying to explain something to Derek."

Engrossed in his culinary skills, Derek only nodded as his wife continued, "It's the look in Chip's eyes. Don't you think they're duller recently? That's one of the symptoms of EO-CLS according to the internet."

Suddenly, Britney stopped talking and gasped. "Wait! Emma, who's watching the kids? You let Esmeralda watch them?" She rushed off to the pool.

"EOCLS?" Emma asked Derek.

He shook his head. "Early Onset Chronic Lethargy Syndrome. She reads these mommy websites and—" He stopped as Emma smiled. "You know what I mean."

Charles came up and put his arm around Emma. She twisted away. Gently, though. She hated to make a scene.

As the guests were filling their plates and carrying them to a long table, Andre arrived carrying something wrapped in wet newspaper. "I just caught it," he beamed. "Bluefish."

Knives and forks dropped onto plates. Everybody looked up to see the person they were waiting for. Andre wore a yellow sleeveless top, skin tight over his well-developed torso, and tight matching polyester shorts that didn't reach much below his crotch. His couture had become less conservative than when Emma had known him in college.

Honestly, she thought, how can Charles not just admit this guy is gay?

Pastor Mitch put his plate down. "Ah, the guest of honor, I presume."

Andre stood there holding the fish out away from his body, letting it drip. He looked so out of place Emma felt a rush of sympathy for him and was glad to see Charles come and make the introductions.

"Just call me 'Pastor Mitch,' is fine," Mitch Rainey told Andre.

Since Andre was holding a dripping fish, no one could shake his hand.

Esmeralda came to the rescue. "Jou bring fish? Is good. I cook. Gracias."

Still, nobody shook Andre's wet hand. Bea put her arm through Andre's and led him to the end of the table. "Oouu, muscles," she cooed.

Charles said he would pass on the steak and wait for the fish that Andre had just caught in the river. He stood next to Emma and lowered his voice. "With the growth hormones they give to cattle, you never know what gets into the meat."

"That's not the kind of hormones I'm worrying about right now, Charles."

Bea called out, "Charles, Emma, come sit over here with Andre. Everybody sit down. It's time to ask the Lord's blessing."

Todd, Chip, Derek, Britney, even Pastor Mitch stopped chewing their food, looking sheepish.

Bea acted as if nothing had happened, nothing had been said in the library. She put Emma on one side of Andre, and she sat on the other, with Charles next to her. "Everybody hold hands, please."

Emma was impressed by Andre's firm grip. Pastor Rainey's hand was cold and flabby.

"Pastor Rainey, would you give the blessing?"

Pastor Rainey swallowed his mouthful, coughed, and called on Jesus to "just bless this food to our bodies," a phrase that puzzled Emma. She looked up, but Pastor Mitch went on, asking Jesus to "just show everyone at the table what he is calling them to do." Apparently, he was making it clear that he wanted just a few things. He wasn't asking much.

The ritual gave Emma the creeps. Both hands holding hers were sticky. She reached for a napkin when the prayer was over.

Ignoring the mounds of food Bea heaped on his plate, Andre launched into a dissertation, aimed at nobody in particular, on the origin of prayer before meals in ritual sacrifices performed in the Hindu, Egyptian, Greek, and Hebrew traditions. Eventually, he looked down at his plate. "This is interesting," he said, and launched into an exposition of the American Indian and other ethnic sources of the food traditionally served at barbecues in America. He never lifted a fork, instead asking if he could have a cup of tea.

"Jes," Esmeralda nodded.

"With a spoon of honey in it, please."

Whenever Andre was well rested and hadn't come out of his house for several weeks, it was hard to get him to stop talking. Bea tried. "Oh, Andre. Sorry to interrupt."

It didn't work. Emma saw Bea put her hand on Andre's leg as she said it again. Andre didn't seem to feel it. He had an amazing ability to focus on his own train of thought. He paused a discourse on the origin of May Day, which he assumed they were celebrating, only to sip his tea.

Esmeralda brought a platter to the table. "Fish," she said.

Andre added, "Fresh from the river."

"Now that sounds good," Charles said, taking a large piece.

The sun was starting to set, giving everything on the patio a reddish glow. Pastor Mitch stood up and looked across the river. "Everybody, you've got to see this."

A huge orange sun was sinking into the river that sparkled with ripples of red and yellow. Everybody turned to watch it go down. "Somebody take a picture," Pastor Mitch called out.

"I have plenty of pictures in the library," Bea declared. She put her arm through Andre's. "It's Pastor Mitch and I together who built this place," she told him. "How do you like the villa? It's quite a change from what used to be here, isn't it?"

"Old Man Grayson and his wife," Andre said. "I used to play pinochle with them in their little house here. With the Trouts, who lived over there." He pointed towards the lots that had been cleared between the villa and his own house. "I wonder what happened to them. One day they just weren't here."

Bea glanced at Pastor Mitch. "Well, as a matter of fact I can tell you the people in both of those houses are now living in condos in Florida. Isn't that wonderful?"

Andre frowned. "That's funny. They always joked about people moving to Florida. They said they were living in the best spot on earth right now."

"Anyway, you've got to admit this place is an improvement."

Andre looked puzzled. "Honestly, I liked it better the way it was before Old Man Grayson's house was torn down. There were trees and honeysuckle and Virginia creeper. The houses blended in. Didn't draw attention to themselves. Like they were part of the riverside. You saw green, not—" He waved his hand across the massive brick and stucco of the villa and the land that had been cleared to make way for its patio, garage, and pool.

"But you can't say you'd rather live in one of those shacks than here." Bea was becoming argumentative. "Good Lord. They didn't even have air conditioning."

"Like my house," Andre said. "I like keeping the windows open. I can smell the evening breeze that comes over the river. I can hear the splash of the water on my pier."

"That's right," Pastor Mitch changed the subject. "You have your own pier. It's tough to get permission to build a new one nowadays, but if you already have one, you can 'enhance' it."

"I wouldn't want any more piers cluttering up the shoreline." Andre frowned. "It's bad enough with all those powerboats churning up waves and scaring the fish."

Pastor Mitch pointed towards the river. "Look at those beauties. You mean to tell me you wouldn't like to have one of those boats yourself?"

"I'm fine with my rowing dinghy," Andre retorted. "I don't need to be spilling gas and oil into the river and contaminating the fish."

Emma heard Charles cough and turned to see him holding his hand over his mouth.

Before Charles dropped his trousers on the floor, he took out his wallet and held out $60. Emma folded her arms. "Now what the heck is that, Charles? For some coaching you did today?"

"It is, actually. Bea says a life coach should charge in ten-minute increments. So for even a few minutes of coaching, she pays me—"

"I know what it means, Charles." She realized she was starting to cry. "So just describe right now what this coaching was that you did for her today."

"I called Andre. Anything I do that helps her towards achieving her goals counts."

Through watery eyes, Emma glared at him.

Charles bit his lip. "Emma, I guess there's something I need to tell you."

She gripped the bedpost, preparing for the worst.

"Bea kissed me. Maybe you saw it. I'm sorry."

"Great. You're sorry." She sniffled. "At the state fair, it used to be a dollar a kiss. Now it's $60?"

Charles ignored this. "Not sure I can explain why she did it. Grateful, probably." He tried to take Emma's hand, but she wouldn't let him. "I know what you might be thinking. It's possible her single life has resulted in frustration of her latent libidinal needs and—"

"Right, Charles. That's what it must have been. You're going to sleep on the couch tonight. You're making a fool of me."

Charles looked hurt.

She kicked his pants out of the way and got into bed with a headache. It was a clear night, and a bright full moon now came through the window, casting a glow on her dresser—and on the white owl vase sitting on it. The owl's eyes seemed to be mocking her.

She put the pillow over her head, turned to one side, then the other. She threw off the sheet. She held her throbbing head in both hands. Finally, she got out of bed, kicking Charles's socks out of the way, and went downstairs to get an aspirin from the kitchen cabinet.

When she walked by the living room, she saw Charles lying on the couch talking on his phone. "Monday?" he was saying. "I guess I can take another day's vacation."

He ended the call as Emma came into the room.

"Charles!"

"Oh, hi, Emma."

"More life coaching business, is it?"

"Yeah. That was Bea. She needs me Monday. For the full day."

"No way, Charles."

"I know. I planned to use the five vacation days I have left to fix the ceiling and paint the downstairs. But with this life coaching we'll be able to hire somebody to do it. Not to mention swimming lessons and—"

"Uh huh. You think you're going to get all that with just kisses?"

13

Trouble in Paradise

Emma didn't speak to Charles at breakfast. Todd noticed something was wrong. "Mommy, you didn't say good-bye to Daddy."

She hugged him and said she was a little mad at Daddy. That was all.

"About what?" Todd pulled on her arm.

"We had an argument about life coaching. Don't worry about it, Sweetie."

As soon as Todd left for school, she got into her car. All night long she'd brooded over Charles's insistence on meeting with Bea again. This meeting was going to be in her office, he told her. "And no more kissing, I promise." Charles had smiled, but Emma hadn't.

The Focus was getting louder every day. When she took off down Shady Park Lane, it sounded like she was driving a race car. The crossing guard at the corner gawked and stretched out her arm to hold the children back. Emma roared out onto North-South Highway towards Bea's office. When she got there, she demanded to sit in on the coaching session.

"These sessions are private. I'm sorry." Bea's secretary took off her reading glasses and dropped them on a chain around her neck. "I could make an appointment—"

Ignoring her, Emma opened the door and went in. Surprisingly, Pastor Mitch was there, too.

"Sorry to interrupt a *private session*," Emma announced.

Pastor Mitch rose and held out his hands. "Emma, dear! Come have a seat. This is fortunate. You may be of some help here."

Charles wrung his hands. "Well, this obviously isn't going to be a life coaching session."

"Don't worry," the pastor told him. "You're on the clock. Right, Bea?"

"Definitely." Bea put some colorful brochures into Emma's hands. Her own villa and views of the Piskasanet River were featured. Nobody spoke. Apparently, Emma was expected to look through them.

Pastor Mitch said, "Looks good, doesn't it?" He gave Emma a wry smile. "But there's trouble in Riverside Paradise."

Bea started, "Trouble, yes. Yet we believe Jesus has sent Charles to us to—"

"Leave all that for a moment," the pastor interrupted. "Now that we're all here, let's get to the point. The trouble in paradise is Andre. His house. And his mother's nearby."

"And from what we saw of him at the barbecue," Bea said, "it looks like it's going to be hard to convince him, and probably his mother, to sell."

"It'll be impossible," Charles declared.

Bea went to his chair and started to put her hand on his but stopped herself. "You're his friend."

"His only friend, from what we can find out," the pastor added.

Bea folded her palms in a prayerful gesture. "And we just think you might be the only one who can convince him to accept a fantastic price for his property."

"You don't know Andre," Charles insisted.

"No," Emma agreed, smiling at their predicament.

Pastor Mitch insisted that everybody must have a price. He turned to Charles. "You, Andre, both of you can profit big-time if we can make a deal."

Charles raised his voice for the first time Emma ever remembered. "Deal? You brought me here to make a deal? I thought I was here as a life coach, not some kind of self-in-

85

terested plotter without a conscience. I could never advise Andre to sell his property. He's perfectly happy as he is. Not only that, next time I see him, I'm going to advise him *not* to sell." He stood up, took Emma's hand, and she followed him out of the office.

In the hallway, Charles was still breathing hard. "I know, Emma. I just messed up a chance for us to move up the ladder. I just couldn't—"

Emma kissed him. "I'm proud of you."

"It seemed like Bea wanted me to put pressure on Andre. I can't believe it."

"Uh-huh. Let's go get some coffee and talk."

He squeezed her hand. "I think I better go back to the office. Sorry."

Charles went to work, and she went to tutor Tran.

Tran's apartment was steamy and smelled of rice and cooking oil, but visiting this family felt like a breath of fresh air to Emma. Thieu had just cooked a kind of rice fritter with powdered sugar on it to serve with tea. Tran and Henry came in from the bedroom and sat on the floor to watch her eat it. The three looked at each other nervously until Emma said it was delicious.

"*Délicieux*?" Tran's wife put three more fritters into a paper bag for Emma to take home.

Tran and Henry were going over something Tran had written in his notebook. Tran read out *You are welcome here, teacher. We thank you for your help.* Henry held up his hand to give his father a high-five.

Even more Vietnamese words were penciled into the margins of Tran's citizenship book. She noticed his wife was now actually repeating aloud the English words as Tran said them. Thieu would probably be as ready to take the test as Tran when it was time.

"You and Mr. Todd coming today for baseball?" Henry

asked.

"Um, sure." Although the Nottingham Estates field was mowed and vacant, the kids weren't allowed to play there unsupervised. So she drove Todd up to Northbrook again after school. She tossed a few balls with Henry, then sat on the bench and talked to Thieu while Todd played out on the big kids' field.

On the way home, Emma's car had a new roar. She noticed a few kids on the lot turn and look. A few laughed.

Soon after they turned onto North-South Highway, Emma heard a quick *Woo-uuu* behind her and saw a blue light flashing in her mirror.

"License and registration."

"I'm sorry. I didn't think I was going too fast."

"Ma'am, it's a violation to drive with an open exhaust." The policeman took out his pad. "I'm going to give you a warning. This gives you four days to get the vehicle repaired. Driving it unrepaired after that will be cause for a $300 fine and impounding. Have a nice day."

She had organic cabbage, and there were organic carrots and mung beans in the fridge. The beef was certified organic. It looked older and grayer than the regular beef, but she'd bought it for the label. As for dessert, there it was in a paper bag. She'd tell Charles it was cooked in canola oil, which he declared was better for you than corn oil.

Todd was still in the back yard throwing himself pop flies when Charles came home beaming. "Guess what. Bea called me back and apologized. The life coaching is still on." He slapped $300 down on the kitchen table, grinning. "And here's the best part. Bea's going to pay for me to go to that life coach conference in New York. She says whatever makes me a better coach will benefit her. She's driving me up. She has some friends she'll stay with during the conference."

"You must be kidding. Charles, you're not going to New York. This Bea thing has to stop."

"You're the one who wanted me to bring in more money, Emma."

"Not this way."

"Listen, Bea says she can get me life coaching jobs in New York after conference hours that could add up to $1,200 a day while I'm there. And she'll help me find more clients when I come back."

"You don't think it's strange she suddenly wants to whisk you away to New York? Right after you told her you'd advise Andre not to sell?"

"It's a life coaching conference."

"No, Charles. You're not going off to New York with some woman."

"Be reasonable, Emma. You never thought Social Services paid me enough. Well, now I'm going to change that. I'm going."

Emma was crying. "If you do, Charles, don't come back."

II

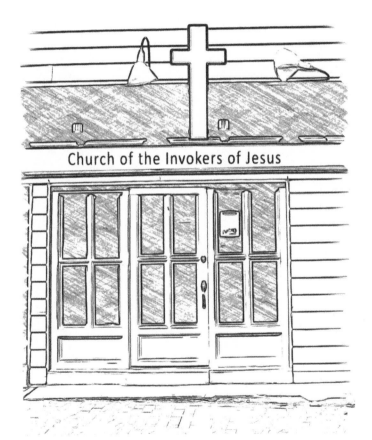

Church of the Invokers of Jesus

14

Stress

A car honk woke Emma from a deep sleep. She jumped up and pulled the bedroom window curtain aside, rubbing her eyes. Charles was getting into a shiny black convertible, its top down. Bea sat at the wheel, her hair in a polka dot scarf. She turned and gave Charles a pat on the knee before speeding off. Bitch.

Todd had a long face when he left for school. "How long is Daddy going to be gone? Will he be back tomorrow?"

Holding back tears, Emma told him it might be a long trip. They'd have to see.

"Bummer."

She kissed Todd and closed the door, then stomped into the kitchen and flipped open her iPad. As she expected, Online Banking said her credit card was maxed out. The checking account was down to almost nothing. The *Piskasanet County Police Department Warning of Violation* lay on the dining room table. Charles, of course, hadn't noticed it. Two days left to get her car fixed. She took the coffee can from the fridge. It probably wouldn't be enough.

The owl vase sat smirking at her. She clenched her hair in her hands. Maybe she really was going crazy. She swallowed hard, and with trembling fingers reached in and took out a handful of cash.

The customers and mechanics all turned and stared when her car roared into Cut-rate Exhaust. She was sniffling when she got out.

"Cheer up, lady. Don't worry. We can fix it." The manager

was shorter than Emma, skinny, with long, greasy hair and black fingernails. He said, "Just give me the keys and take a seat there. Help yourself to the coffee."

She felt like hugging him. "Thanks," she sobbed, fidgeting with her handbag, determined to pull herself together.

When the job was done, like a poor person without a credit card, she paid in cash. She still had over fifty dollars left.

Tran was ready when she got there, in his white shirt and tie. "You and Todd coming back for baseball today?" he asked. "Henry hoping."

"No, not today. Because I have to talk to somebody and—"

Tran's eyes glazed over at her explanation. He smiled and bowed.

On the way home, she stopped at a Tastee Donuts shop on North-South Highway. Then she stopped at Discount Foods and bought two pounds of (regular) ground beef, a head of (regular) lettuce, and some plump red tomatoes that had most likely been nourished with man-made fertilizer. As she started to push her cart towards the checkout counter, she stopped, turned around, and picked up a pound of bacon. She paid for it all in cash.

It was still only one o'clock. To keep from thinking about Charles, she had to keep busy. She dragged a step ladder up from the basement. With pages of the *Ledger* spread over the table and floor, she put a bandana over her hair and started scraping the loose paint from the ceiling with a putty knife. Years ago, a salesman from a contracting company had told them a house as old as theirs certainly contained lead paint and it needed to be removed professionally. Charles had been about to sign a contract for the equivalent of six months' pay to have all the paint in the house removed. Emma stopped him. Charles's problem was he believed whatever people told him. Emma suggested they test the paint for lead first. Charles said, "He ought to know, but OK." The next day, Emma tested the paint herself. No lead.

She took Todd to Britney's when he got home from school. Chip beamed, showing off his new set of golf clubs.

"You look funny," Britney told Emma. "Kind of pale. How about a glass of wine."

Emma brushed off her cheeks and forehead. "I've been scraping plaster."

"What for? I mean, no, it's not just that."

Emma didn't want to talk about Charles and Bea. She told Britney she wanted to go back and finish scraping the ceiling, that was all.

As soon as she got back home, she took a shower, got dressed, and called Andre. He should be up by now. Her hands were trembling.

"Andre, it's Emma. I need to talk to you."

Andre's car pulled into the driveway behind the Beetle that Charles had left there when he took off with Bea. It was easy to recognize Andre's car. He had painted it himself with a paintbrush and a gallon of baby blue interior wall paint. The car had been starting to look a little drab, he'd explained.

"So what's going on?" Andre's eyes narrowed.

"Come in. I have donuts." They were already arranged on a plate beside Charles's chair.

Andre looked around. "Todd's not here? What time does he get home from school?"

Emma ignored this. "Tea? With some honey?"

While she went into the kitchen to get it, he raised his voice and kept talking to her, and his monologue continued as she set the tea on the table, which he didn't seem to notice. It was all about stress—the stress he noted in her and then stress in general as the debilitating force that everyone must avoid at all costs. Apparently he thought we should all live in a constant state of blissful relaxation.

Emma sat on the hassock in front of him. He went on without seeming to see her. There were meditations you could perform to eliminate stress, he said. Certain body positions were effective. People didn't realize the harm that could be caused by stress. From the States, from Europe, bourgeois men and women were going off to join the Islamic State. There could be only one explanation, the stress they felt at home. Some populations like those of Sweden, for example, were less affected by—

"Andre."

The fly landed but didn't bite. She knew he'd heard her, but he kept talking. Maybe it would be too stressful for him to interrupt the flow of his preposterous logic.

She tapped him on the shoulder and said, "Andre, I need you to talk to Charles."

"—real harm caused by letting stress build up to the point that—"

"Andre!" Exasperated, Emma leaned forward and put her hand over his mouth.

He stopped talking, made brief eye contact, then slowly leaned back in the chair with his eyes closed.

She held her breath, letting her fingers linger on his warm lips. An unexpected thrill ran through her body.

Andre reached up, touched her hand without pulling it away. Never in their college days had they shared a moment as intimate as this. She was breathing hard. Andre's lips were trembling. This wasn't what she'd intended.

She gently slipped her hand out from beneath his. "Andre, I'm sorry."

He lowered his hands onto her knees. "It's my fault. I shouldn't be here. Johan's gone. Now you're the only . . . ."

Emma felt a rush of tears welling in her head. All she could manage to say was "I'm sorry about Johan."

Andre's blue eyes were glittery. He shook his head. "I'll get over him, I guess." For a rare moment, he sat there speechless.

A lump of pity rose in Emma's throat.

Andre stood up. "I seem to be feeling a lot of stress right now. I think I'd better go."

She held him as he started for the door. "No. Don't go yet. About Charles—"

"Emma, please don't tell Charles. He's kind of, you know, naïve about some things. He probably likes to think Johan was just a friend. Does he have to know . . ." He looked down. ". . . anything?"

For a moment, the word "anything" kept her speechless. Andre was gripping her hand. Finally, she managed to answer, "No. Charles doesn't need to know. Don't worry, Andre." Then the reason she'd asked him to come returned to her. "But I need you to do me a favor."

15

Illicit behavior

Hamburgers with lettuce and tomato, Todd and Emma's favorite. Everything tasted fresher than what came off the organic shelf. Emma joked with Todd to keep him from thinking about his dad not being there.

"How's the Chipster doing? Still planning to be an astronaut or golf pro or whatever?"

"Heh-heh."

"How about Chelsea? Decided on her life career yet?"

"She got in trouble at school. Something about a paper she wrote."

"I'm sorry."

There was still time to throw a few balls in the back yard before it got dark. Emma was experiencing a surprising new freedom in having Todd all to herself. It was only after she had lain in bed with Todd, reading him an extra chapter until he fell asleep, that the sadness kicked in again. She dialed Charles's number, but there was no answer.

Emma was falling asleep in her bed reading an online article about equity skimming when her phone rang. Charles. "Hi, Baby. Still mad?"

"Are you coming home? Did Andre call you?"

"He did. How did you know?"

"What did he say?"

"Said he was thinking about selling his place to Bea and Pastor Mitch. Strange. Of course, I told him not to. He insisted I come back right away to talk about it."

"Oh. He did?" There was a pause. "So? Are you coming back? There's a train late tonight. I checked. I could pick you up at Penn Station in the city."

"Tonight? No. The conference is barely getting started."

"But Andre needs your support. You have to come back and convince him not to sell." Maybe this was deceitful. Andre had told her he'd never sell. But she knew if she just said, "You're my husband. I want you back," he might scoff and call this "hysterical anxiety."

Charles cleared his throat. "Actually, I wanted to tell you. I might be here in New York a few weeks or more."

Emma was too livid to speak.

"Bea's introduced me to other people here who want me to be their life coach. At least four of them. How about that?"

"Come home, Charles. Come home right now."

"Do you realize what an opportunity this is? I can't let it go."

"Come home."

"Bea says she'll pay for me to stay in the hotel for a while so I can coach my clients here."

Emma raised her voice. "*Bea says. Bea says.* Listen, Charles. If you don't come home right now, don't come home at all."

"But listen, Emma, I'll be bringing in plenty of money. You can get a new car. Get Todd those swimming lessons. Pave the driveway. Who knows? Maybe move to Nottingham Estates."

"I don't care about any of those things. Come home, do you hear me?"

"You're being irrational, Emma. What is this obsession you've developed? You have to get over it."

Emma closed her eyes, said nothing.

"Because this is something I have to do. You'll have to accept it. I'm staying here as long as it takes to get more practice life coaching and develop a network of clients for when I come back to Shady Park. That's final."

"If you don't come back right now, you're not welcome in

this house any more." She hung up.

Within an hour, the phone rang again. It was Andre. "I called him. Told him he needs to hurry back because I need his advice."

A catch in Emma's throat kept her from talking.

"I tried my best."

"Yes. Thanks, Andre. He's not coming back, though."

"I'm sorry, Emma. Still, I hope you won't tell him, you know, I guess he realizes my predilection. He never mentions it, but I wouldn't want him to think—"

"Don't worry, Andre."

She heard him breathe out a sigh. "Is Charles under some kind of stress? He asked if he could stay with me when he gets back. I couldn't believe it. He said, 'just in case.' What's going on, Emma?"

Pastor Mitch Rainey stood at the door, his Muppet mouth flapping—hoped he hadn't caught her at a bad time. "Emma, I have some good news. You're going to thank me." He squeezed her hand between his two clammy palms and held it even as she tried to wiggle it out.

"I was just leaving to go tutor—"

"You probably know what it's about. Charles told Bea that Andre seems to be coming around. Bea asked me to see if you can help reason with him."

"Me? No." She tried to put on an earnest face. "Maybe Charles could. If he comes back."

"Bea's keeping Charles busy in New York. So it's up to you and me." His chin jutted out when he grinned. "Emma, I want you to understand. We can make it worth your while." He looked at Charles's cracked leather chair. "Definitely. Definitely worth your while."

Emma took out her keys and slung her handbag strap over her shoulder. "Sorry, Pastor Mitch. I can't help you. Good luck with your Riverside Paradise. I have to go."

Backing out the door, the pastor grumbled, "This is a big mistake, Emma. I hope you don't end up regretting it."

After tutoring Tran, Emma got a text in the car but couldn't read it until she got home. It was from Andre: *Mitchell Rainey came here. Told him will only discuss sale if Charles is here. Right? He mentioned a job I might like at a youth center. What's going on?*

Emma decided to find out. While Todd was doing his homework, she called Pastor Mitch. He sounded elated. "Oh, yes," he said. "I paid a little visit to Mr. Smyth at his house. I find he's not after money. That's not what drives him." He snorted a chuckle. "I came to realize your Andre is, shall we say, eccentric, if you know what I mean. Covertly eccentric, I have to assume."

"I don't understand."

"I think you do. Anyway, he said he's currently unemployed. So I sent him to the Church of the Invokers of Jesus outreach location in Northbrook tomorrow for an interview. That's our branch that has a Youth Development Center attached."

"He's going to apply?"

"Definitely. He asked for a late afternoon appointment."

The outreach location of the Church of the Invokers of Jesus was very near the Northbrook Apartments, just inside the county limits on North-South Highway next to a Kwik Lube and across from Mike's Used Cars and Hourly Rentals. The church was a former brick hardware store with a cross on the door and a showcase window on either side with scenes from the Bible taped to the glass. A small handwritten sign in the corner of one window read: *Youth Develop Cent. in back.*

Emma drove behind the building. There were a few adjoining lots, one with an enormous blue dumpster in it. She parked in a spot she hoped belonged to the church. She didn't see Andre's pale blue car anywhere. She had time. Maybe she could find out what Pastor Mitch was up to.

She sat in her car and called the number on Pastor Mitchell Rainey's card. No answer. She got out and walked over to the building, stepped up on an empty soda crate, and peeped through a grimy back window.

At first, it looked like a bunch of kids Todd's age fighting. Then she figured it must be some sort of martial arts exercise with all the kids in shorts and T-shirts rather than the white Japanese robes and colorful belts the Nottingham kids wore to their aikido or karate lessons. Some girls in one corner were jumping rope. Two young women in tight-fitting jeans were leaning back against the wall, tapping on their cell phones while the children played.

Somebody touched her on the back. She jumped and slipped off the case, banging her ankle. Two muscle-hardened arms helped her to her feet. Andre.

"Didn't mean to scare you."

Emma's ankle hurt when she put weight on it. She held onto Andre.

"Easy," he said. "Maybe you need to sit down. My car's in that lot over there behind the dumpster."

"I'm all right." She gripped his shirt. "Listen, Andre, I don't think you should work here. That pastor's up to something."

The fly didn't bite. He held her with one arm, leaned down, and felt her ankle. "Not swollen. That's good, I think. The Sanskrit word for ankle is *gulpha*. There's an ancient text that mentions—"

"Andre, OK, let's go sit in my car over there."

He kept his arm around her back as they walked. Her ankle was feeling better already, but the arm on her back was comforting.

Andre had already applied for the job as youth counselor

at the Invokers. Not karate or anything, he told her. Reading books and helping the kids with their homework.

"You applied for a job wearing that?" He sat in the passenger seat wearing sandals, madras shorts, and a long-sleeved pink shirt with a tie. The tie had a green fish on it with a glowing blue eye. Emma couldn't help taking it in her hand. "I remember when we were in class together. You wouldn't have worn something like this then."

"Maybe I gave up trying to fit in."

This made Emma a little sad. "Anyway," she said, "I don't trust the pastor. It's not a good idea to work for him."

"I know. Employers have a limited view of the world, insisting on regimentation. Same hours every day. Five days a week. I told them that would be too stressful for me. I'd get there when I could. It didn't seem to bother them."

Emma started punching him in the shoulder. "Andre, believe me. You can't trust the pastor."

He stared at her as if trying to translate a difficult text in Sanskrit.

"Because, Andre, I think somehow you're being set up."

Emma lay in bed thinking about Charles. She couldn't believe his gall, acting as if it was acceptable to run off to New York with another woman. She called her mother. "I Googled *infidelity.com*, Mom. What Charles is doing is classic."

"Ye-e-s." Her mother drew the word out. "Normally. But Charles is, you know, don't get me wrong. I don't want to say gullible. Maybe trusting is the word."

"I know, but—"

"Hon, I'll help out with Todd. You know, if you need to go look for a job or anything."

Look for a job. That's what had gotten her in this mess to begin with. All she'd wanted was to stay in what politicians called the middle class. Well, that effort had backfired.

She Googled *localjobs.com*. Ugh. Nothing but work-at-home scams. Just the kind of thing Charles might fall for. He hadn't called her since she hung up on him. She picked up her phone but choked up before she could dial, so she decided to send him a text: *Charles, come home right now.* Then she worried that it wasn't strong enough. She sent another: *Or you're going to regret it.*

No response.

In the daytime, it was easier to keep from brooding about Charles. Since Todd liked playing on the Northbrook lot so much, Emma changed the tutoring to afternoons so she would only have to make one trip. Todd could play while she tutored Tran. When Chip found out about it, he wanted to come, too. Worried that Britney wouldn't approve, Emma pretended she was taking them to a Little League clinic, certain that the word "clinic" would satisfy Britney.

As she drove past the "Slow Children" sign on Nottingham Estates Lane which Britney had insisted the county put in near her house, Todd said, "Slow children. Heh-heh."

"What?"

"No. Nothing. Just thinking about Chip with his knee pads."

"Be nice, Todd."

When Britney started loading Chip's knee pads, helmet, batting gloves, and bat into the trunk of the Focus, Emma said he probably didn't need all that. The kids at the "clinic" didn't use anything but bat, ball, and usually a glove.

Britney said he certainly did need his protective gear. "Maybe I need to see this clinic for myself."

Not necessary, Emma assured her. It was a wonderful place to play baseball. The cooler of orange slices and Vita-Juice? "Sure, just put it in the trunk. Don't worry. I'll keep them hydrated."

In the car, Todd told Chip there was a "great guy named Juan" who didn't mind letting younger kids play. "He can pitch and hit really good. I'm going to start holding the bat like he does."

As soon as the car stopped, both boys ran onto the field with their gloves, abandoning Chip's additional gear and provisions. A handsome olive skinned boy of about fourteen waved in the lone outfielder on his side to take second base and motioned Todd and Chip to the outfield. Emma heard Todd yell, "All right! We're on Juan's side."

Tran was making good progress. After a few more tutoring sessions he could answer just about all the questions in the citizenship pamphlet. His pronunciation was a little rough, but Emma figured the naturalization interviewer would get what he was saying. Tran's wife had learned the answers, too—just from listening in—and Emma encouraged her to fill out the Application for Naturalization, as well. She'd help them with it.

"I don't know. I don't know," Tran said.

"No yet," his wife explained.

"Just fill it out and send it in," Emma insisted. "Anyway, it'll take six months to a year or more before they get around to interviewing you."

They knew, they knew.

It took persistent questioning before Emma realized they didn't have the $600 each they needed for the application and fees. "We send later," Tran assured her. "Study now, send paper later."

They had saved almost enough for Tran, they said, from what Tran made at the Grab 'n Go. Tran said he was hoping to become night manager when he became a citizen. "But have to wait and save first."

Emma tossed a ball with Henry for a while until some other boys gathered around to play with him. Then she sat alone on the bench, gloomy thoughts of Charles clouding her mind. The crack of a bat far out in the field where Todd was playing made her start. The ball shot fair inside the first base line deep into the outfield where Emma was sitting. Todd and Chip were too far away even to make a try for it.

"Little help!" Juan, the pitcher, held his hands to his mouth.

Emma jumped up and ran towards the ball. It looked like a sure home run. Her foot hit a dip in the ground, paining her sore ankle, and she fell forward—right onto the ball. She got up, holding it.

"Relay here!" the first baseman shouted as the runner was heading to third.

Emma took a breath, wound up, and got it to him on one bounce.

"Woo-hoo! Woo-hoo!" It wasn't only Todd and Chip. The whole team was excited. The first baseman threw the runner out at home.

"That's my mom," Todd shouted.

"Doesn't count," the other team said.

Juan shrugged. Then he turned and waved Emma onto the field. "We need a right fielder."

Emma wiped the dirt off her scratched arm. Her ankle felt fine. The first baseman was waving her onto the field, too.

Memories of grade school recess flashed through her mind. In softball it had never been like this. Usually they *let* her on their team. Being asked was a new experience. She pursed her lips and jogged towards where Juan was pointing. Somebody on the other side ran out and tossed her a glove. Todd beamed at her from center field.

Grounder to second base. Thrown out at first. Emma's team up. Oh, no. She hadn't swung a bat since probably seventh grade. And that was softball.

The other side had only two outfielders. "What if I just play permanent right field?" Emma called out.

Juan slid his arm over Todd's shoulder, bending down, talking low about something. She saw Todd smile and shake his head.

"Sure," Juan agreed.

A ball bounced into right field. Emma knelt, stopped it with her body, picked it up, and threw it hard to second, preventing a double.

"Way to go," the first baseman shouted.

Emma felt a thrill shoot through her. It was later than she planned to stay, but there was no hurry to get home. Charles wouldn't be coming home for dinner. She smacked her fist into her glove the way she'd seen the boys do.

Todd came up to bat. The pitcher waved Emma in to shallow right. Sure enough, Todd popped up almost right into her hand. She caught it. Hoots and whistles resounded on both sides. Chip was beside himself laughing. She studied Todd's face. Nothing but a proud smile.

A woman's voice from an apartment building stopped the game. "*Hora de cenar!*" Dinner time.

Juan came and gave Emma a polite handshake. His dark eyes were striking. He pointed to a gray brick building next to Tran's. "I live in there. I think you know my mom. Esmeralda Moreno."

"Oh!" Emma put her hands to her cheeks. "You look just like her."

Juan said most of the residents were refugees or immigrants from Honduras, El Salvador, or Guatemala. He added, "You are a good fielder, Ms. Emma." Grinning, he said, "Next time I hope you get a chance to bat."

"Oh, no, I don't think so."

Walking to the car, Todd and Chip talked about sliding into third base and diving for ground balls. Emma worried about some dirt and scratches she saw on Chip's legs and stopped by a water fountain. Just enough trickled out to wet her hand and wipe the dirt from Chip's knees. She pulled his high Adidas socks up over some scratches. Before they got in the car, she opened the trunk and insisted they drink some of Britney's Vita-Juice and eat a few orange slices even though neither boy wanted any.

Whenever she drove kids in the car, Emma loved to listen in as they talked. It was as if they had no idea the driver could hear them.

Todd said, "Did you see how far Juan hit that ball?"

"I thought they were never going to find it."

"He showed me a better batting stance."

Here Emma uncharacteristically interrupted. "How was that, Todd?"

"What? Um, I'll show you when we get home, Mommy."

The conversation changed to their upcoming science projects. Todd wanted his project to be How to Clean up the Bay. His idea was to put a cage of oysters in the river near Andre's house, which fed into the bay.

Chip: "That's crazy."

Todd: "Ms. Heather says oysters filter out the bad stuff."

Chip: "My dad says trying to clean up the bay is a waste of money."

Todd: "Maybe we could go to the Piskasanet and find some oysters for free."

Chip: "Anyway, my mom's working on *my* science project. With a friend of my dad's. An engineer. She says it's going to be awesome."

When they were almost home, Emma stopped by the Grab 'n Go to get some milk. "You guys can look around at the baseball cards or whatever."

The Grab 'n Go was on North-South Highway a mile or so from Shady Park, a long bus ride from Tran's house but a quick drive in a car. Chip said his mother never went in there. She got their milk from Prime Foods.

Todd showed Chip the candy and sports card aisle. Emma went and talked to the tall, dark clerk in a Sikh turban behind the counter. She asked if he knew a man named Tran who worked there at night.

The clerk froze. "I work in the day," he answered. "I do not know the night staff."

After she mentioned she was tutoring Tran, the clerk softened. "Sorry," he said. "I was thinking that you might be with Immigration Services or perhaps a police officer."

"Does Tran have a problem?" Emma said she was sure Tran had a green card. He was hoping to become night manager.

"No, he has no problem," the clerk explained. "Not at all." Waving his head back and forth, he said, "But, you see, there is a difficulty involved in the regulations that have been published in the central office of the Grab 'n Go Corporation, which has its headquarters in Austin, Texas, requiring that managerial positions in each branch location of any business where drugs are available for sale should be supervised exclusively by individuals who are not only permanent residents of the United States but native or naturalized citizens, as well, in accordance with suggested guidelines that have been published for corporations in the United States by the office of Homeland Security in Washington, DC, and because of this it is necessary for any applicant for the position of manager in the Grab 'n Go, if he is not already a citizen by birth, to show evidence that he has undergone the naturalization process and become a naturalized citizen of the United States."

Emma just nodded.

"You understand that the prohibition against Mr. Tran's being promoted to night manager has no relation to his character or work since he has consistently received the highest employee ratings. It is only that the regulations that have been published by—"

"Yes." Emma thanked him and put half a gallon of milk and two cans of mushroom soup on the counter. "Boys." She bought each of them a pack of baseball cards with bubble gum.

The back seat conversation began in the parking lot. Todd said, "Did you see how fast that guy could talk."

"Could you understand what he was saying? Was that English?"

"I guess."

"Look."

Emma couldn't see what Chip was showing Todd.

"Chip!" Todd said. "You didn't buy that."

Emma stopped before pulling onto the highway. Chip had stolen a candy bar.

"So?" he said. "I do it all the time."

He whined as Emma took him back into the store and made him give it to the clerk and apologize. The clerk said nothing, just nodded and turned away.

16

Dinner with Andre

The days were getting warmer. The air inside the house felt hot and stuffy even though it was still cool outside in the evenings. Emma went into Todd's room and opened his window, then came back and opened her own. Still, she had to gasp for air, tossing in the bed with only a sheet over her. She kicked that off and pulled her pajama top up, fanning her stomach with her hand. She turned on her side, facing the nightstand where her phone lay. After a few minutes, she picked it up and called Andre.

"Emma. Anything wrong? How's your ankle?" Andre had a deep, masculine voice. Maybe that's one reason Charles was never really convinced he was gay. Or whatever.

"The ankle's fine. I thought you might still be up."

"I never go to bed until one or two. I'm reading *Walden*. There are some things in here I missed before. Thoreau's grasp of Sanskrit literature is. . . ."

Emma lay there and let him talk, listening to the mellow sound of his voice more than to the words themselves. Instead of annoying, it now felt soothing to listen to his monologue. It must be nice to live like Andre in a world of your own creation, untroubled by mundane things like paychecks, crabgrass, a crumbling ceiling—or a husband who was off in New York with a lewd, devious woman. Andre asked for little and was happy with what he had. He had no aspirations to be in the middle class, which he called the bourgeoisie.

As she listened to him, Emma felt herself absorbing his peace of mind. She put the phone against her ear on the pillow and, for the first time ever, was content to keep quiet and listen to whatever he wanted to say.

She opened her eyes wide and noticed there was no voice coming through the phone. "Andre?"

"Yeah, I said you're usually too busy to listen to me like this."

"Mm. I guess. Sorry."

"Did you want anything special?"

"Um, oh, yes. I wish you weren't working at the Invokers of Jesus Youth Development Center. That's one thing."

"But I love it. It's the best job I ever had."

"It's just, Bea and the pastor want your property, so—"

"Pastor. I guess you could call him a pastor. When you talk to him about theology he doesn't seem to know much. He didn't even realize that the Council of Nicaea—"

"I mean, weren't you surprised that the pastor approved your, uh, flexible schedule?"

"He said no problem. He said he'd give me free rein to nurture the kids any way I see fit."

"It all sounds strange to me."

"He mostly talked about me selling him my property."

"You aren't going to do it, are you, Andre? You're so content living there."

"He wants to set up a meeting."

"Including Charles?"

"No. He told me Charles is busy with some other things in New York and wouldn't be able to come. He seems afraid Charles would convince me not to sell. He wants a meeting with me and Beatrice Doggit. She's coming back in a couple of days hoping to sign the deal."

A familiar catch in her throat kept her from speaking.

"I'm sorry, Emma. I've tried to get Charles to come back. I've called him a few more times, but he doesn't answer."

She swallowed. "It's OK." The energy and fight seemed to be draining out of her. When she noticed Andre was actually listening for her to say something, all she could manage was, "Tell me some more about the Vedic scriptures."

Todd texted Charles, then called. Their conversation was all about playing baseball at the Northbrook lot. Before he hung up, Todd turned to Emma. "Daddy says to tell you he loves you."

She nodded and turned away.

"And there should be some money in the owl vase, he says."

"Let me talk to him."

But Todd had already hung up.

Before getting into bed that night, Emma put her hands on the dresser and stared at the eyes on the owl-shaped vase. She knew there was more money in it but not how much. She'd vowed to replace what she used for the muffler repair as soon as Charles's paycheck was deposited into their account. That wouldn't be for a week. She wanted money now.

She held the vase over the bed and shook it. A bit over $600 fell out. She put it into her purse.

At the Trans the next day, she said, "I'm going to lend you the rest of the application fee so you both can apply for citizenship. Don't worry. No hurry to pay me back. We'll fill the forms out together, and I'll send them in for you. I'll make a copy so you can study the answers we put down."

She folded her legs, leaned back against the warm wall, and looked at Tran and Thieu's clothes stacked in neat piles on the brown tile floor. Every single thing they owned was in plain view in the apartment. She felt justified for taking some of Bea's money and giving it to the Trans. She was a Robin Hood taking from the Sheriff of Nottingham and giving it to the poor.

There wasn't much chance Charles would notice she'd made a $600 bank deposit, then written a check to the Citizenship and Immigration Services. He never looked at their account online.

That evening, Todd was doing his homework upstairs when Andre knocked on the door. He was wearing the fish tie, but now with a blue and white striped shirt and white shorts with white socks and tan leather shoes.

He had news about Charles, he said. He sat down in Charles's leather chair, holding a box of Tastee Donuts on his lap.

Something told Emma that Andre would take his time coming out with what he had to say about Charles. She took the donut box, and he started. "I know you're worried, so I called Charles one more time. The husband-wife relationship is complex. It's probably developed this way since the abolition of primogeniture—"

"Tea, Andre? With honey?"

"Because the Salic Law and the Napoleonic Code—"

Emma walked over to him and gave him the raised-eyebrows face she used for Todd as a final warning. He kept talking but in a lower, huskier voice.

There was no doubt Andre was a good-looking man. She'd thought so when she knew him in college, and, despite his weird change in dress since then, the attraction was still there. It was crazy, but she felt an urge to touch him as she'd done the other night.

Her hand was reaching towards him when Todd shouted from the top of the stairs, "Is that Mr. Andre? I need to ask him something about oysters."

The oven buzzer went off. Tuna fish casserole, made with Campbell's cream of mushroom soup. Andre stayed for dinner. And Todd found out plenty about oysters. Andre was fascinated by his Clean up the Bay project. He said he could get him the oysters.

"Any idea how I can show they clean up the water?"

"Sure. How about putting a bunch of them in a wading pool full of river water. Then you could see if the water in the pool gets clear."

"Yeah! Mommy, can we get a wading pool?"

Donuts for dessert. Todd wolfed down one after another, while Andre went on about oysters. Emma smiled at Todd's interest and let him stay up longer than usual. Before long, though, she noticed Todd's eyes starting to close, like a student's sitting through a comprehensive lecture that might have been interesting at first but just went on too long. She took him up to bed.

When she came back down, Andre was on the couch, his own eyes half closed, a picture of stress-free contentment. It was a new contentment, it seemed to Emma, that had come to replace his grief over the loss of Johan. Emma put tea, honey, and spoons on the marble-top coffee table and sat next to him as he meticulously spooned a level teaspoon of honey into his tea.

"So, you said you had news about Charles? And skip the English Statute of Wills, if you don't mind."

"I called him again. I said you don't like him being with another woman." He eyed her and stirred his tea. "All Charles said was 'Tell her not to worry.' He said he'd be back with plenty of money."

"That's your news?"

Andre shrugged and stirred his tea. "The urge to amass goods and the means to acquire more goods is—"

"Unseemly?"

Andre squinted, cocked his head sideways. "I suppose some people are born with a stronger acquisitive urge than others."

Emma sat staring at the brown lines etched in the marble table top. She hoped she wasn't one of those with a stronger acquisitive urge. Recently, Charles had seemed to assume she was. Now Andre, too? She pulled her legs up under her on the couch, instinctively reaching to put her arm around him, but stopped. "I don't want to be acquisitive, Andre." She rested her hand on his shoulder. "I want to be . . . more like you. That's the truth."

When he only nodded, she asked, "How are you holding up? I mean with your friend Johan gone?"

"Funny. It helps when I come here." He gave Emma a warm smile.

"I didn't really know him. He was a good bit younger than you, wasn't he?"

"Just out of college when I met him. I was about 33." Andre stirred his tea. "It's true. I was attracted to his youth."

"Tell me about it."

"You won't hate me?"

"Andre, how could I hate anybody who comes to see me dressed up in his Sunday best, bringing me donuts?"

Andre fingered his tie. He started biting his fingernails, already pretty much nibbled off. When Emma took his hand, he relaxed and closed his eyes for a moment. He cleared his throat. "All right. Maybe this is how I can explain it. Do you know that statue in the city—it's near the All Saints Episcopal Church—of a man, sort of a rugged hunter type, with his hand on the shoulder of a young man with just the beginning of a beard, guiding him?"

Emma knew it. She'd been moved by the same statue.

"That's what I feel like. I want to guide and protect a young man. That's my thing."

Emma looked him in the eyes. He was trembling, and she squeezed his hand.

"I wish I were different. You can't imagine how much of a problem it is."

The pained, helpless look on Andre's face made Emma swallow. She put her arm around him, leaned her head on his shoulder. "Why is it a problem, Andre? The way I see it, it means you'd make a great father."

"I wish." He put his muscle-hardened arm around her. "In college, remember? I do. I was wrong to let you go." His deep voice sent a thrill through her chest. She pressed her lips against his neck. She couldn't help it.

He held her a moment, perfectly still. Then, in a throaty voice, he said, "I guess sitting here, next to you, it turns out this is what might be a problem."

Her pulse throbbed in her temples. It was wrong, but she pulled tighter against him. "Just hold me," she urged. She watched the steam still rising from her teacup. *Good night, Andre*—that's what she should say here. But when she glanced at him, the words stuck in her throat. She closed her eyes. She might have fallen asleep. When she opened her eyes again, Andre was standing in front of her.

"You're leaving?" At the door she said "Wait" and hugged him. She told herself it was a hug of empathy.

17

Trifle and donuts

The grass in her front yard brushed across her ankles as she slogged to the car. Let it grow. Lawn care was moving lower and lower on her list. She wanted to drive over to Britney's house while the kids were still in school—and before Britney got back from her yoga lesson.

Esmeralda opened the door. "Oh, Ms. Emma. I thinking about you. Ms. Britney not here, but please come in. My son, he say good thing about your Todd."

She poured Emma a cup of Prime Foods café au lait from a chrome coffee maker that had more spouts, dials, and handles than a locomotive in the B&O Train Museum.

"Your son Juan is helping Todd and Chip in baseball, Esmeralda. They idolize him."

"Is good thing?"

"Yes."

Emma didn't know whether one stirred café au lait or not. Esmeralda had put a little silver spoon on the saucer. She held the spoon tentatively, then put it down. "Esmeralda, I didn't tell Britney exactly where I've been taking Chip to play baseball. I thought maybe you should know that."

Esmeralda frowned and tied the apron tighter behind her back. "Si. Perhaps is better she no know." She looked at the chair across from Emma as if asking for permission.

"Please. Sit down, Esmeralda. I'm not used to . . . ."

Emma felt the warmth of Esmeralda's smile. A hint of sadness appeared in her brown eyes as the housemaid sat, at a little distance from the table, with her hands folded in her lap.

"I know Ms. Britney," Esmeralda told her. "What she like,

116

and what she no like."

Emma relaxed.

"She not like Chip play with Juan or city boys."

It was as if Esmeralda had put a soft cushion behind Emma's back. She was never at ease like this talking to Britney. She breathed deeply and sipped the coffee.

"Juan say a man come watch them play. Short pantaloons, funny necktie. I think your friend Mr. Andre, maybe?"

Emma's cup clattered as she set it on the saucer.

"Juan say this man stand there smiling."

"But Andre's working in the afternoons now."

"Yes. In the church. Very close to baseball field."

The church was on the highway. But it did have a parking lot in the back, which adjoined the Northbrook parking lot and field.

"Nice man, but little estrange." Esmeralda smiled.

"Yes. How did you know Andre was working at the church?"

"Some of my friends working there, too. Easy to get job at Invokers even with no green card."

"It is?"

"Jes. Pay is not much, but is job."

Emma turned this around in her mind while Esmeralda released another blast of foamy coffee into her cup. The *ski-yuuurch* of steam made Emma jump.

Esmeralda giggled. "Is funny house, no? Coffee make noise, bacuun inside wall, fireplace burn gas, six television but no newspaper." She shook her head, and a melancholy shadow slowly dimmed her sparkling eyes. "My husband, he say he must read the newspaper every day."

Emma knew Esmeralda had come to the States with her husband a couple of years before Juan was born. "You never mentioned why your husband's not here with you."

Esmeralda's frown reminded Emma of the reaction of the

Grab 'n Go clerk when she'd asked about Tran. "I mean, if you want to tell me. I was just wondering."

When she and her husband had first come to the States, Esmeralda said, he'd taken a job with a roofing company, even though he'd never done that kind of work before. When Juan was only three months old, her husband fell off a roof and broke his leg. The roofer's insurers found out her husband was here illegally. They reported him and he was deported. "His leg still not good."

More often it was the husband who worked in the States and sent money back to the wife and children, Esmeralda noted. For her, it was the opposite. She saved and sent money back to her husband.

"How often do you see him?"

Esmeralda's eyes recovered some sparkle. "Every winter when Ms. Britney family go to ski in the Utah. Sometime he come here, usually I go there. One time he get catch and send back. Me, I never get catch yet."

Britney burst in. Emma spilled some coffee on the table.

"Emma, I saw your car in the driveway. Did you forget I have yoga today?"

With Britney's yoga mat, bolster, and block in her arms, Esmeralda trudged upstairs. Emma glanced at the tall grandfather clock in the hallway that Britney had bought new from Olde Tyme Accessories. "Two-thirty," she said. "I'd better leave before Todd gets home."

"Come on, Emma. Let's have some raspberry trifle. I always need to replenish my carbs after yoga. You'll love this trifle. It's from Sur le Dessus."

"Thanks anyway. I'm just not in the mood for trifle right now."

She texted Andre as soon as she got home: *Need to talk.*
His answer: *Will come by this evening after work.*

He brought donuts. "Where's Todd?"

"He's staying over at my mother's."

"No school tomorrow?"

"Tomorrow's Saturday."

"Ah. Is it?" He scratched his head, still standing in the doorway holding the box of donuts. The setting sun gave a warm glow to his tousled hair.

"Well, come in. You say you're coming from work? No tie?"

"It's interesting the close relation between mode of dress and perception of status in a society based so thoroughly on appearances as—"

"Andre. This is important. I heard you were standing at the Northbrook lot, staring and smiling at those children playing baseball. You can't do that."

He put a finger to his temple. "I did go there once. I felt stupid and didn't go back. I realized I don't know anything about baseball."

"You're avoiding the point. Why were you there? You're attracted to young men, you say."

"Young men? Emma, you don't imagine I was trying to seduce anybody?"

She moved close, grabbing both shoulders, shaking him. "I want to believe you. I'm telling you this for your own good."

"You're crushing—"

She was squeezing the donut box between them. The lid had popped open. Emma didn't care. She pressed closer against him, her chin on his shoulder, clutching his back. "Please understand, Andre." Her face burning, she grasped the donut box and tossed it onto the coffee table, then led him to the couch.

She sat beside him. Studying his eyes, she saw nothing depraved, nothing wicked or wayward. A wave of affection suddenly overcame her. She put her arms around his neck and put her lips against his cheek. Andre closed his eyes and stroked her hair, holding her face against his. She found herself giving him a warm kiss on the lips, a kiss that surprised her as much as it did him.

"Oh," he said. "I thought . . . ."

She turned away, dropping her arms, staring at the twisted Tastee Donut box, trying to catch her breath.

"My predilections," he said. "I thought that's what we were discussing."

Emma took a breath and managed to look at him again. "Of course. Yes. It is." She slid aside enough to pull her knees up on the couch between them.

Andre said nothing for a while. Finally, he leaned forward, straightened the lid of the donut box, and said, "Here's the thing. What attracts me to a young man, or anybody, is if I can tell they're attracted to me. It's not just anyone."

Emma let this sink in, then objected, "Is that really good enough, Andre? How do young men, as you call them, know what they want and what they don't want?"

"I did," he declared. He searched her face with his blue eyes. "You don't think I can tell if people have feelings for me?"

18

Baby blue

Saturday morning. No Charles. A few more paint chips and some plaster dust lay on the kitchen table. The ladder was folded and leaning in a corner. Emma wiped off the table and carried the ladder back down to the basement. Enough dwelling maintenance. She knew Andre would agree. Charles and Todd, too, for that matter. She needed to stop worrying about it.

There was a loud knock at the door. Pastor Mitch stood there trying to shake the dew off his shiny black shoes and black trouser cuffs. "Ah, Emma."

"Yes?"

"I hope you're not busy." He stepped through the doorway. "I came by last night, but I saw Andre Smyth's car in the driveway. Thought I better not stop." His mouth opened in a slow grin like a lid lifting on a row of piano-keys. "Andre's baby blue car is pretty easy to recognize, isn't it? It stands out in the church lot. The girls kid him about it."

"What do you want?"

The pastor looked at Charles's chair, but Emma didn't ask him to sit down. "Funny," he said. "All this time, we thought Andre was Charles's friend. Turns out he's yours."

Emma ignored the implication. "What do you want?" she repeated.

"I wonder if Charles knows about Andre's visits." Pastor Mitch closed his lips melodramatically, then said,. "If he doesn't, he won't find out from me."

"I don't have a lot of time, Pastor Mitch. Is there something you want?" Emma stood between him and the chair.

"What I'm hoping is you'll use your influence on Andre."

"I don't have any influence on him."

"But you do. This is what I've come to realize." His eyes narrowed and he put a hand on each of Emma's shoulders.

Emma squirmed out of his venal laying-on of hands.

"Don't think you won't be rewarded for helping to develop Riverside Paradise. Charles has already received—"

"Please go."

"All right, Emma. I'll give you time to think about it. In the meantime, check your bank account."

He stopped on the porch, looking at her grass. "And I'm going to send somebody to take care of your lawn."

It was the first time Emma had ever slammed the door behind anybody.

She'd left her iPad on the kitchen table, at Charles's place. No need to keep a space clear for somebody who wasn't here. She clicked the bookmark for Online Banking—and couldn't believe her eyes. She refreshed the screen in case there was some kind of mistake. Charles's latest paycheck was there, and listed under it was an additional deposit for about three times what Charles made in a month. "Cash deposit." That's all it said.

She dialed Charles's number.

Busy with a client. Call you later.

She called her mother. "Mom, how's it going with Todd? You two having fun?"

"We sure are. We're making a floating oyster holder out of a wading pool."

"Oh. That's good."

"What's wrong, Hon? You sound funny."

"I just wish Charles would give this whole thing up. That's all."

"I know. Let's hope everything will work out."

"Yeah. Todd's baseball game is at 2:30. I'll pick him up at

2:00. You can come watch if you want. And then stay over."

Emma's mother had wavy gray hair, a powdery face, and glasses. Otherwise, she looked just like Emma. Nobody at Todd's game needed to ask who she was. She sat next to Emma on the top row of the stands behind the backstop and looked around. "Oh, my!" she whispered. "This is serious business."

"My turn, Grandma," Todd called to her as he strode up to the plate.

"Whoa, whoa, whoa!" one of the mothers sitting on the lowest row nearest the kids' bench yelled out. "Helmet, helmet."

Emma had forgotten to bring it. Britney sauntered up to the plate with Chip's helmet. "I guess he can use this. For now." She turned the helmet over and started pulling at the straps. "Time out! Time out! These have to be adjusted right."

Emma saw her mother look away, stifling a laugh.

The teenage coach lobbed a soft underhanded pitch straight across the plate. Todd swung and missed.

"It doesn't look like he can see out of that thing, Hon," Emma's mother whispered. "Does he really have to wear it?"

"It's the rules."

Todd got a base on balls. Luckily, after dropped balls and stolen bases, he made it home before Chip came up to bat and needed his helmet back. Chip seemed embarrassed standing there while his mother put the helmet on him and took it off several times, readjusting. He said something to his mother that Emma couldn't hear. But she heard Britney shout, "What?"

Britney clanged up to the top of the metal stands. "Emma. Is this true?" She might have been trying to keep her voice down, but that was hard for Britney. "You took Chip to play on an unsupervised field? In a questionable neighborhood?

Chip says he was playing with Esmeralda's boy. I can just imagine what kind of things he was learning from the kids who live up at Northbrook."

Emma's mother looked stunned. Emma said, "Britney, you know my mom, right?"

Britney ignored her. "I try to provide good parenting, and this is what happens." She stomped back down to her seat behind her cooler.

"You know, Hon," Emma's mother said. "When you were little, 'parent' wasn't a verb. Guess that goes to show how much we knew."

Emma looked out on the field as the Bears were taking their positions. Todd was in right field, a very short right field, scooping an imaginary ball and pretending to throw it to second base. He twisted and stretched his arms the way he'd seen the older boys do it on the Northbrook lot.

Esmeralda came up to the top row and bowed to Emma's mother, introducing herself. "I am very please to meet you. Is very good lady, your Ms. Emma." Then she said to Emma more quietly, "I sorry for Ms. Britney angry to you. I make Chip promise he no tell about Northbrook baseball, but Chip no listen."

"It's all right, Esmeralda."

Esmeralda bowed again to Emma's mother. "Now I must go get ready the orange and bitamin-water."

Somebody sat down next to Emma and tapped her on the shoulder—Andre in a dirty T-shirt and tattered jeans, smelling vaguely of fish. "There you are, Emma." He nodded to Emma's mother. His hair was windblown and his face and arms were a deeper reddish brown than when she'd seen him the night before. "Emma, I've got something for Todd. In the car."

"What have you been up to? You look kind of scruffy. No youth center on Saturday after all?"

"I don't know. I didn't ask. I got up early—actually stayed up all night reading and thinking about the way Tea Party politicians keep trying to—"

"Can we talk about that later?"

Andre didn't stop right away, but eventually he worked his way around to " . . . and went out on the river at sunrise. I got Todd the oysters he needs."

"Oh, good," Emma's mother said. "And we have the pool he fixed up to put them in. In Emma's trunk."

Andre clapped his hands together almost like a child.

"Could we all help Todd work on it at your house after the game?" her mother suggested to Emma.

Emma glanced at Andre, shrugged. "Sure. Why not?"

When they got to Emma's house, the lawn had been cut and raked. It had never looked so trim. Whenever Emma or Charles cut it, there wasn't time to do anything but leave the clippings there to turn brown and smother the grass beneath. Britney often told her she ought to "get a better lawn service."

They dragged the wading pool out of Emma's trunk and onto the front porch. Todd and Andre got the basket of live oysters from Andre's car and dumped them into the pool.

Todd took charge. "Now I need some river water to see if they can clean it up."

Andre grinned. "No problem. I also have a big bucket of river water in the car."

Todd scooped up a jar of cloudy water. "I'll just take this river water and see if the pool water ends up clearer. Will Daddy be back by Thursday?"

"Why Thursday?" Emma asked.

Andre gave her a funny look. "That's the day of the science fair." Emma knew what he meant: how come I know this and you don't?

Emma's mother gave her a sad look. "Hon, you've been

fretting about real estate tax and mufflers and"—she looked at Charles's Beetle in the driveway—"other things. I think you need to relax a little."

Maybe her mother was right. The lawn was cut—Emma was angry at that, but, still, it was cut. There was money in the bank—she was insulted by that, and determined not to use it, but, still, it was there.

They went inside to fix dinner. "What do you have?" her mother asked.

"Couscous, mung beans—maybe some organic peas, kind of wrinkly. Fava beans—don't know what would go with that. Gluten-free fettuccine."

"Ikh. Why don't we order pizza?"

"And how about some music?" Andre suggested.

"Yes!" Todd ran for his backpack. "Chip's sister lent me a Height CD."

It had been a long time since they played music in the house. Todd turned the sound up, and a steady, thumping beat rattled the window panes. It felt like a party. Emma poured herself and her mother a glass of wine. "How about you, Andre?" He shook his head and swayed to the beat.

Now Andre was dancing with Emma's mother. Emma took Todd's hands and danced with him. They switched partners. Andre had sexier moves than Charles when he danced. Something in the way his hips gyrated. Emma laughed at him, but the truth was she liked it. Before long it was Todd's bedtime. Emma didn't care. After all, it was Saturday night. She let him stay up an extra fifteen minutes. Then another fifteen.

Her mother took Todd up to bed while Emma walked Andre to the door. She turned the porch light on so they could look at the oysters. Of course, the water was still cloudy. But Andre was sure it would be clear very soon.

"Andre, thanks for helping out with Todd." Even though he smelled like the river and sweat, she hugged him and waved from the porch as he got into his car. When she turned to go back into the house, she noticed a note lying on the door sill:

Andre's baby blue car here again. ?? Lots of music. Didn't knock. We really should talk.

19

Muppet preacher

The front door of the Church of the Invokers of Jesus was open. "Come on inside with me for a minute, Todd."

"It's dark. Kind of scary."

"Hold my hand. We're early. That's what I wanted." She'd come right after dropping Grandma off so she could tell the pastor something before any service began.

Fluorescent lights suddenly flickered across the low ceiling.

"Peace be wis you."

Emma jumped.

A pretty brunette teenager came up to them from behind. She wore a pink sundress that came well below her knees. She folded her hands in front of her breast. Emma got the idea she didn't speak much English.

The room was like a small theater, metal folding chairs facing a slightly raised stage. There was a lectern at one side of the stage with a microphone attached. Other microphones hung from the drop ceiling tiles. Chairs, amplifiers, and a keyboard on a stand took up the rest of the little stage. Electric guitars leaned against two of the chairs.

"You think Height plays here?" Todd wondered. "I thought you said this was a church."

"Is church, jes" the girl said. "Is worship room."

Todd laughed, then realized she was serious.

"Come on, Todd." Emma pulled his hand. "I just want to find the pastor before the performance or whatever starts." She led him along a wall covered by red, white, and blue County Executive campaign posters towards a door near the stage marked "Outreach Office. Private." She knocked. She knocked louder—she was angry.

The door opened. "Emma, dear. What a surprise." The pastor ran a comb through his oily hair, slipped it into his pocket, and stepped towards the door.

Emma stood there blocking him. "I came to tell you not to leave me any notes ever again. We have nothing to talk about. Don't come to my house any more."

Todd pulled at her hand. "Mommy, look. The theater's filling up."

"Peace be wis you. Peace be wis you. Peace be wis you."

Emma turned and saw Pastor Mitch's faithful quickly filing in, mostly women. She felt hands grip her shoulders and turned back to see Pastor Mitch beaming out towards the faithful with a smug evangelistic smile on his face. Emma tried to slip away, but the pastor held her, pushed her towards the audience. "Sisters and brothers in Christ, I want you to welcome a new friend of Jesus who has chosen to walk among us. Hallelujah."

"Hallelujah!" the now full theater echoed.

His hands still firmly on Emma's shoulders, Pastor Mitch guided her and Todd to one of the few remaining seats. The room was filled with pastel blouses, skirts, and dresses. Emma, in jeans and sneakers, tried to hide from view behind Todd as they walked down the side aisle.

The performers were already on stage, and the pastor signaled four fingers to the PA man. As he walked to the stage, a recorded sound track blared out, "Change my heart, oh Jesus. Change my heart."

All the Invokers stood in front of their chairs to sing along. Most looked Hispanic. One short man might have been Britney's landscaper, but she couldn't be sure. An attractive woman with brilliant red lipstick took Emma's hand and held it up, but when the woman next to Todd reached for his, he folded his arms. Now the whole audience was swaying from side to side, waving their joined hands in the air as they sang. "Change my heart, oh Jesus. Change my heart."

"Amen. Amen," Pastor Mitch boomed out from his podium microphone as the song came to an end. He nodded to the sound man, who switched the amplifier over to the guitars with a sharp feedback squeal. Each person in the audience turned to the person on her right, then on her left, saying "Peace be wis you."

Emma looked back. The outside door was closed. It would be hard to leave without making a scene.

". . . our visitors today."

Emma had missed the beginning of what the pastor said.

"Welcome in the name of Jesus," everyone sang out, and Emma realized all eyes were on her and Todd. There was no escape.

Warm-up chords from the guitars brought the room to silence.

"Sisters and brothers, will you sing with Brother Elijah? *Who at my door.*"

Todd whispered, "Can we sit down?"

"Doesn't look like it. Not yet, anyway."

The guitars twanged out the introduction, and the whole room burst out in song again. Pastor Mitch, eyes lifted, walked to the center of the stage and sang, too.

> *Who at my door is standing,*
> *patiently drawing near?*
> *Entrance within demanding,*
> *whose is the Voice I hear?*

"Will you open your door to Jesus?" Pastor Mitch moaned, his palms uplifted. "Will you hear the word of the Lord?" He closed his eyes, pressing his fingers against his forehead as if to channel the Lord's words into his head.

"Jes," some of the women said. And again, "Jes."

The pastor picked up a black leather Bible from the podium, and everyone sat down in silence.

"Finally," Todd grumbled.

Pastor Mitch opened the Bible. "We need the guidance of the Lord. Today I find guidance in the Proverbs." He read the lines in a powerful voice.

> *One gives freely, yet grows all the richer;*
> *another withholds what he should give,*
> *and only suffers want.*

After a pause in which he stared at the audience with narrowed eyes as if he had scolded them, he repeated the lines, this time very slowly, in an almost whispered voice, pausing between phrases. He drew out the word "withholds," closing his eyes with a pained look. He put the Bible back on the podium and began:

"What do we understand from these words of God? What is he telling us that we need to know? He says *grows*. The one who gives *grows*. And we know what it takes for something to grow. It takes a seed. Sisters and brothers, when I go into my garden, I plant a seed, a little seed, and with the power of Jesus, guess what happens? That seed grows. It grows into something much bigger than itself. My garden grows *rich* with the fruit of my seed."

Pastor Mitch's chin bobbed up and down when he preached.

Todd pinched Emma's arm and whispered. "He looks like Statler."

"Shh. What?"

"You know. One of those Muppets in tuxedos at the opera."

Emma held her hand over her mouth to keep from laughing and felt her eyes watering. Yes, that was the Muppet he looked like. But with his hair dyed black. When the lipstick lady next to her looked over to see what was wrong, Emma coughed and pointed to her throat. The woman nodded her head up and down slowly, satisfied that Emma was overcome with emotion at the pastor's words.

". . . if you plant a seed. I know some of you, many of you, perhaps, can only plant a small seed. The amount—that is, the size—of your seed is not important. It will grow. The Proverb tells us it is only important that you *give freely*. This is what the Lord demands. And what does the Proverb tell you will happen if you *give freely*? A wonderful miracle will happen, the Proverb says. You will *grow all the richer*. Yes, people of Jesus, you will be rich. But you must first plant the seed."

There was some shuffling of chairs on the stage, and the lady next to Emma went up and stood at a microphone. Pastor Mitch closed his eyes and bowed his head. "Will you pray with me? Christians, will you pray with me?"

Everybody except Emma and Todd bowed their heads with their eyes closed. There was a long silence.

"This is creepy," Todd whispered. "Let's get out of here."

Emma, too, thought it might be a good chance to escape while everybody had their eyes closed. But suddenly Pastor Mitch's voice boomed out:

"We pray that you would lead us, Lord Jesus, on the path of Christian righteousness. We pray that you will help us to shine the light of faith upon the unredeemed, upon all those misled by humanism and prideful human logic."

A silence. Then everyone opened their eyes and said, "Amen." There was a feedback squeal on stage, and a thump on the mike.

"Sisters and brothers in Christ," Pastor Mitch intoned. "Please join together in song with our beloved Natalie as she leads us in worship of the Lord."

The sisters and brothers in Christ stood. Natalie's thick cranberry red lipstick didn't look so outlandish up there on stage. She was a full-figured woman with a beautiful, powerful voice. When she got to the chorus, everyone sang along:

> *On fire, hallelujah!*
> *On fire with the glory of the Lord.*
> *I will plant my seed, hallelujah.*
> *I will plant it for the Lord.*

The guitars started a lengthy instrumental interlude while a woman on each aisle brought a basket to be passed along the row. Everyone sat down, swaying from side to side to the rhythm of the guitars.

The collection was the only part of this religious service at all familiar to Emma from her childhood. "Todd," she whispered. "My wallet's in the car. You don't have any money, do you?"

"The five dollars Grandma gave me."

"Lend it to me, will you? I'll pay you back when we get home."

When the basket was passed to her, she held it for Todd to drop in his five-dollar bill.

At last, it was time for the Invokers to gather on the sidewalk outside the church door. They shook each other's hands, hugged, and chattered, mostly in Spanish. Natalie, the singer, put her arm around Emma. In English, she announced, "We have a new friend."

Emma found herself and Todd encircled by smiling women speaking both English and Spanish—and every one of them wanted to shake her hand. Natalie told Emma, "I think maybe you know my friend Esmeralda."

Todd perked up and asked her where Juan was now.

Natalie made a face. "Playing baseball, of course. The

boys don't like coming to church. Some come, when their parents make them, but—"

The women saw Pastor Mitch approaching and scurried aside to let him into their circle. He was supporting a stern-looking woman in a dark dress who limped beside him. Her slightly graying hair was done up in a bun, and a black bag with a padlock hung from her shoulder.

The pastor moved towards Emma with an extended hand, but she slipped aside. He ignored the slight. "Well, ladies, I need to be on my way to Bay Hills, to my congregation there."

He opened the passenger door of a black Mercedes parked at the church door and carefully helped the woman he was supporting into the seat, buckling her seat belt and checking to make sure it clicked tight. The woman stared straight ahead as the pastor tooted the horn and waved good-bye to his flock.

Todd shifted from one foot to the other. Emma could tell he was bored.

Natalie had an idea. "Maybe Todd would like to play baseball with Juan? If you have time. The field is very close."

Feeling guilty for putting Todd through the church ordeal, Emma agreed. Todd knew how to get to the field through the parking lot behind the church. He ran off.

Natalie suggested, "Maybe your Todd could come to youth center sometime. We have new worker in afternoons, Mr. Andre."

"Oh," Emma said. "I know Andre."

"He is wonderful. Kids love him."

"They do?"

"You want to see? Come in with me. Security camera in the youth center. I am office girl, have key."

Natalie took her back into the church and unlocked the door to the pastor's office. His large metal desk was piled with papers and political bumper stickers. Emma recognized the name of the man now running for re-election as Piskasanet County Executive, Andrew Mauer.

Natalie opened a door in the back of the office so Emma could look in. "Youth center in there."

From the doorway, Emma got a better look at the mostly bare room she had seen from the back window when she'd come looking for Andre. Blue and green shag rugs were scattered over a worn gray vinyl floor. Wood and plastic toys, or parts of toys, were piled up against one wall. A cardboard box overflowed with a mound of clothes that children presumably had left behind. A beige beanbag chair sat beside an orange throw rug, stacks of children's books piled next to it.

Natalie pointed to a camera on the youth center wall. "Camera over there come on by itself if anybody in the room. If anybody move." She closed the youth center door. "Monitor here over office door. You see." Emma turned and noticed for the first time a small monitor on a shelf facing the pastor's desk. It was showing a view of the empty youth center. Natalie tiptoed up and rewound the video. "Here. Friday."

The video was black and white but clear. The camera slowly panned around the room. In a corner, a woman was telling some children stories about Jesus. Boys were trying out martial arts moves on each other. And over by the pile of books, there was Andre in the beanbag chair. A girl about four years old sat in his lap as he read her a book. A boy about five sat on the floor with his hand on Andre's knee, listening. The sound track was filled with noisy children, but you could clearly hear Andre's voice reading *Winnie-the-Pooh*.

Emma concentrated on the video. Andre was clearly enjoying the story himself. He laughed sometimes before the children laughed. And then they laughed because he did. "He seems to fit right in," Emma said.

"Yes. Now watch."

As Andre paused at the end of a chapter, the girl on his

lap lifted her head and kissed him on the chin. The boy on the floor laughed and taunted, "Celia loves Mr. Andre. Celia loves Mr. Andre." Andre put on a mournful face and, in the voice of Eeyore said, "I know it's hard to believe, but I do have my friends. Somebody spoke to me just yesterday."

Thieu and her baby Byu were sitting on a bench by the Northbrook lot when Emma went to pick Todd up. Her son Henry came running up. "Hello, Ms. Emma." He sat beside her. "Todd says he went to church."

Emma nodded.

"I ask a question?"

"Sure."

"You have God, yes?"

Emma nodded.

"And you have Jesus, too, yes?"

Another nod.

"So what is Jesus?"

Emma hesitated.

"Does he take over if God dies?"

Emma smiled. "I can't help you, Sweetie. It never made any sense to me, either."

That night Todd wanted Emma to call Charles. She refused. "But, here, *you* can."

The conversation started off with baseball. Then Todd told Charles about going to church. "The head guy looked like a Muppet. They sang songs."

Todd listened. "Yeah, I guess so. It wasn't worth five dollars, though."

20

Following the rules

Emma missed Charles. But she was keeping busy managing things without him. It was Todd she was worried about. No father to watch him play baseball. No father to help him with his science project. She appreciated Andre stepping in.

The oysters cleaned up the water in the wading pool so fast that Andre had to keep bringing back more river water for them to feed on. He didn't seem to mind. It might have been more practical to transfer the whole project to Andre's house until the science fair, but Emma liked having him around.

The project annoyed Britney. When she dropped Chip off at Emma's to play, she held her nose. "Ugh. You better get that stinky mess off your front porch before the neighbors start complaining."

This gave Todd a new idea. At the school science fair, he would put oysters and river water in one Tupperware container and river water without oysters in another. By the time the fair was over, he hoped people could see the difference just in the amount of time they were at the fair.

Todd explained the project to Chip as he put the containers on a kitchen counter.

"I don't get it," Chip said. "Your project's just going to be some oysters sitting in a container?"

"And I'll write a card to explain it."

"Sounds boring to me. Sorry. Mine's going to be awesome. It's got these two cars, one red and one blue, and they run on batteries and go up in a loop, around and around without falling off the track."

"Wow! What keeps them from falling off?"

"I don't know."

"What kind of track are they on?"

"I don't know. Wood, I think. Maybe metal."

By the time Emma got back from driving Chip home, the water in the container with the oysters was definitely a little clearer than the one without the oysters. There was a fishy smell in the kitchen now. Emma smiled to herself, realizing she didn't care.

Britney phoned as soon as the children were off to school. Her voice was quivering. "Emma, I can't believe that woman. I'm going to need you to back me up."

"That woman" was a teacher who accused Chelsea of plagiarism, and Britney had set up a meeting with her. She wanted Emma to come over to discuss her strategy. "That bitch is going to pay for this."

Esmeralda let Emma in. "Maybe you calm her?"

"That's what I was hoping."

Britney was on the phone to somebody else. "I'm going to need a bulldog. Are you the right person? Fine." She hung up and breathed out an exasperated sigh. "Esmeralda, get us some coffee. Come on, Emma. We'll talk in Derek's den."

Emma looked at Chelsea's paper. The grade was F, and there was a comment: "Copied directly from *Freereports. com.*" The paper began: "Kate Summers, a *New York Times* best-selling author, has hit the mark again with *The Doctor Is In*, a novel which provides children with a captivating look at the medical profession and may well inspire them to enter the field of medicine themselves. In scene after scene, Molly, the disadvantaged but resilient and determined protagonist . . . ."

Emma looked at Britney.

"So? Anything wrong with that paper?"

"No. Except a seventh-grader didn't write it."

"But is it an F paper? That's the question here."

"Mm, I don't agree. The question is whether Chelsea handed in a paper she didn't write."

"Come on, Emma. Don't you understand doing research? That's all Chelsea did. I mean, I helped her, of course. I found it for her."

"Wouldn't reading the book be all the research she'd need to do? It's a book report."

"Whose side are you on, anyway? I'm glad Derek suggested I get a lawyer."

Esmeralda knocked on the door and brought in two cups of latte. Britney told her to close the door behind her. "Come on Emma," she said. "You mean to tell me you didn't take your high school papers from the encyclopedia and your college papers from the internet?"

"No. Never."

Britney slammed her cup down, spilling some coffee on the saucer. "Well, I did. And I got through school just fine. Who does this woman think she is?" She breathed out a sigh through her teeth. "Derek knows people on the School Board. She's not going to get away with this."

Esmeralda knocked on the door again. "Ms. Britney, Mr. Starkezahn here to see you."

While Britney conferred with her lawyer in the den, Emma took her coffee to the kitchen. Esmeralda sat across from her. "I hear you meet my friend Natalie in the church."

"Yes. She's very nice. Beautiful voice."

They could hear Britney's voice all the way from the den, although they couldn't hear what she was saying.

"Lot of my friends, they like to sing. That's why they go to pastor's church. Natalie is good singer. So is pastor's wife."

"I saw a woman get in his car after the service and drive off with him. Was that his wife?"

"Yes. She keeps collection for him. She comes to Northbrook church, also goes with him to Bay Hills church. You ever see it?"

"No."

"Is a big church, Natalie says. Overlooks the bay. Stone walls and high roof. Air condition. Big cross on top, very high. Trumpets, too, and drums. Many people coming in cars. This what Natalie tells me. Much money in the offering. All checks, not cash. Natalie helps pastor's wife to write down names, keep record."

"Bay Hills," Emma said. "It's beautiful out there. Rolling green fields, white fences, horses—"

"Horses?" Esmeralda's eyes glimmered. "Natalie tells me. She says pastor calls those people his Horsey Invokers. Maybe that is why."

Emma chuckled. "Yeah." She hadn't thought all his money came from the Northbrook Invokers.

Esmeralda gently tapped her fingers on the table. "Something about pastor I no like. Don't know why. But most of my friends, they like him. They happy to work at youth center and at church."

"You like it better working for Britney and Derek?"

"Mr. Derek, he likes money. Not interested in women. He never touch me like bad husband in house where some of my friends work. This why I am happy."

The coffee maker hissed, and Esmeralda got up to turn a dial and flip a switch. From the den, they could still hear Britney's voice.

Emma wondered if Charles should be considered a "bad husband." She felt the need to confide in someone. "I'm worried about my own husband, actually."

Esmeralda gave Emma a pat on the arm. "I understand. He is in New York with Ms. Bea. I hear Mr. Derek and Ms. Britney talk about this. I am sorry."

"What did they say?"

Before Esmeralda could answer, Britney came into the

kitchen. "Ugh. I can't believe that teacher is causing me so much trouble. And expense. On top of that, I missed my yoga lesson."

"Yeah, Britney," Emma said. "That is a problem."

The walls of the seventh-grade classroom were covered with drawings of book characters with quotes from the children's reports pasted below each. Chelsea's teacher looked nervous. Alone, the tall, thin Ms. Ernst faced Derek, Britney, Britney's lawyer, and Emma. Britney had insisted that Emma come along as a "character witness" for Chelsea.

Ms. Ernst was holding a paper first in one hand, then the other, as she dried her palms on her pleated skirt. Emma noticed a quiver in her lips.

Britney's lawyer, Mr. Starkezahn, wore a tan gabardine suit and had perfectly round frameless glasses. He began with introductions, formal and polite. Emma expected to dislike him, but she was changing her mind. They all managed to squeeze into seventh-grade-sized desks, Britney having the biggest problem. "We're here to discuss your accusation," Mr. Starkezahn began.

Ms. Ernst put the paper on the little desk in front of Britney. "This was the assignment."

Mr. Starkezahn picked it up. "I see. 'Write your own analysis.' And did you explain to the students what this means?"

"Yes. We talked for two days about how to write the report—and how it was wrong to take words from another person, book, or website."

"And are you certain that every student understood what you meant by 'take words from another person, book, or website?'"

"Yes."

"And what makes you certain of this?"

"I used our computer, here, to show a website on the screen, there. We composed a dishonest report on a book we'd all read using the website. Then we composed an honest report."

"I see. And was Chelsea present for all of these classes?"

"Yes."

Emma immediately saw what the problem was. The children had heard and understood the explanation of what was honest and what was dishonest before writing their reports. This would work if the school system's assumption that the children would be writing the reports was correct. Unfortunately, some parents, like Chelsea's, wrote the reports for their children. And these parents had not attended the classes explaining how to write an honest one. Emma looked at Britney, squeezed into the little chair, and thought she would do well to repeat Ms. Ernst's seventh grade.

"I see," Mr. Starkezahn said. "But the grade of F presumably, since the quality of the writing is good, was given because the student copied the paper from the internet. Is that right? Good. Then if it can be shown that Chelsea herself did not copy it from the internet but someone else did, can the grade of F be justified?"

Ms. Ernst picked up the assignment sheet from the desk, her thin fingers trembling. "Um," she said.

"Yes?"

"It says here that the students are to write the paper themselves. If someone else did it for them, it's still an F—for handing in somebody else's work."

Britney strained to dislodge herself from the little chair, holding down her skirt. "I've heard enough of this. You're telling me the way I did papers all through middle school, high school, and college was wrong?"

Ms. Ernst made no comment.

"I'm going to file a complaint with the School Board. Let's get out of here. Emma, you were certainly a great help."

21

The art of the deal

Charles called. "I know you're mad, Emma. Don't want to talk to me. But please listen. I can probably come home soon. This is just something I have to do while I have the chance."

The eyes of the owl vase glowered at her.

"Are you listening? I love you. I have some good news."

"I'm listening."

"Check our bank account. There should be plenty of money in it now. Maybe you can put a down payment on a new car."

"I don't know who you are any more, Charles."

"There should be enough to pay the real estate tax right now."

"I don't want money from Bea."

"It's not just from Bea. I told you. She set me up as a life coach for some of her real estate friends. Then they recommended me to *their* friends. I'm working out of the hotel room. Bea's paying for it, so don't worry."

"Yeah, Charles? I thought you did your best work in a swimming pool."

"Seriously, Emma. I'm getting leads on clients who live in Shady Park. It's only a matter of time before I can set up an office there. I told the county welfare services I'm taking the rest of my vacation now."

"I think you need a life coach yourself, Charles. I'm going to hang up."

"Wait, Emma. One more thing. You know I don't want Andre pressured into selling his land, right? I heard Bea tell Pastor Mitch on the phone to 'turn up the heat' this week. That's what she said. Can you find out what that's about?

And if he's meeting with Andre, could you go?"

"He's *your* friend, Charles. You should go."

"I just thought—"

"Come home, Charles. I'm not going to say anything more."

Almost as soon as she hung up, Andre called. "I don't know if you agree with Jeremy Bentham's method of determining the morality of an action by—"

"What is it, Andre?"

"Huh? Oh. I got a message from your friend the pastor."

"What does he want?"

"He said now you want me to change my mind and sell. But, Emma, I have to think of the people he's displacing from their houses, the trees he's cutting down, the wildlife he's driving away—even the fish and *oysters* that are going to be killed, with the river becoming more polluted and—"

"Andre!" She wasn't sure he would stop, but he did. "Back up, please. He said I wanted you to sell? Where did he get that idea?"

There was a pause as if he were rewinding the tape of his thoughts. "He wouldn't tell me. He said he needs to meet with you and me together, and I'd find out."

Emma got to Andre's house before Pastor Mitch. The outside was clapboard of a grayish color. It wasn't paint. That had all worn off long ago. It was the silvery gray of the weathered wood itself. She stepped over a puddle in the dirt driveway and wiped her feet on the sagging front step.

Andre stood inside the door of the dimly lit room, a half-eaten donut in his hand, which seemed to be shaking slightly. The house smelled like pizza, not fresh pizza but the stale, cardboardy smell of piled up boxes. The walls were brown—there wasn't enough light to tell whether it was paint or wallpaper. A chair by a small window held a book opened across the arm. Gradually, Emma's eyes adjusted enough to make out a table with more books piled on top of it and one straight-backed chair.

"Andre, I wanted to talk to you before the pastor gets here."

The light from the window reflected in his eyes. He seemed more vulnerable than she'd ever seen him before. If Todd had looked this confused, she would have thrown her arms around him. "I'm here to back you up, Andre."

He picked up the book from the chair arm and nodded for her to sit down. "I don't like the tone of that man. This is going to be the last time I talk to him."

"He came to my house," Emma told him. "Twice he saw your car there and drove away. He's been spying on us."

"Why would he do that?"

She gave Andre time to come up with an answer to his own question. But he just put the book and donut on the table and came and sat on the arm of Emma's chair. He leaned towards her. "Why, Emma? I don't get it."

"Maybe he thinks . . . you and me . . . ."

"What?"

They heard a car coming down the gravel road towards his house.

"Anyway," Emma breathed out. "Here comes the Scourge of God himself."

Pastor Mitch didn't wipe the mud off his shiny black shoes. He trailed it into the house. Emma stifled a laugh when he stumbled over one of Andre's dumbbells.

Andre didn't offer anybody a seat, maybe because there was only one chair in the living area. Or maybe he was hoping the "meeting" could be concluded while they were still standing. The pastor held a briefcase, looking around for some place to put it. He said, "Cozy little house."

With an ironic flourish of his arm, Andre offered the pastor the chair. He turned over two buckets, which he and Emma sat on like acolytes at his feet.

"Well," the pastor began. "Here we are together." He opened the briefcase on his lap and took out a large drawing in blue ink. "I hope you can see in this light. This sketch shows the remarkable improvement we plan to make to Riverside Village. 'Riverside Paradise,' we're renaming it, as you know by now." The large building plan wrinkled as he spread it over his briefcase and pointed. "Here's where we are now. What do you think?"

At the edge of the high ground looking down to the river, just where Andre's house stood, the sketch showed a building as big as Bea's villa. Similar mansions were drawn along the river between Bea's villa and Andre's house, all set much closer together than the houses they would replace.

"I have to wonder what kind of people would live in them," Andre said.

The pastor frowned. "I don't follow you."

"I'm guessing not people who grew up catching crabs and minnows in the river. Not people who even know how to fish, how to clean and cook fish and crabs themselves. Not people who care about how construction runoff and lawn fertilizer cause algae blooms that kill crabs, oysters, and fish and make the water smell like rotten eggs."

The pastor's mouth flapped. "I can assure you we comply with all construction regulations."

Andre simply glared at him.

"And as for the people who will live in these homes, the County Executive, for one, has already been given an option to buy. One of our state senators was very interested when we approached him. We have a car dealer, a bank president, an electrical contractor. All first-class citizens."

Andre continued to stare.

"I can see you're not impressed. So maybe we can get to the point." The pastor pulled out another paper and showed it to Andre, tapping it. "One million dollars. That's what we're prepared to offer you for your property."

"No thanks," Andre said. "Anything else."

The pastor turned and peered out the window. "I see. This is how it's going to be."

Emma couldn't help making a remark. "Pastor Mitch, the land itself is assessed for just over a million dollars. I checked online. Andre could get a construction loan, build his own mansion, sell it, and make twice as much if he wanted to."

The pastor's jaw stuck out as he took in a deep breath and let it out slowly through his teeth. He glowered at Emma, shaking his head, then turned to Andre. "All right, then. Two million dollars. We can't have a fishing shack sitting at the edge of Riverside Paradise."

"No thanks."

The pastor studied Andre, then Emma. "It's clear you two are a team, sitting there on those buckets. I can't help wondering, Emma, does Charles know about Andre's visits when he's away earning money for the family? What would he think? You should know that, as a Christian, I'm offended by lascivious behavior."

Andre stood up. "You're questioning our behavior?"

"Calm down. I'm hoping we can make a deal. And then Charles doesn't have to know."

Andre took hold of the pastor's lapel. "Just to be clear. I'm gay, you realize?"

The pastor smirked. "Not bi-sexual, then? You certainly seem very *close* to Emma, I can't help noticing. Closer than Charles is aware of, I'm assuming."

Now Emma stood up. "Enough." She took out her phone. "I'm calling Charles right now. Let's see what he has to say about all this." Luckily, Charles answered.

"Charles, I'm with Andre and Pastor Mitch. The pastor wants to talk to you." She handed over the phone.

"Charles, good to talk to you. I hear your New York trip is quite a success." He gave Emma a warning glance. "I just made Andre an exceptional offer. No, he hasn't accepted—yet." A glance now at Andre. "I hope those deposits to your account went through all right. Emma hasn't thanked me yet." He listened for a while. "Well, let's not talk about that money now. We're still in the middle of our negotiations with Andre. I'll call you back and let you know how things went." He glared at Emma. "One way or another." He tapped the phone off and handed it back.

"Call him back right now," Emma screamed. "Tell Charles whatever you want about me and Andre." She thrust her phone into the pastor's hand and folded her arms, daring him.

The pastor looked at the screen, then waved the phone at Emma like a teacher threatening a child with a ruler.

"What money?" Andre asked Emma.

"Money? Oh, it's money Charles made from life coaching. At least, that's what he thinks."

Andre was silent, staring out the window. He seemed to be in a daze. "I need some air," he said and walked out of the house leaving the door open.

"Pastor Mitch," Emma said, "you've gone too far."

"Emma, dear. I can go farther."

The pastor's car sped away, spraying up gravel behind it. Emma ran across the road to the river bank where Andre stood looking down at the river, his eyes glassy. She tried to put her arm around him, but he stepped aside.

"Andre, about the money. I haven't spent it—at least, hardly any. I plan to give it all back. I don't even know who to give it to. Please don't think—"

"I know I always annoyed you a bit. I know you never approved of my lifestyle. Then, lately, it seems you sort of warmed up to me a little, as if you understood me better. At least, that's what I thought."

22

Missing person

A gray-haired man sweating in a polyester suit stepped through the doorway and introduced himself to Emma as a "special investigator." He took a small notebook with curled-up edges from his breast pocket. "I'm trying to get information on one of the employees at the Invokers of Jesus Youth Development Center and heard you know him. Andre Smyth?"

"What's this about?" Emma tried to avoid staring at a black mole almost on the tip of the man's nose.

"His employer said you know Mr. Smyth." The investigator tapped his notebook. "There's been an anonymous complaint about him from one of the youth center children's parents."

"A complaint?" Emma's voice came out at a higher pitch than she expected. "What about?"

"All I can tell you is it's quite serious. His employer wants to investigate this further before notifying the police. We have Mr. Smyth's mother's address, but I was told to contact you first."

"You say the complaint came from a parent? When was that?"

The man looked at his notebook. "The complaint was received . . . the day after he disappeared."

"After he what?"

He looked at his notes again. "That's what I have here. He's missing."

The moment Pastor Mitch's investigator left, Emma sank to the floor, holding her face in her hands. Had Andre fled because of the complaint by a youth center parent? Impossible. He'd disappeared the day *before* the complaint was made, the investigator said. A tightness rose in her chest as she remembered Andre standing at the river after hearing about the money she and Charles got from the Riverside Paradise developers. "Andre," she whispered aloud, "it's not what you think."

She couldn't think of anywhere Andre might have gone. With Johan out of his life, he didn't have friends except her and Charles. She called Andre's phone. *No service available at this time*. She texted him. Waited. No reply.

Maybe she should call Andre's mother before Pastor Mitch's investigator got to her. She might know where Andre was. Emma shuddered to think what his mother might say to the investigator.

She found the phone number among some scraps of paper next to where the landline used to sit on the kitchen shelf.

"Who? He doesn't live here." Andre's mother was a little hard of hearing—and a little suspicious by nature.

"Yes, I know. I was wondering—"

"Who did you say is calling?"

"It's Emma. Emma Bovant. Do you know where Andre is?"

"I'm sure he paid all his bills."

"Yes. I'm just trying to find him."

"Who is this?"

Emma realized getting information from Andre's mother was impossible, at least on the phone.

As soon as she ended the call, her phone rang, and she jumped. Pastor Mitch said, "Emma, now listen. I'm considering filing a charge against Andre for child sexual abuse."

The phone felt slippery in her sweaty hand. He was waiting for her to say something. In her most stern voice, she managed, "You'd better think carefully before making a charge like that."

"I have an incriminating video that could put him in jail."

He waited for a reaction.

Emma's hand was shaking so much she needed her other one to steady the phone. Her cheeks were hot.

"Now, Emma, you're his friend. You have some influence over him. That's clear."

"I don't—"

"Let's not waste time denying anything. I'm not interested in your affairs. All I'm asking is for you to find him and get him to reconsider the offer. This Riverside deal is bigger than you imagine. If Andre signs, we'll see that you have enough to move into Nottingham Estates near your friend Britney. Charles can do his life coaching or whatever he wants. Bea will keep feeding him customers." He paused. "Or you can take Todd and run away to Florida with Andre, if that's what you prefer. There's lots of good fishing down there."

It was Britney's day to get her nails done, so Esmeralda would be there alone. She might have heard something about Andre from Natalie. She answered the door in an apron, her hair tied up in a white scarf.

"Yes," Esmeralda told her. "Natalie say Mr. Andre quit the youth center."

"She didn't say why? Nothing about . . . ."

"Yes?"

"Uh, nothing. He's missing, it seems."

Esmeralda's dark eyebrows rose. "Fishing, maybe?"

"I wonder. Could you call Natalie at the youth center? Maybe she knows something."

Esmeralda called from Emma's phone. She said something in Spanish, then handed the phone back.

"Um, Natalie. It's Emma. I talked to you after church last Sunday. I'm calling about the new teacher at the center, Andre? I hear he's missing."

"Missing?" Natalie said. "All I know, he call and quit."

"Do you know why he quit?"

"No."

"Were there any . . . complaints about him, or anything?"

"Pardon? Hard to hear." There was a distant sound of hammering and sawing. "Big meeting in Northbrook tomorrow. I must help set up on parking lot. We talk later, maybe."

23

The American dream

Emma caught Todd staring gloomily at the Tupperware containers on the kitchen shelf. Andre had been so enthusiastic about the project, she knew Todd was disappointed he wouldn't be here to go to the science fair with him.

"Crazy Mommy!"

She forced a smile and brushed her hair back down with her fingers. "Come on, Todd. Want to go to Northbrook and play some baseball? I need to tutor Tran first. Then maybe I can see if Natalie has any idea where Andre is."

The entrance road to the Northbrook apartments was lined with parked cars, old pickup trucks, and some motorcycles. She couldn't get into the parking lot. It was crammed with people, some of them holding little plastic American flags. The only spot Emma found to park was back behind a Java Hut. She looked in the shop window as she and Todd walked by and saw men in new red baseball caps and faded T-shirts, most of them sipping coffee. All the caps said *Mauer for America.*

She led Todd around the crowd in the parking lot towards the baseball field and Tran's apartment. They had to move aside to let people carrying crudely-lettered signs push by. One said, "Cut off there Welfare and theyl' go home." Some of the men had long pony tails and wore sleeveless shirts with old punk rock logos on them. The women wore shorts and lettered tank tops—Emma read "Girls Just Wanna Have Guns" and "Native-born Boobs."

"Stay over there on the field and play ball, Todd," she said. "Keep away from that crowd on the parking lot. I'll come get you when I'm finished at Tran's."

She was tutoring Thieu along with Tran now. Both of them seemed to know the citizenship answers well enough to take the test.

"Look, Teacher." Smiling, Tran showed her a letter from the U. S. Citizenship and Immigration Services. "Interview appointment in six months."

Thieu offered her tea, but Emma said she didn't have time today.

When she left the apartment, Henry followed her outside. The crowd in the parking lot was bigger and louder. They heard a hoarse shout. "Keep America Christian."

Henry tugged at Emma's sleeve. "I ask you something, Teacher? *Christian* means *good*?"

"No, Sweetie. What makes you think that?"

"Kids from the center, they say, 'That's not Christian.' And 'It's Christian thing to do.'"

She tousled his hair. "They're just kids, Henry. They don't know any better. When they grow up, they'll realize—"

A long, undulating squeal blasted out from a microphone. The crowd was starting to chant. They sounded like fans at a football game when the referee had made a bad call.

"You better go back inside, Henry. It seems a little crazy out here today."

She made her way around the crowd towards the field and called over to Todd. "Stay there, Sweetie. I'm going into the youth center and see if I can talk to Natalie for a minute."

But the crowd had spread across the parking lot almost to the door of the youth center. Emma tried to work her way through with people pushing against her on both sides. A cardboard placard scraped her face. She had to give up and squeeze back to the rear of the crowd. They were shouting, "Stop taking our jobs," "Build a wall," "Send them all back."

Two men climbed up onto a platform. One was Pastor

Mitch, sweating in a black suit, a smile plastered on his face. His voice echoed out from a loudspeaker. "Yes. Yes. What a wonderful turnout. Thank you. Thank you."

Emma recognized County Executive Andrew Mauer standing beside him.

"We want Mauer. We want Mauer," the crowd chanted. "We want Mauer, not taxes." A man with a shaved head standing in front of Emma cupped his hands at his mouth and shouted, "Mauer for guns! Mauer for America!" Another shouted, "America for Americans! Shoot 'em if they cross the border." A fat woman with long grayish hair and a missing tooth yelled, "Cut off their food stamps." She slurped up some cola through a straw sticking out of a mammoth pink Java Hut cup. A wizened little man wearing a red *Mauer for America* cap held up a sign. "Bomb the turrorists-Keep the Muslims out."

The pastor's microphone squealed. "—introduce the man you've been waiting to hear from, the man who will lead this county back to its fundamental Christian values, who will roll back taxes, keep us safe from terrorism—and give us our freedom. That man is Andrew Mauer."

The crowd roared as the County Executive now running for re-election took the microphone. In a surprisingly squeaky voice for a large man, he sang out, "Do you want your taxes cut?" They roared, "Yeees." "Do you want terrorists in our country?" They roared, "Nooo." "Do you want the government to take away your guns?" The roar was deafening: "No, no, no." They tramped on the ground as they shouted. "Do you want your sons to marry men? Your daughters to marry women?" More stamping. "Nooo." A man up near the platform started shouting, "No mo ho mo. No mo ho mo," and the crowd took up the chant.

Emma glanced towards the ball field to check on Todd and noticed a young man standing beside her with teased-up hair, writing in a notepad. He wore a short-sleeved button-down shirt, and had a chain around his neck with an ID tag. A phone or possibly a recorder hung from his belt. Like her, he seemed to be strictly an observer. She got a glimpse of the ID tag and saw that he was from the *Shady Park Ledger*.

The microphone squealed again. "Fellow Americans, I tell you I'm here to put tax money back into your pockets. I'm here to stand up for your right to carry a gun. I'm here to give businessmen the break they deserve to achieve the American dream."

Emma turned and quickly walked out onto the ball field.

Todd ran up to her. "Mommy, you look all messed up."

"Yeah," she said. "A lot of people seem to be."

24

Cheap labor and tax liens

The next day, Natalie looked confused when Emma insisted on meeting her in the parking lot. "Why you no come inside, Ms. Emma?"

"I don't want . . . I don't want anybody to know I was here asking about Andre."

Natalie's brown eyes opened wide.

"The pastor told me a parent complained about Andre. You don't know anything about that?"

"No. I never hear about this. Mr. Andre call and say he quit. He don't say why."

"Can you tell me when he last worked here?"

"Couple days ago. Is important? We can check video."

"I'd like to see what's on the video. But I'm afraid—"

"No tell anybody. Better we go around to front door. Video camera in youth center always running."

Emma was nervous as they made their way down the dark aisle, past the stage, and into the pastor's office. "You don't think he'll come in?"

"Here. You watch video. Tape for last two weeks." Natalie rewound until she got to the first day Andre worked there. "Press here, you play. Press here, you stop. You watch and I go back to youth center, check for the pastor car come into parking lot."

Emma's hands were sweaty. She pressed Play, then had a thought and pressed Stop. She took out her phone. It might be a good idea to make her own video of the tape. She pressed Play again, capturing the screen on her phone. In the video, Andre was reading, then helping a boy with his arithmetic homework. Emma fast-forwarded it to the next afternoon. Andre was reading to some children again and then giving them a spelling quiz. Then came the day Emma had seen—the kiss after reading *Winnie-the-Pooh*.

The video rolled on, with some stops and starts as one day ended and a new day began. No more Andre. She was about to turn off her phone when a new clip started. There were no children in the room. It must have been after the center closed. The video showed Pastor Mitch coming into the center from the outside door by the parking lot alongside a big-boned man with a huge head. Andrew Mauer, the County Executive.

"I have a hundred Invoker names to attach to the donation," the pastor was saying in the video. "Mostly from my Horsey Invokers." He chuckled. "A thousand dollars each. That's the legal limit." He patted Mauer on the back. "Of course, they don't know they're making the donations. So don't send them any thank-you notes."

Mauer smiled. "I owe you for this."

"Speaking of that," the pastor said, "I have a request. All this uproar about illegal immigrants."

Mauer nodded. "My base wants them all deported."

Pastor Mitch grimaced. "I know. They think they're taking their jobs, think they're getting welfare." He grabbed Mauer by the shoulder. "But you know we need them. I refuse to pay minimum wages to workers at either of my Invokers sites. And I know you can't afford to pay union rates to all the day laborers you use for your construction projects, either. We need illegals to keep operating at a good profit."

Mauer glared at the pastor. "There's no way I can be re-elected if I talk like that in public. Leeches on the U.S. taxpayers, that's what I have to call them. We need to round them up and send them back where they came from, that's what my supporters want me to say." He frowned. "In fact, I might have to call for some immigration control—you know, put on a show."

"That would be bad," the pastor advised. "The Horsey Invokers would be furious. You know how things are. They'd have to pay legal maids and gardeners more."

"Understand." Mauer put his arm on the pastor's back. "I'm thinking we'll have a limited raid, just the folks in these tenements here."

"No. That's where all my workers come from."

"No problem. Give me a list of the illegals you don't want bothered." Mauer gave a squeaky laugh as the men went into the office and the video stopped.

Emma turned the tape off, then her phone. There was a sound at the office front door, and Emma looked around for a place to hide.

Natalie's voice rang out. "Just me. I check in office. Mr. Andre only here three days. Nice man."

When her heartbeat slowed, Emma realized how much Natalie had helped her. "Can I ask you something?" she said. "Do you like working for the pastor?"

"Not much pay and no Social Security, but at least is a job."

"Pastor Mitch doesn't pay your Social Security? You're a legal resident. He has to pay."

Natalie laughed. "He no pay for nobody. If he going to pay Social Security, he would hire people with better English. That what he say."

Natalie's phone rang. "Si? Qué puerta? Gracias." She told Emma, "Pastor's car. He coming in back now. Better you go out front."

Gas was expensive, and Emma was using a lot more lately with all the driving around. She stopped at a gas station near the Invokers of Jesus church where the price was a few cents less per gallon. What a pain to have to worry so much about money. But as she watched the pump meter turning up, she thought that even people like Bea and the pastor and his County Executive friend worried about money. Worried more than she did. She wondered who didn't worry about money. Charles—that is, before he got a taste of it. And, of course, Andre. But now he was missing.

That night the *Shady Park Ledger* contained a two-page supplement published by Piskasanet County listing the homes on which real estate taxes were overdue, along with homes for which the county had sold a tax lien. It also listed the buyers of the liens. Several along the Piskasanet River were bought by INVOKIM, LLC.

Emma grabbed her iPad. On the county website she saw that after six months, if the owner failed to pay the tax plus interest and legal fees, the purchaser of the tax lien could seize the house. Her own tax was due in a week. Of course, it would have to be overdue a year before the county offered her house to tax lien purchasers. But the thought of losing it was frightening.

She looked at her checking account online and got a shock. Four more cash deposits had been made, bringing the total now up to more than Charles earned in a year. She checked the dates of the deposits. All before the day Andre had flatly refused to sell. None after that date. No doubt about it. The pastor and Bea meant the money as a bribe so she'd convince Andre to sell. All right, she thought. You gave it to me, Ms. Executive and Mr. Invoker. I'm using it. She wrote out a check for the amount of her real estate tax and sealed it in the envelope.

25

An angry wafture of the hand

Todd was disappointed that neither Charles nor Andre could come with him to the school science fair. On the long table that held the students' projects, his—basically two plastic containers of water, one with a few oysters in it—didn't attract much attention. Esmeralda set up Chip's whirling-car edifice near the oysters. Most of the kids as well as their parents huddled around it the whole time. You could push a button to make the cars go faster or slower.

At the end of the fair, there was a vote by the parents for Best Science Project, and after a quick look at the ballots, the principal announced, "It's almost unanimous. Best project is the centripetal force demonstration." He presented Chip with a two-handled silver cup set on a plaque engraved "Excellence in Science."

The parents and children all applauded. Todd let out a "Woo-hoo" and gave Chip a pat on the back. But when Esmeralda was packing Chip's project into a box, she whispered to Emma, "I see trophy in Ms. Britney's house. I think she bought for school to give. She pretty sure Chip gonna win."

As everyone was starting to leave, Britney and Derek stood aside talking with the principal, Mr. Prosterner, who shot dark, beady eyes from one of them to the other like a cornered mouse.

"Ms. Ernst, would you come over here a minute, please," Mr. Prosterner commanded.

Chelsea's teacher looked flustered as the principal spoke to her with his puckered mouth lifted in the air. Although Emma couldn't hear what they were saying, she could guess.

It was about that paper Britney had copied for Chelsea to submit. After some discussion, Ms. Ernst nodded in agreement to something the principal said. She seemed about to cry. Derek reached out and snatched her fingertips in an awkward attempt at a handshake.

Outside, Britney seemed unusually animated. She turned to Emma. "Well, we showed that bitch. Definitely. Chelsea's F is now an A, I'll have you know." She gave Emma two short taps on the arm as a wake-up warning. "Parents need to develop connections on the county school board who can step in and protect their children's rights when the teacher is being unfair."

Emma couldn't stop herself. "Got that from *mom24-7. com*, Britney? You say parents should limit their children's 'screen time.' Ever think you should limit your own mommy-screen time?"

Britney wasn't listening but glaring disdainfully at Todd putting his oyster project into the trunk of the Focus—Todd insisted on keeping it to show to Charles and Andre. Britney sniffed. "You ought to throw that smelly thing out as soon as you can."

"Just one of the jars smells," Todd pointed out cheerfully. "The one with the oysters doesn't."

Britney looked at him as if he were mentally challenged. But she insisted that Emma bring Todd over to her house to celebrate. It wasn't clear whether she meant her achievement in the science fair or her victory over Chelsea's teacher.

It was Friday evening, no school tomorrow, and Todd begged her to go, so Emma reluctantly agreed, despite her feeling of revulsion at Britney's dishonesty and bullying.

While Derek opened a bottle of red French wine on the patio, Esmeralda brought Power Drink juice boxes for the boys. Britney explained, "Got to build up stamina. Game tomorrow. A prime cause of lethargy in children, according to *bestmoms.com* is electrolyte deficiency." She poured herself a large glass of wine and drank half in one swallow as if to prevent some kind of deficiency in her own body, an antioxidant deficiency perhaps.

They were all sipping their drinks when Chelsea came downstairs—her hair dyed purple. She nonchalantly picked up a sausage link with a toothpick, slipped it into her mouth, and sat down on a narrow wicker chair next to Todd and Chip.

"Noooooo," Britney screamed, pointing to Chelsea's hair. "Noooooo!" She put her hands over her eyes, gasping. "Chelsea, you can't do this to me. Look at—you can't do this. You're grounded until you find a way to look like a normal young lady again. Up to your room, you understand?" She pulled Chelsea by the oversized sleeve of her Bohemian off-the-shoulder blouse and it slid down over her training bra, mortifying her. With a red face, Chelsea raced back upstairs.

"I thought her hair was cool. Come on, Mom," Chip whined. "That's what the middle school girls do to their hair. Right, Todd?"

Todd sucked some green Power Drink up through his plastic straw, glancing at Emma. She knew he was a little afraid of Britney and didn't want to get in trouble. "Yeah. Some of them, I guess."

Britney was standing in front of her husband, breathing hard. "Derek," she shouted. "You see what I've been telling you? We need to get members on the board who will bring these schools under control. We need—"

Derek's phone rang. He looked at the screen and raised his hand for Britney to stop. "Hold on. This is just the person who can do something about it."

Bluetooth earpiece flashing in his ear, he walked towards the patio door. "Andy Mauer, my man. I hear Mitch's Horsey Invokers have been good to you, heh-heh. Great support from that Bay Hills hand-waving crowd. Sounds like things are looking good for the re-election. Listen, I'm with Britney here, and she's fit to be tied over the Piskasanet schools." He listened. "No, that grade was taken care of, thanks. But the school's going all to hell according to Britney. Kids bused in from who knows where, looking like they live on the street. Kids raised in homes without a father. Bad influence on the decent kids."

He listened. "I know. But we need at least one more vote on the board if we're going to clean things up. Yeah, I do have somebody in mind." Derek lowered his voice and looked back at the guests. Still on the phone, Derek took a glass of wine from Esmeralda and kept talking, too low to be heard.

Britney poured herself another glass of wine and squeezed into the chair next to Chip. She patted Chip on the knee. "How's my little Excellent Scientist? You're never going to disappoint me like that sister of yours, are you? Letting teachers take advantage of her, marking her late for school almost every day just because she can't decide what to wear. As if looking respectable isn't just as important as being on time. And now this, this hair. What are my friends going to say when they see my daughter like this?"

Chip glanced at Emma, possibly hoping she would come to Chelsea's defense.

"Well, Emma?" Britney challenged.

The truth was that Emma thought Chelsea looked cute in purple hair. Yet she was unwilling to stir Britney up any more by saying so. As Emma's mother always told her, you will seldom be sorry for holding your tongue.

Chip turned away, discouraged. "Oh, Todd's mom doesn't approve of me, either."

"What?" Emma was shocked. "Where is that coming from, Chip? That's not true at all."

"You made me take that Snickers bar back."

The wicker chair squeaked as Britney twisted her hips the best she could to turn and confront Emma. "I don't believe I'm hearing this. What is it you made him do?"

"Nothing, really. It's nothing to get upset about."

"Well, I am upset. And you're going to tell me everything right now."

Emma knew this was the time to use the popular phrase "Chip made a bad choice," but she couldn't make herself say it. He hadn't made a choice. He had done a bad thing.

Britney said, "You mean you've done something to my little Chip you can't tell me about?" She turned to Chip. "You tell me the whole story yourself."

"She made me go back in the store and give the candy back to the scary man with the thing on his head. I only took one piece."

Britney was incensed. "And where did this take place?"

"At the Grab 'n Go."

Britney exploded, "Emma, I need to know. What were you doing taking my Chip into a place like that?"

"It's just a store," Emma reasoned.

"I'm sure you're aware what kind of people you find in those stores along the bus route. Anyway, the point is you embarrassed Chip. If you would ever take the time to watch programs like *Doctor Pill*, you would know that allowing children to be publicly embarrassed can cause psychological damage later in life."

Now Emma was getting angry. "Well, I wouldn't have embarrassed my daughter like you just did. And what about the damage caused by being taught you can get away with stealing?"

Derek ended his call and came over. "Stealing? What's this about stealing? Emma, you need to be careful what you say."

Britney chimed in, "I won't have it." She pointed towards the door. "Emma, I want you to leave. Now."

26

Getting by

When Todd finished talking to Charles, Emma quickly took the phone from his hand before he ended the call.

"Jeez, Mommy."

"Sorry, Sweetie. Go finish the book you were reading, would you? I need to talk to Daddy."

She tried but couldn't speak in a calm voice. "Charles, are you going to miss another one of Todd's games? You know, you missed the science fair. Todd needs his father."

Charles sounded gloomy. "But what about you, Emma? The pastor tells me you're doing fine without me. 'Having a grand time'—that's what he says. What does he mean by that?"

She stifled a sob. "He's a liar, Charles. You know I want you to come home."

He seemed to cheer up. "I will, Baby. It shouldn't be long. I'm going to set up an office in a wing of the Executive Homes building when I get back." He cleared his throat. "And here's the best news. I quit my job at Social Services. From now on, I'll be life coaching full time."

"You quit your job? Are you insane, Charles?"

"Life coaching is going to put us solidly in the middle class where we belong. Money won't be a problem any more."

"You never cared about that, Charles. What's happened to you?" She wanted her old Charles back, the Charles who seemed to float on a plane above practical concerns. Not the Charles biting at the lure of easy money. To give him credit, it probably wasn't the money itself. It was probably how money seemed to confirm his counseling skills. At least, she hoped that's all it was.

"Emma?"

"I'm still here. Listen, Charles. Be realistic. The money won't keep coming in the way it has. Have you checked our account? There were some big deposits, sure, but none since Andre rejected the offer."

"Nothing this past week? Because I did a lot of coaching."

"Coaching? Don't you get it, Charles?"

"No. What are you saying?"

"I'm saying all they want is to get Andre's property. They'll do whatever it takes. They knew you didn't think Andre should sell, so they've been keeping you in New York. Now it doesn't matter. Andre is—"

A sound in the background came over the phone. Charles stammered, "Uh, um, sorry. I'll have to talk to you later." The phone icon switched to red.

Todd came back into the room and sat on the bed beside her. Emma used a pillow to wipe the tears from her face. Todd pursed his lips. "I don't want to go to the baseball game tomorrow."

She pulled him to her, rocking him. He'd been talking about the game all week. He loved baseball. It was always a struggle to get him to leave the Northbrook lot and come home. Juan had showed him a way to change his batting stance, and he felt like he could hit better. "Cheer up, Todd," she whispered. "You'll feel different in the morning."

Todd struck out in his first at-bat. He looked back at Emma and shrugged. She didn't know how to cheer him up. She had taken her usual seat at the top of the stands before Britney, Chip, and Esmeralda arrived, and when they did, Britney made a point of sitting on the bottom row, farthest from Emma. Clearly, she still wasn't speaking. Emma was actually relieved.

Todd was in the field at second base when a boy hit a high popup just over his head. Emma heard someone shout, "Backstep, Todd! Backstep!" She looked. It was Esmeralda's son Juan, walking up to the grandstand. Todd caught the ball.

"Sorry if I scared you, Ms. Emma. I came to see Todd play." He looked towards the other end of the stands. "And Chip, too." Esmeralda waved, but Britney didn't.

Todd beamed as he threw the ball to the coach on the mound. Juan nodded to him. "Nice catch, Todd."

And that was it. Todd was himself again. He ended up hitting two home runs—in the park, of course, and, technically, he came home on errors both times. But the team won. Chip got a hit, too. Both boys ran up to Juan to get high-fives.

"Come on, Chip." Britney called him over to where she was sitting and her equipment was set up. "Esmeralda, hydrate Chip, then carry the cooler and his gear back to the van, will you? Maybe you can get your son to come over here and help."

"Excuse me." Juan went off to help his mother.

"See you at the field next week," Todd called out.

Juan turned and came back. "I hope so. I might have to go back to Guatemala. My father's sick."

Emma took in a quick breath. "Oh, no. Is it serious? Ask your mother to call me, would you?"

On the way home, Todd seemed glum again.

"What's wrong, Sweetie?"

"First Daddy goes away. Then Mr. Andre. Now maybe Juan." He leaned his head against the car window, gazing out.

"Tell you what, Todd. Want to go swimming?"

"Where?" He knew the Nottingham golf course pool where Chip took lessons had a long waiting list for membership—even for people who could afford the fees.

"We'll go down to the Piskasanet River and swim on the beach in front of Mr. Andre's house."

The river was cold but felt good. They stood in shallow water by the shore feeling the soft sand squish up between their toes. Emma held her arms under Todd, letting him practice turning his head to breathe while he swam. The water was brackish from the bay, and this probably helped her hold him up. Now and then, she dropped her arms, and Todd kept on swimming. Not very far, but he was actually swimming. He kept at it with a determination she had to admire.

If you stood still and let the yellowish silt settle, you could see minnows swimming at your feet. The raucous calls of seagulls broke the silence as they hovered and dove after fish. One flew over her head with a clam in its mouth and dropped it on the pier, cracking the shell. The gull picked it up again, flew higher, and dropped it again, this time shattering it, then dove down to pick out the clam with its beak.

Emma floated on her back and looked up at the sky. The thick, white clouds were swollen and distinct, drifting very slowly in from the bay. She heard a loud *peep-peep* and saw a brown and white osprey flap up into the sky from its nest on a buoy out in the river. It was looking for fish to bring back to its young.

Farther down the shore, some children were playing with a bucket, trying to catch minnows. Todd watched a while, then asked to go play with them. Emma walked him down the shoreline. There were two boys who looked about Todd's age and two girls a little younger. All had tanned skin and brown hair bleached almost blond by the sun. Their bathing suits were stained a yellow-brown from the river. The boys emptied something into the bucket, then ran into the water, swimming fast. The girls followed. Emma could see Todd was impressed. They all swam out to where the water was deeper. "Cold!" one of the girls giggled and started swimming back.

The rest followed. Emma and Todd stood waiting for them.

"You live around here?" the younger-looking boy asked Todd. His knees were scratched, and Emma noticed red marks on his arms.

"No." Todd was peering into the bucket.

"Minnows," the taller boy said. "We made a sieve from a piece of screen and some boards we found in the dumpster up at the construction site."

"Cool." Todd stuck his hand in the bucket to feel the little fish swirling against his fingers.

"What school do you go to?" one of the girls wanted to know. She said they all went to Southside Elementary. Her name was Beth. She was eight. And her brother's name was Bill. He was the oldest—nine. And the other two were Alan and Fran. They were both seven.

"Seven and a half," Fran said. She had curly hair and a sweet smile.

"Sometimes we catch crabs," Bill told him. "Old Man Grayson gave us a crab net before he moved. Not so many crabs now. He said the big boats going up and down the river scare them away. Can you make a sailboat? I'll show you. Just get a stick, like this one, and two gull feathers. Stick the feathers in like this. You have to turn them like this. See where the wind's coming from. Then just drop it in and give it a little push."

Todd made a little boat with Bill's help and watched it sail away.

"Look at this," Alan, the other boy called out to Todd. He ran with a piece of plywood towards the beach, dropped the board, and jumped on it, skimming along the shore over a couple inches of water.

"Cool." Todd tried it. "Woo-hoo!"

Emma asked Alan what the red marks on his arms were. He said they were stings from sea nettles. "You just wipe sand on them, and they stop hurting after a while." He shrugged.

Todd wanted to know if any of the kids knew Mr. Andre.

"Yeah," Beth said. "Alan lives right behind him." Emma presumed she meant one of the original fisherman houses far enough back from the shore that Riverside Paradise wasn't interested in the property. "And Bill and I live next to Alan."

"We catch bait for Mr. Andre to fish with," Bill said. "If he catches something, he always gives us some."

"Have you seen him lately?" Emma hoped the question sounded casual enough.

"No." Beth shrugged her shoulders. The others shook their heads, too.

Todd asked, "Are your fathers fishermen?"

"No more," Fran told him. "See how muddy the water is? From tearing down houses and digging up the ground. Almost no fish. My dad had to go up north looking for work. I live with my grandmother now."

A gleaming blue and white yacht sped by, sending brown waves crashing against the shore and shaking the piers. Along the side of the yacht was a huge sign: *Waterfront properties. Contact Executive Homes.*

Fran said, "Alan's dad still catches some crabs and takes them to restaurants to sell."

"Not many now, though." Alan watched the waves capsize his little boat.

"My father used to be a fisherman," Beth put in. "Now he drives a truck. He's away a lot."

"Mine is, too," Todd told her.

Emma and Todd sat wrapped in towels when they drove home. As they passed Bea's villa, there was a small gray car in the driveway that she didn't recognize.

27

The ICEman cometh

Emma was used to Britney's outbursts, usually aimed at Esmeralda or the gardener or somebody who'd exasperated her. If it was Emma she scolded, Britney forgot about it in minutes, and Emma was able to ignore it. But this time Britney had gone too far. She had actually kicked Emma out of the house.

It was Sunday, the day Britney often brought Chip over to play with Todd. Emma turned off her phone. She felt sorry for Todd, but she couldn't handle Britney right now.

Todd said he'd help her take care of the lawn. It was growing fast these days. Emma had to lean forward to push the power mower through the tall grass and weeds while Todd raked up the rows and clumps of cuttings left behind.

"Now you can tell Chip's mom you got a new lawn service, Mommy."

Lines of sweat rolled down her face, stinging her eyes and tasting like salt in her mouth, but the physical exercise invigorated her. Britney talked about cardio workouts and muscle toning and ab flattening yoga exercises—all done in an air-conditioned gym with pricey membership fees. Apparently, she never thought that just doing some actual productive work could accomplish the same thing. Besides, it was fun working with Todd.

When they were finished, they sat on the back porch drinking Cokes, something Charles wouldn't have approved of. They gave each other conspiratorial looks. "Ahhh," Todd breathed out. "That's good."

Emma turned her phone back on, intending to try calling

Andre again.

It rang immediately. It was Esmeralda—the first time she had ever called. "Ms. Emma, can you meet me at the bus stop at 8:30? I can't talk now."

"Who's that? Daddy?"

"No. Listen, Sweetie, I need to talk to Esmeralda when she gets off tonight. How about if I ask Grandma to come and stay over?"

"Cool."

Emma pulled to the curb within sight of the bus stop, turned off her lights, and waited for Derek to come and drop Esmeralda off. It wasn't long before Derek's new Jaguar that had one headlight dimmer than the other appeared in the mirror. It swerved past her, let Esmeralda out at the corner, and sped on through a yellow signal as it turned to red.

Emma pulled up to the bus stop. Esmeralda leaned in the window. "Is OK. Just want to talk. You no have to drive me home." She was sobbing.

"Get in, Esmeralda. Of course, I'll drive you home. What's wrong?"

"I just want to tell you I fired."

Emma couldn't believe she'd heard her right. "What? How long have you worked there?"

"Five years."

"But why? You do everything Britney wants. You work seven days a week and never complain."

"Is my husband. He is sick. I must go back. I tell Ms. Britney I going to wait another week till Juan school finish, then go back for maybe a month. She say no."

"What do you mean?"

"She say she need me more in summer than other time. She say if I go back, I fired." Esmeralda wiped her eyes on her sleeve. "Then she say if I going back in a week, I fired right now."

North-South Highway became more lit up with neon signs and store front lights as they got nearer the Northbrook apartments. Emma noticed new signs on telephone poles, light posts, and the sides of liquor stores and auto body shops.

America for Americans
Build a dam wall
No welfare for illegals

"Something going on," Esmeralda muttered. "Yesterday a man come through the apartments. He knocking on doors and asking where everybody work. Funny-looking man. He say not Immigration, but I don't know."

Emma had a thought. "What do you mean, funny-looking?"

Esmeralda giggled. "Black mark on nose."

They sat in the car in the apartment parking lot. Emma said, "If you go home, will you be able to get back into the States?"

"Is not easy. But I do it three times. It cost money."

"Listen, Esmeralda. I can give you the money you need. I'm coming back to these apartments tomorrow afternoon to tutor Tran. Tell me your apartment number, and I'll bring it there."

Esmeralda insisted she couldn't take any money but gave her the address.

A national news network van dominated the Northbrook parking lot, and cameramen were filming a pretty blond woman in heavy makeup who stood holding a microphone. There was a bigger van identified as Immigration and Customs Enforcement nearby. Stern-faced agents in blue shirts and tan pants were getting out and walking towards the apartment building. Their shirts said POLICE. They all wore blue base-ball caps emblazoned with ICE in yellow letters. A woman's dark brown ponytail hung from the back of one of the caps, and an earplug on a wire coiled down under her padded black vest. Pistols in black holsters were strapped to everyone's belt.

Emma held Todd's hand as she pushed her way through the crowd to the baseball field. Beside the news van she heard the blond TV woman, with the illogical emphasis favored by news-personalities, intone the phrase "the federal crackdown on illegal IMMIGRATION called for by Andrew Mauer." Reporters were filming the Immigration and Customs En-forcement team in action.

"Stay out here on the field, Todd," Emma told him, "until I get back from tutoring Tran. Play with Juan and the boys. I'll come and get you when I'm finished." She was glad to see some of the boys calling him over.

The entrance to Tran's building that Emma normally used was blocked by the ICE police. She went around to the other end. A clean-shaven young man with teased hair followed her and introduced himself as Anthony Mansfield of the *Shady Park Ledger*. It was the same reporter she'd seen at the rally for Mauer in the Invokers parking lot.

"Sorry. No. I don't know what's going on," she answered him.

He gave her his card.

Thieu opened her door just a crack and peeped out be-fore letting Emma in. She and her husband wrung their hands. Realizing something was wrong, Henry sat silent against the wall, eyes wide-open. Baby Byu was crying.

"Man come here yesterday," Tran said. "Ask me where I work."

"Now iceman outside," Thieu added.

"You'll be fine. You have green cards and a work permit. Immigration isn't looking for people like you."

Immediately, their faces softened into smiles. Henry said, "I am American."

Just then, a thunderous banging rattled the apartment door. "Immigration and Customs. Open up."

Thieu took her baby into the bedroom and closed the door. Tran looked at Emma as if asking what to do.

"Warrants for N-gok Dung Tran and Thee-yoo Tran. Immigration. Open the door."

Through the high half-window on the back wall of the apartment, they saw black boots scraping across the sidewalk. Then a knee bent to the ground, and they saw a gold badge strapped around an ICE agent's thigh. Two huge hands touched the sidewalk, and then a face in an ICE cap looked in, shining a powerful flashlight around the room.

"I guess you better let them in, Tran."

As soon as Tran turned the knob, a bulky agent pushed the door wide open, almost knocking Tran down. A taser gun in one hand, the ICE agent yelled, "Hands up and against the wall. Everybody, hands up against the wall." A woman agent followed him in. She wore pale blue rubbery-looking gloves.

"Anybody else here?" the woman demanded. "Open that room door." When Tran opened it, the woman shouted to Thieu, "Get your things. We're taking all of you to a processing center. Now."

"This is all a mistake," Emma gasped. "These people have residence permits."

"We follow our orders, Ma'am."

Within seconds, Tran, Emma, and Thieu had their hands bound with yellow nylon straps, and Henry and the baby were crying on the floor.

The ICE man wrote each of their names down on a pink pad and made them line up facing the door. The ICE woman picked up the baby.

"Stand right there," the man snapped. He bent his head,

pressed a button on his radio, and said, "743. 743. Subjects apprehended and ready for transporting."

His radio squawked. "One male, one female, two children?"

"Affirmative," the agent said. "Additional female also in custody. Name: Emma Bovant."

There was a pause. Then the radio voice said, "Emma Bovant is not on warrant. Release and bring the others."

The ICE woman made Emma stand against the wall, her hands still bound. After the ICE man had taken Tran's whole family away, the woman spoke into her radio. "743. 743. Clear to release Bovant?"

"Affirmative."

She cut the strips off Emma's wrists. "Remain in the apartment, Ma'am. Do not come out."

Emma rubbed her wrists a few seconds, then opened the door and peered out. The hallway was clear. She tiptoed down and pushed the building door slowly open. The parking lot was filled with bystanders watching the ICE van drive away. The news frenzy was in full swing. Now there were two blonds in heavy makeup talking to two different cameramen. She looked towards the baseball field, and it was empty. A brief panic, then she found Todd with the other children standing in the crowd, watching.

"What's going on, Mommy?"

"I'll tell you later. Where's Juan?"

"He didn't come today."

Emma checked Esmeralda's apartment number on her phone. "Come on, Todd. Let's go see where he is."

Nobody answered when they knocked on the door. She kept knocking until an old woman came out of another apartment. "Esmeralda, she not there. Nobody there."

28

No-fault

Todd wanted to know if the blue-shirt men had taken Juan. All Emma could say was she hoped not.

A small gray car kept an annoyingly close distance behind her as she drove down North-South Highway, almost bumping into her once as she stopped quickly for a yellow light. The car stayed behind her as she turned onto Shady Park Lane and only passed her when she slowed down and turned into her driveway.

When they went inside, she and Todd both glanced at Charles's empty leather chair.

"So. I guess it's just you and me, Mommy." Todd started tossing his baseball up and catching it in his glove again and again.

"You have any homework?"

"A little. I don't feel like doing it now."

"Let's go out back and play some catch."

Emma concentrated on throwing the ball straight, trying to think of nothing else. Todd seemed to be doing the same. He threw harder and harder. Both of them were tired when they came in to eat a sandwich. Todd went upstairs to do his homework, and Emma went out front to look for the newspaper.

It wasn't in the front yard. As she retrieved it from the hedge along the driveway, she noticed that same gray car that had been following her earlier. It was parked in front of the house next door. There was a man behind the wheel with his head thrown back on the seat, mouth open, asleep. She wasn't sure, but it looked like he might be the investigator

Pastor Mitch had sent to ask her about Andre.

The paper had a story headlined "ICE Raid in County." The byline was Anthony Mansfield. There was a quote from County Executive Andrew Mauer: "Our county can no longer continue to harbor and support illegal aliens who come here to take advantage of our welfare system. At the request of many of our county citizens, I have asked the federal government to perform this roundup." There was also a quote from a Northbrook Apartment resident, Isabel Rodriguez, saying the ICE agents carried away "mothers and their crying babies."

Emma lay in bed thinking of Tran and his family. She'd try to help them if she could think of a way.

The next morning, after Todd left for school, there was a knock on the door. The mole-nosed man stood there, hair all messed up, his gray polyester suit more wrinkled than before.

"Ah, Ms., uh, Bovant. I'd like to speak to you, if you don't mind."

Emma put her foot behind the half-opened door. "I told you. I don't know where Andre Smyth is."

"Uh, this is not about Mr. Smyth. It's in reference to your current husband, Mr. Bovant."

"What?"

"Yes, I have now been retained by Ms. Beatrice Doggit. I believe you know her. She is at the present supporting your husband, as I believe you know." He took out his notebook. "You also need to know that I have seen your car parked near Mr. Andre Smyth's house at the Piskasanet River recently, which I am sure you will agree is something that might arouse suspicion, that is, given the reports of Mr. Smyth's car being seen in your driveway multiple times."

Emma tried to push the door closed, but the man stood his ground. "Please, Ms. Bovant. Hear me out. You see, Ms. Doggit and the pastor don't care about your affair with Mr.

Smyth. They want your cooperation. If they get it, they believe they can convince your husband not to take you to court."

Emma pushed harder on the door.

"If you could just let me tell you what Ms. Doggit proposes. She will suggest that your husband agree to a no-fault divorce so that the affair can be settled peaceably." He drew a line in his notebook. "Otherwise, things could get ugly."

It was all Emma could do to get the door closed on him.

She pulled the phone from its charger on the kitchen table and brushed a flake of ceiling paint onto the floor. A white light was blinking on the bottom of the phone screen. She had a message:

Emma, it's me. Bea told me something that's hard to believe. Is it true? She thinks we should divorce. Call me.

III

29

Meet the press

Emma had a pretty good idea what Bea had told Charles. Let him believe it if he was stupid enough. After almost ten years of marriage, he meets a woman who tells him he has beautiful eyes, begs him for counseling—and he lets her take complete control over him. The owl vase smirked at her. She picked it up, lifted it over her head, and smashed it on the floor, kicking the shards across the room. A wad of bills lay on the floor. She kicked that, too. But then picked it up.

She noticed a business card she'd left on the dresser. Anthony Mansfield, *Shady Park Ledger*. News Reporter.

With Tran and his family in detention somewhere, Charles could wait. She called the *Ledger* reporter and arranged to meet him at Tastee Donuts.

A mix of men in T-shirts and suits looked up from reading the sports section of their papers when Emma walked in. She felt like an interloper in a male retreat. The young reporter was at a table by the window, paging through some notes. He stood up, pulled out a chair, and held out his hand. "Anthony Mansfield." He spoke in a low voice as the coffee drinkers eyed them with barely disguised curiosity. "Can you spell your name for me?"

She was relieved when Anthony mumbled, "Maybe . . . would you mind if we talked in my car?"

She described the scene in the Trans' apartment when they were arrested. "They didn't even get a chance to show their residence permits."

Anthony jotted down the names. Emma looked at his notebook. "It's T H I E U," she corrected.

He wrote down Emma's description of the arrest. "Do

you know of anybody else who was taken in the raid?"

"No." It felt like a lie since Esmeralda was also missing, but she didn't want to mention her name. And, in fact, she hadn't seen anybody else being taken away. "Does that seem strange to you?" she asked the reporter.

"Does it seem strange to you?"

"I mean, the apartments are filled with immigrants. Not saying any of them are illegal. But only one family was taken, as far as I could tell. And they were definitely legal. They were waiting to become citizens."

He drew a firm end-quote with his pencil. "The authorities say that one other person was arrested. Esmeralda Moreno."

Emma swallowed.

"Do you know her, too?"

She nodded. "Where did they take them? I want to see them."

He checked his notes. "The press release from the County Executive's office says they're being held at the Enforcement and Removal Operations city field office. That's downtown."

Emma sighed.

"You seem quite emotional." He tapped his pencil on his notepad. "Do you know anything more about these people? Or about this raid?"

A mosquito in the car whined past her face, and Anthony smashed it between his hands. "Got it. Almost bit you." He wound up the window, started the car, and turned on the air conditioning. "If you want, anything you tell me can be kept in confidence."

"I just want to go see if I can get them out. It's not fair."

"Might not be possible. At least, not without a lawyer." He must have noticed that Emma was holding back tears. "Hold on. I'll call the city field office." He Googled the number and patiently went through an elaborate phone tree until he got to speak, first with one human, then another, then another, repeating each time his name, newspaper affiliation, and the names of the people he was asking about.

"All of them are there," Anthony finally told Emma, "but none of them have been processed yet. Unless you're a family member or an attorney representing them, you have to send a written request to visit. And you can't do that until they've been processed."

Now she felt the tears coming down her cheeks. "They don't have any money. I guess there's some kind of public defender who can help them."

"Not for noncitizens." He started searching on his phone. "Here. The name of a lawyer who specializes in Enforcement and Removal. I can email you the link if you want."

Emma gave him her phone number and email address.

"His office is near the jail. I should say near the 'field office.'"

As Emma was about to get out of the car, Anthony stopped her. "One more thing I want to ask, if you don't mind. Do you know the names of anybody else living in the apartments?"

"No," she lied. Natalie was here legally, but she didn't want her to be questioned about any friends of hers.

"I guess I can find out," Anthony said. "They're probably mostly people getting rental assistance from the Department of Housing and Urban Development, and there's a public record of that. He gave her his card again. "May I call you back after I look into this a little more?"

She drove up to Northbrook. A few mothers were watching their toddlers play in the dirt at the edge of the lot. Walking past the bench Thieu usually sat on, Emma felt a tightness in her chest.

The hallway in Tran's building was empty and smelled like cooking oil. Emma's sneakers squeaked on the brown vinyl floor. For the first time, she noticed that none of the doors had a name in the slot under the apartment number. She stopped at Tran's door, her hands shaking, and looked around. She hadn't thought to lock the apartment when she left after the raid. She tried the doorknob. It turned, and she went in.

A basket with some cloth diapers and a baby blanket sat on the floor by the door, perhaps forgotten as Thieu was rushed out in handcuffs. A stack of noodle packages had been tipped over. Everything else looked the same. Not that there was much else. There had obviously been no need to lock the door.

There was no place in the outer room where valuable papers might be kept. Emma went into the bedroom. The piles of clothes were in disarray as if Tran and his wife had rummaged through them picking up a few things to take along. There wasn't a single piece of furniture—no chest of drawers, no cabinet, not even any kind of box in which they might have kept their important papers.

Two mattresses lay on the floor covered by sheets and pillows. Emma knelt and lifted the side of the bigger mattress. She held the heavy mattress up with her head and slid her hands under until they reached something that felt like a towel. She pulled it out. Wrapped up neatly inside were school report cards, passports, and some official-looking papers. Among them were two permanent residence permits and Henry and Byu's birth certificates.

She put everything into her handbag, peeped out the door before locking it behind her, then squeaked quickly down the hallway and out of the building.

In her car, she checked her bank account from her phone. Still plenty of money. Plus she had a wad of cash. She called the number of the lawyer Anthony had emailed her.

"Initial consultation fee is cash only," Edward Donnelly told her. "No credit cards or checks."

It was challenging for a suburbanite like Emma to drive downtown. Cars were constantly blowing their horns. Lanes suddenly changed into turn-only lanes. The traffic was always bumper to bumper, with cars squeezing over into your lane. The street signs were so small they couldn't be read until you were passing them—and lots of them were twisted, facing the wrong way. If you found the location you were looking for, there was never a place to park.

Emma slammed on her screeching brakes to avoid hitting a car that cut in front of her from the right-most lane. The car behind her blasted its horn and tapped her rear bumper. She drove on.

The lawyer's office was in the southeast part of the city, near the harbor. The Google map on her phone said to turn right, but it was a one-way street. Her lane came to an abrupt end, leaving her stopped behind cars parked along the curb. She gritted her teeth and forced her way back into traffic. It seemed to take forever to circle back around to the three-lane street the lawyer's office was on. Her phone map said the building was on the left, and so she did what everybody else seemed to do. She edged in front of a car in the next lane, making him brake and hit his horn, then edged in front of a car in the lane beyond that. But there was no parking on the lawyer's street.

She turned down a brick-paved alley, came out on a narrow street, and parked by a sign that said "One Hour Parking." She stepped around a homeless man with shoulder-length gray hair who was slumped on the sidewalk, his back against the wall of a row house. His chin was dropped onto his chest, his legs were stretched out in a V, and he was holding a bottle in a brown paper bag. He peered open-mouthed at her as if expecting to be told to move on. She had to make her way around a woman, also with long gray hair, sleeping in the shadow of the white marble steps of a boarded-up brick row house. Charles had told her these were the people who had no place to go after the mental hospitals were forced to turn them out.

The address for Edward Donnelly, Esquire, was a sooty granite building around the corner. She saw the number that had been chiseled into the stone a century ago, but there was nothing else to indicate the building was occupied until she climbed up the stone stairs and saw a sign on the door: "Ring bell for service."

She rang, and a buzzer sounded as the door clicked open a few inches. Nobody was inside. There were handmade signs pointing to the offices of various bail bondsmen and lawyers. Donnelly's office was up a creaky, winding staircase on the second floor.

The lawyer looked like Pastor Mitch and Bea's rumpled investigator, except without a mole. There was no secretary. He pointed to a chair beside his hefty mahogany desk—which had nothing on it but a telephone and the newspaper he was reading—and lifted himself from his own chair slightly, extending his hand. "Donnelly. And you must be Mrs. Emily Bovant."

"Emma," she said.

"Pardon?"

Emma took out the papers she had found in Tran's apartment. Without looking at them, Donnelly reminded her that the first half-hour session would be $300. "I believe I explained that the payment must be made in cash." She handed him the money, and he stuffed it in his pocket.

The lawyer wrote down what Emma told him in a tiny spiral notebook like the ones school children used to put their homework assignments in. Unlike the reporter, he didn't bother to ask about the spelling. When Emma showed him the Trans' passports and permanent residence permits, he broke into a grin, nodding.

"I feel confident that I can secure the release of Mr.—" He looked at his scribblings. "Of Mr. Train, is it? And his family. Now, as for Mrs., what is it? Morello. That would be more difficult."

"Tran," Emma said. "And Moreno."

"Yes. If you would like to retain my services, I am willing to take on both cases. My initial retainer is $10,000."

Emma's jaw dropped.

He waited. "For the retainer, I can accept a credit card."

Emma put her hands on her cheeks. "Maybe I could take the residence permits to the field office myself?" she asked. "And I could hire you just for Esmeralda Moreno."

"That's what you'd think. I'm afraid the system doesn't work that way. Enforcement and Removal only allows family of detainees or their attorneys admission. Maybe if you kept at it you could get somebody to look at the permits, but you say there's a baby and a young boy detained along with the couple. You wouldn't want them held in what is basically a crude jail for any length of time."

She bit her lip. "You say Esmeralda's case will be difficult because she's not here legally?"

"Yes. But I've had some success." He pointed proudly towards rows of pictures on the wall—himself posing with immigrants he had won appeals for, some of them hugging him. "At least I can delay the deportation, which they now call 'removal.' He sneered at the term. "Sometimes for a very long time."

Emma found herself staring at the lawyer's gray hair, shorter but as straggly as the hair of the homeless people she'd passed on the street. This wasn't her picture of a lawyer. He seemed confident, though. She told him Esmeralda was planning to go back anyway because her husband was sick.

"Ah-ha. So maybe she won't mind being removed?" Donnelly put his chin in his hand. "Still, you must realize it's not a good thing to have a removal order on your record." He looked at the pictures on the wall. "I'll tell you what, Mrs. Bovant. We'll make it $7,000, and I'll see what I can do for all of them."

Yet another of Anthony Mansfield's cards was sticking out from the crack of her front door when she got home, "Please call me" written on the back. She called. Anthony had some information. He could come to her house if she wanted.

She thought of offering him one of Charles's organic beers but wondered if he was too young. His smooth face looked like it never needed shaving. He sat down with an earnest half-frown.

"I hired that lawyer. He seemed a little sketchy. Who knows if he'll be able to do anything?" She tried not to sound like she was pouting.

Anthony shrugged. "They say he's—"

"But if you put a story in the paper about permanent residents and American citizens being arrested and detained, maybe that would help."

"I will. But I'm trying to make sense of the whole raid first. I'm like you. I find it curious that only the Vietnamese family and one Guatemalan woman were arrested." He unfolded a sheet of paper. "I've confirmed that almost all of the apartments are rented with Housing and Urban Development assistance."

The names on the list were mostly Hispanic.

"Do you recognize any of these people?"

Esmeralda was there. And Natalie. "I don't really want to say," she objected. "I mean, what if any of them are here illegally? Even if I know any of them, I'm not going to turn them in."

"Of course. And you realize it's not my job to turn anybody in, either. But here's my problem. Chances are, quite a

FIRST WORLD PROBLEMS

few of the apartment residents are here illegally—you know, running from the violence in Central America over the past few years. You have to wonder. Why weren't a lot more taken into custody?"

Emma tapped idly on the screen of her phone. "Have you asked the County Executive's office? Your paper says Andrew Mauer is taking credit for the raid."

Anthony's eyes closed briefly as he nodded. "Got no more information from his office. And my publisher doesn't want me bothering them any more. We'll see, though."

Emma realized she was holding her cheeks and pushing her hair up crazy-mommy style.

"Mrs. Bovant, can you just tell me yes or no whether you know that any of the people on this list are undocumented. You wouldn't have to say who."

She remembered Esmeralda saying most of her friends were here without documentation. "It's as you say. Some of them probably are."

Anthony sat there scratching his head with the eraser of his pencil. "I'd just like to know more before I go with the Tran family story. I have a feeling they're just part of it." He put his notebook away. "Thanks for you help. I left messages with ICE. Maybe they'll get back to me. I'm not optimistic, though."

"Wait." She took a breath. "I have something to show you."

He sat spellbound watching the video of Pastor Mitch and Andrew Mauer's conversation on her phone. His face was flushed, Emma couldn't tell from anger, embarrassment, or what.

"What do you think?"

"Let me replay something." He listened again to "Give me a list of the illegals who shouldn't be bothered," his pale green eyes darkening. He sat twisting his pencil.

191

She wanted to make sure Anthony understood. "It was the illegals who work for rich people that shouldn't be bothered."

"That's what it sounds like. Who are the Horsey Invokers? Do you know?"

"Wealthy evangelicals in Bay Hills. Pastor Mitch Rainey has a congregation there, too."

Anthony opened his notebook back up. "Just one thing. Let me ask you. You say you know—" He flipped through his notes. "Esmeralda Moreno. She doesn't work for 'rich people?'"

"She did, but she got fired before the raid."

He made more notes murmuring, "This is, I have to say, outrageous." He sat tapping his pencil on the side of his head. "So, let me get this straight. You didn't actually take this video. You copied it from the security monitor onto your phone?" He scratched his head with the pencil again. "Couple of possible problems. One, it's against the law in this state to record somebody's conversation without their knowing it."

The thought of breaking the law made Emma's hand tremble, but she said, "Does that go for recording a recording?"

"That's what I'm wondering. It's a question for the *Ledger*'s legal advisor." A determined grin gradually spread over his face. "Anyway, we could argue the pastor recorded it himself. It was his own video system."

"I don't want to get in trouble."

He ignored the comment. "We could use AirDrop to copy the video onto my phone, if you'll let me."

Emma said "um" a few times, but handed him her phone. In seconds he had copied the video onto his own phone, which he clipped back onto his belt. "Don't worry," he assured her. "No one will know who I got this from."

"I trust you." This was what she wanted, but she was nervous. "You said there were a *couple* of possible problems.

What's the other one?"

He seemed hesitant to say. "Just that the *Ledger* has come out endorsing Andrew Mauer for re-election. Let's not worry about that for now."

30

The elephant not in the room

Todd stood looking at the broken pieces of vase on Emma's bedroom floor. "It fell off," she lied. "I haven't had a chance to clean it up yet."

He pulled her tight, arms around her waist. "I called Daddy today on Chelsea's phone."

"Oh."

"He said you don't want him to come back." Todd was sobbing.

"Todd, that's not true. I'm a little mad at him right now. That's all."

"I think Daddy was crying."

Emma knew her hands were trembling. "What did you tell him?"

"I said Mommy needs you, Daddy."

"I'll call him."

But she had to leave a message. Todd was standing beside her, so she didn't want to say Bea was lying about her and Andre. She only said, "I *do* want you to come back, Charles." Todd seemed relieved as she tucked him into bed.

In her own bed, she wept to think Charles might suspect her of being unfaithful. How had it come to this? Somehow Bea had managed to turn the tables on her. What nerve, trying to make it look like Emma, not she, was the guilty one.

As for Bea, Emma had convinced herself some time ago that her thing with Charles *looked* more like an affair than it actually was. That Bea was more interested in money than sex. That Bea was keeping Charles in New York to make it easier to get the property from Andre. It'd better be true.

Then she thought about Andre. Andre suspected her of being a different kind of unfaithful. Poor Andre. Unlike her, he didn't have much use for money. He never worried about something like slipping below the middle class. He simply took it for granted that people at the top sucked their lavish life—his words—out of those at the bottom. And it didn't bother him. He was completely content at the bottom. Or, rather, he considered the "executive" one-percent type to be beneath him. She wanted to be more like Andre. She missed Charles, but she missed Andre, too.

Chip came home with Todd after school. It wasn't long before Britney called, frantic. "Is Chip there? Did he dare go to your house when I told him not to?"

"They're in the back yard playing catch."

"He should call me. He knows that. That's why I gave Chelsea an iPhone, so I'll always know exactly where she is. That does it. I'm getting Chip an iPhone tomorrow."

"Don't worry. Chip's fine. They're having fun." Then Emma added, "Even if we don't get along, what's wrong with our kids playing together?"

"Ugh. You wouldn't believe what a hassle it is taking care of two kids, cooking, washing dishes, washing clothes, all without help. Derek says he can get me a new girl—Pastor Mitch has some contacts. But I'm still waiting."

Emma couldn't resist: "I didn't think you were speaking to me any more."

Britney ignored this. "Anyway, Chip can stay there for a while. I have to take Chelsea to her therapist."

This was new. Todd had told her Chelsea was "getting in trouble a lot" at school. "Therapist?" Emma asked.

"Tutor, I should have said. I have to improve her grades. Listen, Emma, just promise me you won't take Chip up to that so-called baseball clinic again. You can't fool me any more. I know it's just a bunch of scruffy kids playing on the Northbrook Apartments lot. I found out about a lot of other things, too." When Emma didn't respond, Britney went on, "Derek is in contact with Bea and Pastor Mitch, you know."

Emma pursed her lips.

"I know about you and Andre."

Emma started to hang up but didn't. She wanted to hear her out.

"Bea's keeping Charles away from you to make things go smoother in a divorce. That's what she told Derek. Something about getting a no-fault divorce after being separated for a year." Then Britney added, "I don't get it, Emma. Andre's good-looking, sure, but he doesn't have any income at all as far as anybody can find out."

Anthony Mansfield called, then came over. "I wanted to ask about another part of the video."

A while ago, Anthony said, he had received an anonymous complaint about a worker, a man, at the Church of the Invokers of Jesus Youth Development Center. The caller said the worker had made sexual advances towards his child. "I tried to follow it up," Anthony explained, "but couldn't get the father who called to agree to meet me in person or even give me his name or the name of his child."

Emma avoided his look.

"I contacted the pastor of the church. He wouldn't give me the name of the parent or the child either, but he confirmed there was a complaint against an employee and said he fired him. He gave me the employee's name: Andre Smyth."

Emma tried to keep a poker face.

"I found out where he lives, but he seems to be missing." Emma fingered the hem of her blouse, and Anthony went on. "I checked with the police. No missing person report. No charges filed against him, at least not yet, they say. So now

I'm trying to find out if that was him in the video, the man reading to the kids. Can you help me on that?"

Emma could feel the blood pulsing in her temples.

"I mean, you made the video, so I just thought you might know."

A seedy lawyer she had to trust, and now a callow news reporter? She took a breath. "It was."

"So you know him?"

"Yes. And I know he did nothing wrong."

The reporter flipped to a blank page in his notebook and waited for her to explain.

Emma said, "You saw the video of the only days he worked there."

He ran his pencil eraser through his hair. "Let me see. So you're saying the whole time of his employment at the youth center is recorded on this video? Meaning whatever he might have done is recorded here?"

"Exactly."

"The parent who called me referred to his 'child.' Do you think it's the girl who was sitting on Mr. Smyth's lap while he read?"

"I didn't see anything wrong there, did you?"

He ignored her question and asked if there was anyone who could confirm that all of Andre's employment was contained on the video. She said there was. "But, please, I don't want her to get in trouble. She works for the pastor." When Anthony promised to protect his source, she gave him Natalie's name and phone number.

Emma's mother called to say Pastor Mitch had phoned her. She wanted to come talk about it. Emma was pacing in the hallway when she arrived.

"You look nervous, Hon."

At the kitchen table, her mother discreetly picked up a

flake of paint with a fingernail. "The pastor asked if I knew where Andre was."

"Because Andre's missing. The pastor's trying to force him to sell his house by the river."

Her mother made a tisking sound. Emma asked if she'd like some tea.

"Do you have a beer?" Her mother folded the paint flake in a paper napkin. "I told him I had no idea where Andre was." She sipped some beer from the bottle, then looked at Emma. "He said you and Andre were having an affair."

"Oh."

Her mother took another sip. "He said, as a Christian, such a thing disgusted him."

Emma's heart was pounding. "I'm not having an affair with Andre, Mom."

"Of course, not, Hon. Why would he say such a thing?"

"Andre came here a few times after Charles went off with that woman." Emma looked away. "I have to admit, with Charles gone, I liked having a man around."

Her mother smiled. "A *man* around. Poor Andre."

So her mother realized Andre was gay. It wasn't something they'd ever discussed. Emma had a close relationship to her mother, but it wasn't like that of some women she knew—who told their mothers every single concern they had on an almost daily basis. As for Emma's mother, she shuddered at the thought of being nosey or prying. She didn't ask for details about every new person Emma met. She didn't feel the need to know where Emma was at every given moment of every day.

Now, though, Emma wanted to confide. "I'm worried about Andre, Mom. Nobody knows where he is." She took a breath. "I'm afraid he thinks I betrayed him somehow."

Her mother frowned.

"Because in front of Andre, Pastor Mitch mentioned money I got from him and Bea. When Andre heard that, I could tell he was hurt."

"You got money from them?" This seemed to shock her mother as much as it did Andre.

"They put it in our bank account. Charles insists he earned it. You know, life coaching." Emma could hardly get the phrase out of her mouth.

"Ah, Charles," her mother said, as if that explained everything. "I see." She picked at the label on her beer bottle. "So you mean Andre thought you'd taken some kind of bribe to help convince him to sign? I'm sorry, Hon."

Her mother sipped her beer while Emma explained the whole Riverside Paradise scheme. "First, they threatened to tell Charles that Andre and I were having an affair unless I convinced Andre to sell. I called their bluff. I didn't think Charles would believe it. Now I don't know."

"Of course, he doesn't, Hon."

"We'll see. Now they've told him he should divorce me. It makes me mad to even think he'd listen to them. I've been too angry at him to call. He should call me."

"Oh, my."

"Now it looks like the pastor's trying something else. Threatening to accuse Andre of child sexual abuse if he doesn't sell." She'd never used the words "sexual abuse" with her mother before and she felt her face and neck flush.

"Oh, Emma, I don't believe Andre is capable of such a thing."

"He's not. Believe me."

Her mother rolled part of the beer label into a tight little ball between her thumb and forefinger. "Well, I'm sure he appreciates having a good friend. That must be a help."

"I don't know where he is, Mom." Emma was holding back tears.

Her mother gave her a kiss. "Well, Hon, maybe until you

find him, the best thing you can do is make sure that pastor and his partner in crime don't find a way to get his house away from him."

"I'm working on it."

"And call Charles."

31

Take my picture

Edward Donnelly, Esquire, beamed a yellow-toothed smile. Esmeralda's case would take some time, he said, but he'd gotten Tran and his family released. "They're downstairs in the conference room," he told Emma. "I'll take you down as soon as the press arrives.

"Press?"

"I called the *City Paper* but they don't have a reporter available. So I called the *Shady Park Ledger*."

His phone rang. "Ah, the *Ledger* is downstairs."

Anthony Mansfield was waiting for them in the lobby.

"I see you know each other." Donnelly raised his graying eyebrows and shrugged. He pointed to the end of the hall. On one of the doors, a yellow page torn from a legal pad read "Conferenceroom." They entered the long, narrow room in single file. At the end of the room was a card table—and there were Tran, Thieu, Henry, and baby Byu.

Emma rushed to give them hugs. Thieu cried and gripped both of Emma's hands.

"Pictures, please," Donnelly piped to the reporter. He went and stood between Tran and Thieu. "Mrs., uh, Bovant, would you mind?" He wanted some pictures with just the husband and wife. He posed with his arm on Tran's shoulder, then with an arm around both of them.

"Mind if I look?" He reached for Anthony's camera. "Ah, use this one for the newspaper, please." He pulled a camera from his desk drawer. "And would you mind taking a few more with this? For my wall."

Anthony followed Emma as she drove the Trans back to

their apartment, and Emma asked if she and the reporter could come in. Thieu put some blankets down on the floor for them to sit on. It wasn't easy explaining that Anthony was neither a policeman nor a lawyer but a friend who wanted to help them. Thieu started to boil a pan of water on her little electric burner.

"Thieu, no tea, thanks. Tran, could you just tell Mr. Mansfield about the man who came asking where you worked, the man who came the day before you were arrested?" Emma knew the reporter would want to get the description directly from the Trans.

"And . . . something about his nose?" she prompted.

Neither Tran nor Thieu seemed willing to comment on a physical defect, but Henry stepped in. "Black thing on his nose. Funny."

"I know who he is," Emma informed Anthony. "An investigator hired by Pastor Mitchell Rainey and by Beatrice Doggit."

"Hired by the pastor who's friends with the County Executive, you're saying? Hired to ask, before the raid, who everybody worked for?"

"Yes. At least, I know the pastor hired him for . . . something else. So I'm assuming he hired him for this, too."

"And the only people arrested were the Tran family, presumably not on the pastor's do-not-arrest list, and"—he checked his notes—"this Mrs. Moreno, presumably removed from the pastor's list when she was fired?"

"Seems like that to me."

As she and Anthony left, Emma assured the Trans they were safe. "Your arrest won't show on your record, the lawyer told me. Don't worry." She used her mother's phrase. "Everything will be just fine."

In the parking lot, Anthony said, "There's something else, Mrs. Bovant, if you have time. I've looked into the anonymous child abuse charge against Andre Smyth. Ms. Natalie at the youth center confirmed that the video you gave me shows the only days Mr. Smyth worked there. She didn't know why he quit or where he is. I found out his mother lives in a house near his and went to interview her."

Emma wondered how that might have gone. It was hard to imagine what Andre's mother might have told the reporter.

"She said she doesn't know where her son is. She's never heard anything about a charge against him. She didn't even know he had a job."

"I didn't get much more out of her when I called her earlier."

Anthony turned a page in his notebook. "When I mentioned the Church of the Invokers of Jesus Youth Development Center, Mrs. Smyth said she'd recently received a check for $60,000 from 'a nice pastor.' She wasn't sure of his name."

The word "pastor" hit Emma like an icicle down her back.

Anthony went on. "It was hard to get clear information from Mrs. Smyth. So I searched the records at the courthouse. It seems that Mrs. Smyth has donated her house to the Church of the Invokers of Jesus."

Emma tensed. "Why would she give her house away?"

"The pastor, probably Pastor Rainey, by her description, explained that churches are exempt from real estate taxes, so if she signed the title over to them, she wouldn't have to pay taxes any more." He tapped his notebook. "This is a scam I know about."

"So she won't have clear title to her house until she pays the $60,000 back?"

"It's worse than that. She's already signed the title over to the church. The church can evict her whenever it's convenient. The $60,000 is on record as a personal loan. If she doesn't pay that, they can seize whatever other assets she might have."

"Does she realize any of this?"

"It's hard to get a clear answer from her. She acts like the $60,000 is a gift from heaven."

Emma felt her pulse racing and needed to close her eyes.

Anthony gave her a moment. Then he asked if she knew how Andre Smyth came to be employed at the youth center.

She took a deep breath. "Have you ever heard of Riverside Paradise?" They sat in her car and she told him everything she knew.

Chip stood in Emma's front yard beside Britney's white SUV, which was parked at an angle in the street. The CD player blared out *Animal Instinct* so loud Emma could hear it in her own car. Britney sat behind the wheel, waving her head up and down to the beat, too absorbed to notice Emma pull into the driveway. Emma tapped on the window and was met with a glassy stare.

"Britney, turn that down. What's going on?"

The window slid down. Britney put on a child's pouty face. "Tell me the truth, Emma. Do you think I'm losing any weight with all of Punchy's tantric yoga?" She opened the door, and her fleshy thighs squeaked across the leather as she eased herself down from the high SUV seat. "I hear you thinking *no*. Well, now I'm doing something about it. Chelsea's going to get straight A grades, and I'm going to lose weight. I've taken care of it."

She didn't seem to be drunk. Emma suspected she was high on something else.

"See me now? Just wait two or three weeks. I'll be as thin as, I'll be as thin as Chelsea."

"I don't think you want to be as thin as a twelve-year-old, Britney. You're acting strange."

"You'll see. They'll think we're sisters." She worked her phone out of her pocket. "Here. I need a couple Before pictures." She held her hands by her side and struck a pose first from the front, then from the side, almost as if for a mug shot.

She took the phone back. "Let me see. Ugh. Ugh."

"Is that all you wanted, Britney? Me to take your picture? You kicked me out of your house, remember? How can you act like we're friends again?"

Britney's eyes flashed an empty glare. "What? Don't be so sensitive, Emma. I need you to watch Chip while I take Chelsea to the hairdresser's."

Chelsea was in the back seat, ear buds and iPhone blocking out all but her own private world. Britney climbed back into her car. "Got to go. Mind bringing Chip back about five?"

"Why not come in for a minute, Britney? Maybe you could use some coffee?"

"No time. Got an appointment with Jermaine—finally. You wouldn't believe how hard it is to get an appointment with that man. Meanwhile, I've had to suffer with Chelsea's purple hair." Her eyes studied Emma's hair. "You ought to go see Jermaine yourself. That mousey look isn't doing you any favors."

Emma ran her palm over her hair. She'd just washed it, and Todd had said, "You look pretty, Mommy." And she'd noticed the gas station attendant eyeing her that morning. No way her hair was mousey. She said, "Well, Britney, Chip's welcome any time, but you'll have to pick him up and take him home yourself. You can't be friends only when it's convenient."

Britney leaned her head out the window, an amused look on her face. "Come on, Emma. I'm sorry. Please. I have to go straight home after the hair salon to get dinner ready."

"You're cooking?"

"Well, yeah. Who else is going to do it with Esmeralda gone?" She gave a high-pitched giggle. "Actually, no. I'm having it catered from Sur le Dessus. They bring it early and I warm it up just before Derek gets home. Chicken Kievsky tonight. Last night ratatouille Niçoise. Derek says I'm a better cook than Esmeralda." She laughed out loud. "I have more energy these days. I feel like a teenager."

She drove away with the CD player blaring and her arm hanging out the window. A car cruised down the street behind her, and a rolled-up newspaper flew out the window to land on the roof of Emma's car.

Local U.S. Citizens, Permanent Residents
Arrested by Immigration Authorities

The story focused on the unwarranted arrest of Tran and his family by the Immigration and Customs Enforcement. The Trans' lawyer, Edward Donnelly, was quoted castigating the federal agency for "roughhouse tactics" and "false arrest." There was even a quote from Thieu: "We so scare."

Anthony Mansfield knocked on the door while Todd and Chip were in the back yard. "Guess you read the article?"

"I'm glad you didn't mention Esmeralda Moreno."

"I didn't mention the County Executive's role in the raid, either, you must have noticed. That doesn't mean I won't. I need to get more information first." He shifted in the chair. "As I told you, our publisher has a relationship with the exec. But if there's a major abuse of power, he'll have to let us print it. For now, I'm trying to keep the pastor-exec aspect to myself. That way I can come out with it first if it turns into something."

Emma was less interested in going after the County Executive than going after the pastor and Bea.

Anthony went on, "I did look into Riverside Paradise, as you suggested. And its developer, Beatrice Doggit of Executive Homes." He rustled through his notebook. "Here's the interesting thing. The Riverside Paradise project began five years ago—at the same time an LLC by the name of INVOK-

IM started buying tax liens."

"I remember seeing in the *Ledger*'s list of sales that a corporation called INVOKIM bought a lot of tax liens."

"And all the property INVOKIM seized along the Piskasanet River was immediately transferred to the Riverside Paradise project. It seems Beatrice Doggit's Riverside Paradise was made possible by INVOKIM buying those tax liens, then transferring the property to them."

"INVOKIM. I get it now. That must be the Church of the Invokers of Jesus, don't you think?"

"That would be my guess." Anthony unfolded a Riverside Paradise brochure. "INVOKIM is listed here as an investor in the project."

"Meaning the pastor's church is an investor. That makes sense. The two of them work together."

"There must be other INVOKIM partners, though. Riverside Paradise is too big a project to be funded just by donations to a church."

Emma reminded Anthony of the Horsey Invokers. "The main church branch, out in Bay Hills. They donate lots of money."

Anthony produced a grim smile. "I'll bet these Horsey Invokers aren't aware of where their donations are going. Still, there are probably more partners in INVOKIM."

"Can you find out?"

"It isn't listed as an LLC in our state. So I'm going to check—"

"Delaware."

"Right. The world's home of shell corporations and LLCs." Anthony squinted at Emma. "You surprise me."

"Got that from *realestateventures.com*. The billionaire's tax shelter state, they call Delaware. The money-laundering capital of America."

Anthony smiled. "Reason I haven't checked yet, Delaware

makes it near impossible to find out who benefits from an LLC. Our editor Ralph tried for months once, and the trail dead-ended at a post office box in Kenya." He tapped on his pad again. "But it might not matter. If the public hears about what INVOKIM is doing, everything'll probably all come out."

Pictures flashed across Emma's mind. Bea kneeling in front of Charles, her hands folded in his lap. Bea driving off for New York with Charles in her convertible. Then Charles's message on her phone: *She thinks we should divorce.* Anthony Mansfield didn't know how personal her battle against Bea was. She wondered if it was only fair to tell him.

"Anthony, I want to help you expose the pastor and Bea. But you need to know it's partly personal with me. Bea lured my husband away to New York, and he hasn't come back yet. And the pastor has threatened to wrongfully charge my friend with a sex crime."

More scribbling. "Mr. Smyth, I take it you mean?"

She nodded.

"You mean it's the pastor who called me with the accusation, not a parent?"

"I'm sure of it. Setting up Andre for blackmail."

Anthony looked her in the eye. "I'll definitely check into that, too."

Immigration Apologizes for Local Arrest

In the next day's *Ledger*, a follow-up article by Anthony Mansfield gave the federal Immigration and Customs Enforcement agency's response to his previous story. They were "deeply concerned" about the incident and "pledged to look into how the mistake could have been made." The Department of Homeland Security spokesperson wanted to "make it clear that all of its agencies took the rights of American citizens extremely seriously and had their safety and welfare in mind."

Emma drove straight to Tran's apartment. He was holding a letter when he opened the door. "Mrs. Bovan, I so afraid. Please. What is this? We must go jail again?"

It was an express letter from the Department of Homeland Security apologizing for the inconvenience to Tran and his family and moving up the date of their interview.

"This is good news. They've moved up your citizenship review. You don't have to wait. You can go for fingerprinting next week and the interview is set for the week after that."

Tea and rice fritters—the Trans' way of thanking Emma. And celebrating. Even Henry drank tea, and the baby was given a little taste of fritter. Emma took a copy of their citizenship applications from her handbag. "Maybe we need to go over what we wrote on these applications and make sure you can answer questions about them."

For a moment, a *will this never end* looked passed over Tran and Thieu's faces. Emma put the papers aside. "Not now, though. Now we can just talk."

With the prospect of citizenship in sight, Tran became animated. He would apply for a promotion at the Grab 'n Go. He would work overtime and save money. Maybe he could even buy his own store in a few years.

Thieu couldn't stop smiling. Maybe she could sponsor her sister to come live with them. She was a seamstress and could make clothes for "fine ladies."

It was peaceful sitting on a blanket and talking with Tran and Thieu. But the thought of Esmeralda wasn't far from Emma's mind. She didn't stay long.

In the lot outside, she stood by the bench and phoned Natalie. At first, Natalie seemed leery of talking to her, almost as if wondering if Emma had anything to do with Esmeralda's arrest. "You give my number to newspaper man?" she whispered.

"Yes. After the raid. Not before." Emma paused. "I'm your friend, Natalie."

That assurance was all that Natalie seemed to need. She said she was "worry to the death" about Esmeralda. "I don't know where she is. I don't know when I see her again."

Emma explained there was a lawyer supposedly working on her case.

"Her Juan, he stay with me. Is too bad. Only one bedroom. He sleep on floor. He don't want to go out. I think afraid."

"Natalie, I'm going to try to find a way to talk to Esmeralda. I'll call you back later."

She called Edward Donnelly.

The number you have dialed is not available. Please check the number and dial again.

Her heart pounded as she remembered Donnelly had given her a credit card receipt for the payment but they'd never actually drawn up an agreement.

The traffic in the city was terrible, but this time she knew exactly where she was going. Using the speakerphone, she auto-dialed Donnelly several times as she drove. Same recording. She found a place to park on the same side street near Donnelly's office.

An old woman with her hair wound stiffly up into a horn like a unicorn bumped into her with a shopping cart full of cardboard and blankets. Emma stepped around a gooey-looking red spot on the sidewalk and crossed the lawyer's street in the middle of the block. Horns blared, but this seemed to be the only way to get across the street.

She pushed the "Ring bell for service" button. The door clicked open a crack as before. The huge lobby was empty, and dustier than she'd remembered. She coughed as she climbed the circular staircase. The lawyer's door was closed. She knocked. No response. All the doors along the high-ceilinged hallway were closed. She listened. Not a sound. She knocked louder. "Mr. Donnelly. Mr. Donnelly, it's Emma Bovant."

The ancient rosette-inlaid brass door knob was worn but gleaming, the only item on the second floor not masked by a layer of dust. Emma wondered how many hands had touched it. "Mr. Donnelly?" She turned the knob. The door opened. No one was there.

The large mahogany desktop was completely empty except for a black telephone that looked like one she remembered from her grandmother's house. She looked around for a filing cabinet, something. Except for the desk and two chairs, the office was empty. Maybe it had been like this the other two times she'd been here and she never noticed. But the whole impression was that Donnelly had moved out.

A wave of panic made her breathe in gasps. For the first time, she wondered if he was really a lawyer at all. She scanned the green papered walls above the darkened walnut wainscoting for a diploma. Her eyes stopped on one of the pictures. Donnelly posing with Tran's family.

Her phone rang and she jumped. "Ah, is this Ms., ah, Boven? Donnelly here."

Her voice came out several octaves higher than normal. "Yes. Bovant."

"Pardon?"

"What is it, Mr. Donnelly? I've been trying to reach you."

"Ah, yes. Where are you now?"

She looked around as if he might be watching her.

"I say, where are you now? This is important."

"Actually, I'm in your office. The door was open and—"

"Can you get to the airport? I'm with Ms. Morello here. Voluntary departure. No record of deportation. She wants to see you and her son before she leaves."

"When? When does she leave?"

"Hour and a half."

"Juan's living in an apartment that's on the way to the airport from here. I'll try."

"Who?"

"Juan. Her son."

"Good. Good. Did you say you were in my office?"

Emma thought of denying it—he seemed so scatterbrained she might pull it off. But she said yes.

"Would you mind getting my camera out of the top right drawer of my desk and bringing it?"

Juan, Natalie, and Emma ran from the hourly parking garage across the causeway to the airport departure area. Emma was breathing hard when they arrived at the gate for the plane to Guatemala. Esmeralda, Donnelly, and two uniformed ICE police sat near the entrance.

Esmeralda jumped up when she saw Juan. "Mi hiho. Mi chico." She threw her arms around him. Natalie clung to her arm. "Volveré pronto," Esmeralda said, which Emma took to mean "I'll come back soon." Juan's face glistened with tears in a beam of LED lights.

An ICE woman separated them from Esmeralda. "No contact with the departing passenger, please."

Donnelly, who seemed to speak a kind of broken Spanish, explained to Natalie he'd arranged for Esmeralda to be able to get a visitor's visa when she wanted to come back and see Juan.

Emma said, "Esmeralda, I told Juan on the way here he can stay with me while you're gone. Natalie doesn't have much room, but we do. What do you think?"

Esmeralda kissed her. "Si, Si. Yes. Gracias."

The ICE woman pulled on Emma. "Stand back, please, ma'am. Everybody stand back from the departing passenger."

Emma opened her purse. "Esmeralda, this is for you. I wanted to give it to you before, but—"

"Ma'am, stand back. I need to examine that."

"It's money."

The ICE woman took it, sniffed it. She looked at the ICE man next to her. He counted it. "Not over the limit." He shrugged.

The woman gave it back to Emma.

"No." Esmeralda shook her head. "You are too much kind. I cannot take."

Emma dropped it into Esmeralda's bag.

"Please, ma'am, no contact with the departee." But the ICE woman let the money stay in the bag.

Donnelly tapped Emma on the shoulder. "Ah, Ms. Bove, did you bring the—"

"Camera. Yes. Here it is." She took a picture of Donnelly standing next to a grateful-looking Esmeralda, her son, and her friend Natalie. At his urging, she took four more in different poses.

32

On the warpath

Todd was ecstatic helping Juan move his bundle of clothes, backpack of books, and duffel bag of whatever into the spare room. All they talked about was baseball. Right away, they ran to the back yard with a ball, bat, and gloves. From the window, Emma saw Juan hitting grounders to Todd.

School was almost over. Emma drove Juan up to North-brook in the mornings so he could finish school there. They hadn't heard from Esmeralda yet. Emma hoped her husband would get better and she could come back soon to "visit." But if she was going to be away for a long time, Emma would see if Juan wanted to enroll in Shady Park High School.

Juan came with them to Todd's last game. The season didn't extend into the summer—when baseball is traditionally played—because Nottingham parents complained they had to take their children on vacation.

As Britney drew near the stands, she was already shouting. "Come on, Bears! Don't let those Sharks tie you."

Emma had to ask Todd what that meant. Apparently, Todd and Chip's Bears had won two games and lost one. The Sharks were one and two.

"Bears! Bears! Bears!" Britney shouted.

Chip looked embarrassed. He walked to the plate without putting on his kneepads.

"Oh, no. Oh, no. Time out!" Britney held up one hand, Chip's knee pads in the other. Emma felt sorry for Chip as she strapped them on him, but what could she do?

Juan, who was constantly trying to improve his vocabulary, turned to Emma and muttered, "*Over-parenting*. I get it now. We don't have this problem in Guatemala."

Chip tipped the ball and it landed halfway to the pitcher's mound. He ran as fast as the knee pads would let him and made it to first just as the first baseman dropped the throw from the coach-pitcher.

Todd knocked a dribbler down third-base line into the outfield. Emma assumed he and Chip would both score, but in the short season, all the boys had improved. The Shark left-fielder got the ball and held Todd and Chip on second and third. It wasn't long before they scored, though.

Todd got three hits, actual hits, and made it to base every at-bat, either on a hit, a walk, or an error. The Bears won 17 to 15.

"Bears win the season!" In front of the stands, Britney was stomping around in what could have been some kind of tribal dance, lifting her head now and then to hydrate herself with a plastic bottle of Perrier.

"My mom's crazy these days," Chip mumbled.

Juan looked confused. "Is there a prize or something for the team that wins the most games? It's just kids playing baseball, no?"

At the Northbrook field, baseball didn't stop when school was over for the summer. It went on unfettered by league rules, sign-up fees, uniforms, coaches, parent input, or knee pads. Emma drove Todd and Juan there whenever she could. When they wondered why Chip couldn't go with them, Emma just said he was busy with golf and swimming lessons. That and Physics Camp, which Britney had signed him up for after he won the award for Excellence in Science.

It wasn't clear whether Britney was on speaking terms with Emma or not. She'd kicked her out of the house and sat apart from her at the kids' next baseball games, yet later she'd come and asked Emma to watch Chip for a while.

215

Emma was surprised when Britney called her. She was talking fast. Something about the Board of Education. She wanted to get Emma's support for somebody she thought would be perfect. "All these school shootings you hear about. We need somebody who can step up and make sure the teachers can defend our kids."

"Defend?"

"I've always said, and Derek agrees, the teachers should be armed."

"Now, there I don't agree with you. I'm sorry."

Britney raced on, talking about children shot by "kids who brought guns to school." She veered off that topic onto "our kids sitting with kids whose parents get food stamps" and finally onto "teachers who don't appreciate our kids and give them unfair grades." She was talking so fast she had to catch her breath. "So, here's what I want. I can get you on the nominating commission. They vote for candidates the governor picks from. I want your support for a Board of Education member."

"Is it somebody I know?"

"I'm calling all the parents of Chip and Chelsea's friends. I want you to be objective. Objective, right? You know a tough business woman is what we need to straighten things up. Beatrice Doggit is the best person for the job. Derek agrees. Can I count on your vote?"

"Britney, no. You can't be serious?"

"OK. I see how it is. I don't know why I even called. I need to stick with women who have their kids' welfare in mind." Emma's phone went silent.

County Homeowners Lose Their Houses

An article in the *Shady Park Ledger* by Anthony Mansfield described how twenty or more county residents had lost their homes to an organization that specialized in purchasing tax liens and taking claim to the houses when the owners couldn't immediately pay their back taxes, utility fees, legal fees, or interest penalties. INVOKIM, LLC, was identified as the lien purchaser. The article said titles to the houses it seized along the Piskasanet River were transferred to real estate developer Executive Homes.

This was to be the first of a series of articles on the topic. It focused on the Grayson family, who had been forced to move from their house on the Piskasanet River into a trailer on a relative's lot in the Florida panhandle. The article quoted Adam Grayson saying he lost his house because he hadn't paid a $320 late fee on his electric bill that he didn't know he owed. "They say it was published in the paper, but I never saw it. One day I just got an eviction notice."

The article said a sizeable new villa now stood on the former site of the Graysons' house. It was owned by Ms. Beatrice Doggit of Executive Homes, which had begun to build an exclusive riverfront community along the Piskasanet to be called Riverside Paradise. It said that INVOKIM was listed on Riverside Paradise brochures as an investor.

The houses were "legally seized," the article was careful to point out. But it created sympathy for the homeowners and was a blot on the reputation of Bea's real estate agency.

Maybe that was enough, Emma thought. The story was out there. The public knew. She hoped Bea and the pastor were reading it right now. How about Britney? Definitely not. She didn't read the newspaper. The only news she got was from Reddit and Facebook.

She called Anthony's number and left a message complimenting him on the story, adding that she'd met children along the Piskasanet whose families had been disrupted by the Riverside Paradise construction, if he was interested in talking to them.

Local Family Loses Home to Corporation

This story focused on the Trout family, who had difficulty paying their second mortgage when the crabbing business dried up. They signed over their home to INVOKIM with the provision that they could buy it back as long as they kept up with the rent the corporation was charging them to stay there. At first, the rent was lower than the mortgage. But when the rent kept going up, they were no longer able to pay the full amount, and INVOKIM had them evicted. Their house was torn down to make room for a villa to be part of the Riverside Paradise project.

That night Emma got a call from Charles, his voice quavering. "What's going on, Emma? I thought you would call me."

"I've been busy with a lot of things." She cringed to think how that must have sounded, then softened her voice. "I love you, Charles. No matter what lies Bea told you. That woman's making a fool of us both. Come home."

"But what about Andre?" His voice was almost a whimper. "Aren't you with him now? That's what Bea says."

"She's a scheming, lying woman, Charles. Nobody even knows where Andre is."

"Oh." His voice was husky. "Andre's missing? Maybe that's why . . . . Bea's furious at something. She called me from Shady Park. She says she's on the warpath. Says I can't use a suite at Executive Homes when I get back. And my New York clients aren't showing up any more."

"Come back right now, Charles. Your affair with Bea is over. She's going to be sorry for everything she's done. I'm on the warpath, too."

"Don't say affair, Emma. I've been stupid, maybe. I'm starting to see it now."

"Starting?"

"I was trying to move the family up into the economic level you always thought we should be in. I saw a chance and took it. But I let you and Todd down, I guess."

The tremor in his voice softened her. She still loved him, after all.

Lying in bed later that night, Emma felt a rush of physical desire for Charles. It had probably started when she heard his voice on the phone. Anyway, there it was. Memories of making love to him aroused her as she lay there. Love-making was Charles's way of pushing all problems aside. If he were here beside her right now, that's what would happen. She longed for it.

Now that school was over, Chip was being driven to Physics Camp every day and couldn't play with Todd. Luckily, Juan quickly became part of the family. Emma kept driving the boys to Northbrook to play baseball while she made sure Tran and Thieu were ready for their citizenship interview.

Juan was fourteen, almost fifteen, and tried to help Emma around the house. He started cutting the grass for her and washing the dishes. He kept his room neat and even started bringing in the newspaper and putting it on the table next to Charles's chair.

Local Realtor's Connection to Evictions Being Investigated

There was a third article about home owners being evicted by INVOKIM. Apparently, Anthony's stories were encouraging more victims to come forth. This story concluded, "The District Attorney's office is conducting an investigation and would not say if it knew the identity of the partners in IN-VOKIM, which is listed as an investor on the Riverside Paradise brochures of Executive Homes, owned by real estate developer Beatrice Doggit."

Emma also worried about Andre's mother. Apparently, she hadn't owed any back taxes, and so there had been no tax lien for INVOKIM to buy. So, according to what Anthony had found out, Pastor Mitch had simply tricked her into signing over her house to the church to avoid paying real estate taxes. She could be evicted at any time. Plus, she had a $60,000 loan from the church to repay and didn't seem to realize it.

Situated as it was back from Riverside Road, Mrs. Smyth's property couldn't be used for a waterfront house. But eventually her lot might make a nice place to put a swimming pool or tennis court for whatever villa was built in front of it. Andre's mother had called the $60,000 a gift from heaven, not realizing it was more like an attack from hell.

Emma sat in Charles's chair, her head in her hands.

Natalie called. There was a sound of wind in her phone. "Ms. Emma, I thank you again for help Esmeralda and Juan. Now I watching Pastor drive away from church with Ms. Bea. I think you know her?"

"Yes."

"Why I call: I hear them talking about you and your husband. They afraid of something."

"Could you hear what they were saying?"

"Jes. I stand near door. Bad, I know, but—"

"What did they say?"

"Pastor, he tell Ms. Bea stop going to see Mr. Charles in New York. He say he is starting to get jealous. She say it is nothing; she never sleep with him. She say anyway no need to keep Mr. Charles up there no more. They got bigger trouble now. They talking about it, but I no understand."

Emma needed a moment to take this in.

"Then," Natalie continued, "also bad, but I watch in parking lot when they leave. Ms. Bea get into his car and they kissing."

"What?"

"Is true. Lot of kissing. I go closer and take picture with my phone. Why? I also hear pastor before. He talking about me and other workers at church. He call us 'dam spic.' He say he going to fire anybody who is legal, like me, and save money by hire only illegal and pay less."

"Natalie, if he fires you, I'll try my best to find you a job."

"Thank you, Ms. Emma. You very kind." She seemed about to end the call.

"Natalie, one more thing. You say the picture's on your phone? Can you text or email it to me? Don't worry. I'll never say where I got it. But I know who to show it to if he fires you."

"Even he don't fire me, I looking for new job. Why? I respect for Pastor's wife. She teach me many songs. This is not good pastor, I think."

Emma wanted to warn Andre's mother about her loan from the pastor's church. Since school was out, she took Todd and Juan down to the Piskasanet to wade and swim while she went to see her. Todd was excited about showing Juan his newly acquired ability to surf-glide on pieces of plywood.

Construction along River Road had stopped. Piles of plowed-up rubbish sat in cleared lots, but the trucks and bulldozers were gone. Driving past Bea's villa, she noticed her black convertible parked in the driveway. She dropped the boys off at the beach where Todd had played with the children before, telling Juan to make sure they didn't go in over their heads. She wanted to talk to Andre's mother and would be right back.

But as she started to drive down the dirt road to Andre's mother's house, she changed her mind. She drove to Bea's villa instead and rang the doorbell.

She had to ring a few times before Bea opened the door. Bea's hair looked stringy and frazzled, and her makeup blotchy. "What do you want?" she demanded. She put her hand on the door to close it.

"I want a job."

Bea stood with her open mouth forming an ellipse bordered by sparkling pink lipstick.

"I came to ask for a job, a job in real estate."

"Jesus give me strength. What kind of sick game are you playing?"

"I'm sure you remember. I came to your office to apply for a job. You never got back to me, so I figured it was because I didn't know that much about the business. So I've been studying up on real estate and know a lot more now than I did then."

Bea clenched her fists, driving long opalescent nails into her palms.

"The real estate code of ethics gave me some problems at first—it's so detailed, you know. But I think I understand it now. Actually, it seems the very beginning sums most of it up. Where it says agents have to *protect and promote the interests of their client.*"

"You came here to lecture me? I want you to get off my property."

"Lecture you? Not at all. I just thought now that I'm more knowledgeable about real estate laws and procedures and sanctions you might be willing to hire me."

Now the sparkling pink lips were trembling.

Emma couldn't believe her own courage. "Go ahead. Ask me some questions. See if I know what can cause an agent to lose her license. What problems there can be getting loans or building permits once that happens? That kind of stuff. I'm ready to pass a test on it now."

"How dare you come to my door and talk about losing my license?"

"I'm only talking about agents who have done something wrong. I read online about this case where an agent did something that wasn't actually illegal but might have seemed unethical. When it came out, she realized she had three choices. Give back the houses she conned the owners out of. Pay the owners a fair price for their property. Or lose her license."

A red flush spread from Bea's throat down across her chest to the exposed top half of her breasts. She gripped the gold cross hanging around her neck. "As Jesus is my savior, I know what this is really about. You want your husband back."

Emma stared at her, trying to control her anger.

Bea went on, "Your sinful husband who has been pursuing me shamelessly. He needs to beg Jesus for forgiveness. And you need to keep that man away from me."

Emma shrugged. "I'll try. But there's not much I can do to keep other people's husbands away from you."

Mrs. Smyth's bungalow was on a short dirt road that ran behind where the Trouts used to live before their lot was cleared for the Riverside Paradise project. The paint looked like it used to be light gray or maybe white, but most of it had peeled off. Mrs. Smith didn't have a car. A derelict wooden skiff was upturned on cinder blocks at the end of the road. Emma peeped into the door window through a lace curtain. She knocked, wondering if Andre's mother would recognize her.

"Emma, dear. Mercy. I can't believe it. Is Andre with you?" Mrs. Smith wore a lace-fringed apron over a brown jumper. Curls of gray hair hung down each side of her face.

The house smelled of furniture polish. Everything made of wood was gleaming. There was lace everywhere. Lace doilies covered two end tables, and lace antimacassars covered the arms and back of the couch and her one armchair. A lace tablecloth covered the small table in the corner of the single room that served as entrance hall, living room, and dining room. They walked by a gleaming walnut console half as big as Mrs. Smith herself with a tinted dial and large knobs. It was a radio like some she'd only seen in old black-and-white movies.

Mrs. Smith took her to the kitchen, sat her at a porcelain enamel table with green legs, and offered her a cup of tea with honey. She said, "You look troubled, dear. I know how it is for young people trying to get by, so I'll come right out with it. Do you need money?"

Emma was too surprised to speak.

"Now don't be bashful, dear. I know it's what my Andre would want." She widened her blue eyes and nodded. "He's very fond of you. Always was."

"Where is Andre?"

His mother put a mason jar of some yellow vegetables on the table in front of Emma. "I've just canned some squash from my garden. It's Andre's favorite. I want you to have some."

"Thanks. Where is Andre?"

"He loves squash."

"Do you know where he is?"

"I don't know where Andre is. He called me, but when I asked where he was, he didn't seem to hear me. He's like that, you know?"

"Yes."

"Are you sure you don't need any money? I have some I could give you."

"I wanted to tell you about a church that gets people to donate their houses and lends them money. I was wondering if you got any money from them. The Church of the Invokers of Jesus."

"From the nice church pastor. Yes."

"Mrs. Smyth, I think you should repay the loan. And, more important, try to get the title to your house back. Maybe I can help."

Mrs. Smyth smiled. Her eyes had the impish gleam she sometimes saw in Andre's. "A loan? Oh no, dear. The pastor said I could keep it."

33

Learning opportunities

Her phone rang just as Emma was starting dinner.

"Mrs. Bovant? It's LaKisha. From Social Services? I wanted to check on something Human Resources told me. They say Charles called and quit his job. They say they gave him some time to think it over and change his mind. But he never called back, and now they've replaced him. I tried calling Charles to make sure this was true. But he didn't answer. It's kind of a shock. I thought he was on vacation."

A picture of a Social Services Christmas party she had gone to with Charles came to Emma's mind. LaKisha was there, looking beautiful in a low-cut white satin dress covered with beads. Everybody had been drinking a strong punch, and LaKisha was dancing with Charles. When the music stopped, LaKisha looked up, and she and Charles were directly under a sprig of mistletoe hanging from the hall doorway. She put her arms around his neck and kissed him. It wasn't just a little peck on the cheek.

"I'm afraid that's right, LaKisha. He says he wants to be a life coach."

There was a silence. Then LaKisha ventured, "I left messages for him, but he never called me back." She lowered her voice. "The thing is, our Human Resources department, well, sometimes we think they aren't too bright. And so I just wanted to make sure they got Charles's message right." She paused as if giving Emma one more chance to say it wasn't true, then went on. "Sorry to bother you. I just didn't think it was like Charles to quit by telephone like that. You know, and not come in and say good-bye. I mean to everybody."

Emma knew LaKisha liked Charles. They worked closely together, and Charles clearly liked her, too. She was another woman in his life. But Emma also liked and respected LaKisha. She didn't see her at all in the same light as Bea. Yet Charles acted as if Bea was another LaKisha. It was unbelievable that he didn't see the difference.

"He's still in New York, LaKisha. I'm sure he'll go to the office and say good-bye when he comes back." When LaKisha was silent, Emma added, "I'll make sure he does."

Todd and Juan were looking at baseball cards on the kitchen table.

"You'll have to clear that off," Emma told them. "Dinner's almost ready."

"What is it?" Todd must have been hungry. He was scooping the cards into a shoe box fast.

"Hot dogs and canned beans."

"Are the hot dogs organic?" Todd teased.

"You bet. They're made from all kinds of organs."

"When's Daddy coming home? I mean, I like eating hot dogs and beans and stuff, but I want him to come back."

"We both do." She meant it, even though there was no denying she'd begun to appreciate her recent independence, the feeling of being in charge of her own life. She promised herself never to give this up, no matter what.

And then, when she brought the boys home from North-brook the next afternoon, there he was, sitting in his cracked leather chair, a spaced-out look spread over his face. Emma didn't know whether the pounding of her heart was because she was furious with him or still stupidly in love with him. She took a breath and did her best to give him an ironic look.

"Oh, hi, Coach."

Charles hugged her and Todd together. Emma hadn't used

227

mascara for some time—good thing because it would now be running down her cheeks onto his white collar. "Emma, Todd, can you forgive me?"

"It's OK, Daddy," Todd said. "You're back now."

Emma was still angry but held her tongue. Her mother would have approved.

"Daddy, Juan's staying here. He's Esmeralda's son. She's in Guatemala." Todd then exploded into descriptions of the Little League games Charles missed and playing baseball with Juan at the Northbrook lot and the rookie baseball card he had of . . . .

Emma was glad Todd was doing the talking. She didn't know what to say. She wanted Charles to talk first. He was holding her hand the whole time he was listening to Todd's baseball stories, clinging to her as he often used to do when he felt nervous or insecure.

"Mommy, can we go out back and play catch with Daddy?"

Emma nodded, giving Charles's hand a squeeze. She watched them through the window. Every now and then Charles would look back at her.

Now what would she fix for dinner? She'd been slacking off since he went to New York. Lots of tuna fish sandwiches, scrambled eggs, canned soup. Todd ate these meals with more relish than he ever ate organic mung bean sprouts or whatever. Well, she was more in charge of things now, right? She served Heat 'n Eat Pizza, giving Charles a look that dared him to comment.

Charles picked up a piece and ate it with the same blank stare he'd had when she found him sitting in his chair. He didn't seem hungry and didn't seem to notice or care what he was eating. He hardly said anything during dinner. When Todd told him Andre had helped with his science project, Charles's face turned red. He couldn't look at Emma.

"Let's go for a walk," Emma suggested. It was then she realized his VW Beetle wasn't in the driveway. "Where's your car?"

"I wanted to see if the battery was dead. You know. After all that time." His face reddened again. "It started, but the engine ran rough. Had to get it towed to a garage in Northbrook."

"So there's repair work to be done? That's what you're saying?" She gave him a pat on the behind. "We'll have to get working on that."

"Heh-heh."

The houses on Shady Park Lane were all built in the 1940s or 50s and had towering pines and maple trees in the yards. It was early July, and orange daylilies and pink tea roses bloomed in the front yards. The smell of roses and fresh pine needles calmed Emma as they walked along the sidewalk.

Charles seemed distracted. He glanced at her sideways. "So, you really don't know where Andre is?"

"I'm not lying to you, Charles. Why don't *you* try calling him? I've tried, but I always get *The number you are calling is not in service.*"

"Always?"

"What do you mean?"

"You know. You and Andre. You call him a lot?"

"Gosh, Charles. You and his mother seem to be the only people in the world who don't realize Andre is gay." She knew this wasn't quite an honest reply—more of a red herring.

Charles frowned. "I know he's different, but the best research shows it's more complicated than just gay or not. You assume just because he never married—"

"Or had a girlfriend, or ever went on an actual date with a woman." She left it at that for now.

They passed twin Japanese maple trees glowing red in the sunset against the dark brown of an old cedar shingled house.

"Look at that, Charles."

"What?"

"The trees."

"Yeah. Beautiful." He took in the view. "Don't you think we'd miss this street if we ever moved to a place like Nottingham Estates?"

"Move? I never said I wanted to move there. I'm sorry if you thought that."

Charles nodded noncommittally. He said almost nothing else during their walk. That evening, washing the dishes, he stared into the sink in silence.

"Thinking about Bea, Charles?"

He flushed. "Sort of."

"She wanted you to divorce me, you said in your text."

Charles dropped a dish with a crash into the sink. "Yes. Because she said you and Andre . . . you know."

"What happened? Did she change her mind?"

He started picking up the pieces of the broken dish. "I guess. I don't know. She left after the conference was over, but she came up a few times and took me to dinner to meet new clients. And she called me every day to see how the coaching was going. Then recently she stopped. And my clients stopped showing up. I don't know why."

Emma was pretty sure *she* did. But she left him alone with his thoughts. Charles was what her mother called a "simple soul." No denying that. He never suspected people wanted to harm him, and the idea of harming somebody else never entered his head. He was a social worker, after all. Emma wondered if getting close to Andre while Charles was gone had harmed him. It was obvious that Charles was upset by whatever Bea told him. There must be some way to put worry about her and Andre out of his mind.

After Todd and Juan were asleep and it was time for bed, she showered and put on the black negligée she hadn't worn since the night of the Fontainbleau reception. Charles was already in bed. She moved towards him and looked into his hazel eyes, putting her face closer and closer to his until he blinked. She touched his cheeks, and he pulled her to him and kissed her. "Emma." His breathy voice excited her.

Climbing on top of him, feeling him under her thin nightgown, she said, "I'm out of shape, Coach. Is there any kind of workout you know of that could help me out?"

The next morning, Charles seemed contentedly dazed. He chewed the bacon she put on his plate—laced with who knows what chemical preservatives—with a face that expressed nothing more than a dull satisfaction. "Mmm."

With the analytical concentration of a budding biologist observing a subject in an experiment, Todd watched him eat it. "Good, huh, Daddy?"

"Hmm? Oh, yeah. Delicious."

Charles stayed at the kitchen table scrolling down through several screens on his cell phone. Emma leaned back against the stove and watched. They'd made love last night, passionately, but they hadn't talked much, and she really didn't know what was going through his mind.

"I don't understand," Charles muttered to himself.

Emma waited.

"Nothing from Bea since I left New York."

Emma wrinkled her nose, but he wasn't looking at her.

"Strange. My clients don't respond, either."

"That is strange." Emma tried to control her sarcasm.

"Maybe I can get in touch with their friends who live down here."

"New clients?"

"That's what I'm hoping."

Charles put his phone on the table and looked at his empty plate.

"More bacon, Charles?"

"Yes. Thanks, Emma."

"Here you go. It's not organic, but—"

He gave an embarrassed snicker and munched it greedily. "I've been mostly skipping breakfast in New York."

"More eggs? Not organic, either. I've been economizing."

"Yes, please."

"I've been trying to save money here and there. You know, since you quit your job."

He swallowed a huge mouthful of scrambled eggs. "You think I quit Social Services prematurely. I know." Looking at his phone, he mumbled, "No answer from the few potential clients I've called in our area."

"Maybe you could put an ad in the paper." She opened the *Ledger* to the Features section. "See here? Look at these ads. Ads for Mommy Makeovers, Cool Sculpting, Breast Augmentation, Glycolic Peels, Medi-Spa Sessions. . . let me see . . . an Integrated Aesthetic Center, Intense-Pulsed-Light Weight Displacement Seminars, Seniors Dating Bootcamp—I wonder what that is—ah, here. Astrological Advisor, Fashion Coordinator, Personal Fitness Trainer. See what I mean? You'd be the first Life Coach to advertise."

Charles's blush surprised her. She'd expected a rebuttal in defense of the life coaching profession. Instead, he put his hand on the table and declared, "I'll prove myself to you yet, Emma. If the life coaching doesn't work out, I'll find something else."

Emma's throat felt tight. "Prove yourself? Charles, there's nothing to prove. I was so proud of you when you were helping people at Social Services. Don't you know that?"

"But you said I didn't get paid enough."

"I said you weren't paid what you deserve. Nobody at Social Services is. I said pay should be determined by the value of the work we do, and it's not. Instead, people like Derek get rich by making deals, sometimes with dishonest people."

"So you mean I should go back to my Social Services job? I kind of miss it."

"You do, Charles?" She swallowed. She didn't have the heart to tell him he'd been replaced at work. "Tell you what, Charles. Let's talk about that later. How about coming with me this afternoon to Tran's apartment and helping me get him and his wife ready to take the English and citizenship tests?"

"Mr. Charles! You are return from the business."

"Mr. Charles! We are so happy."

Henry burst out, "See how much English they've learned since you've been gone, Mr. Charles?"

Emma dropped familiarly onto the folded blanket they set on the floor for her, but a slight groan escaped from Charles as he bent down to sit on his. Tran laughed. "You long time in big New York chair. Maybe you forget how to sit on floor." Thieu echoed her husband's laugh. Emma was loving this.

"Yes," Charles admitted. "I've forgotten a lot of things."

They served tea and Vietnamese snacks on a plastic tray. Emma watched as Charles, smiling more than he had since he came back, ate a ball of rice containing a red dyed plum without even asking what chemicals were used to preserve it. He picked up a slimy green thing with his fingers—an item that even Emma declined—and dropped it into his mouth.

Tran and Thieu tried to explain how Emma and her "important friend" had "saved" them. Charles just nodded. He was only half-listening. He took a piece of dried squid, laced with "MSG for flavor" according to the cellophane it was wrapped in, and chewed and chewed until it was soft enough to swallow. "Mmm." He sounded like a cow, and Emma waited for the Trans to laugh again, but they were too polite.

Before they left, Thieu took Emma into the bedroom and unfolded a shimmering white dress from a pile on the floor. "I

233

sew," she told Emma. "For take oat of areegeance." She was like a bride showing her maid of honor her wedding dress. Emma scanned the room. No sewing machine. Just a basket with scissors, needles, and thread.

"It's beautiful, Thieu." Emma ran her hand along the embroidered neckline.

Thieu nodded solemnly and folded the dress carefully back on top of the pile of clothes. As far as Emma knew, the swearing-in ceremony was far from formal, but she didn't mention this to Thieu. She said, "You'll be the most beautiful person there."

They pulled over onto the dirt strip that served as a parking lot for Domestic Foreign Motors, where the VW had been towed. A door with a barred window hung open. Men in greasy white T-shirts turned and stared when Charles, Emma, Todd, and Juan walked in together. It was impossible to tell who was in charge.

"Wondering about the Beetle," Charles ventured.

Two of the men turned and walked away down a narrow aisle lined with dim shelves of metal parts. Another sighed, set a can of Dr. Pepper down on a high black counter, and walked behind it. He burped. "Beetle, you say?"

"I hope you had a chance to look at it."

Without a word, the man pulled a white form out from under the counter, leaving a black thumb print on it as he slid it over to Charles. "Blew a cylinder head." He tapped twice on the form where it said so, each time leaving another smudge.

"So. How much will it cost to fix it?"

The mechanic acted surprised at the question. "How much to fix it? That's going to be hard to say. Have to see if we can get parts, first. It won't be cheap."

Charles aimed a wary glance at Emma. Todd did, too.

"Probably not worth fixing a car that old," the mechanic declared. "You can junk it and get a much newer car for less than it would cost to fix this one."

Emma knew if they used some more of Bea's money, they could even buy him a brand new car, but she wasn't going to mention that. Charles wanted his old car back. And she wanted her old Charles back. "Let's fix it," she urged. "It's a classic."

Charles's face beamed a look of relief like an injured athlete who has been told he can get back in the game.

Emma avoided talking about Bea's money until they were alone again. She didn't think they should keep it.

"Why not?" Charles objected. His feelings seemed hurt.

"Because . . . I mean, what is it a payment for?"

"For my services. I made out bills and Bea took them to give to her friends that I coached.

"You don't think it was Bea who made all the deposits?"

Charles shrugged. "If she did, my clients reimbursed her, I'm sure."

Emma felt as if she were walking a delicate line. She didn't want to imply that Charles's coaching wasn't worth what he was paid and cause him to get all depressed again. But she wanted to get him to see the money as a bribe. She frowned. "Andre was upset when he heard about the deposits."

Charles was taking a sip of the last of the organic beers and coughed. "So you've been close enough to Andre to discuss our finances with him? I know you insist he's—"

Emma fought to control her mounting exasperation. "Gay. He's gay. Homosexual, Charles. And no, I didn't tell him anything about our finances. He was standing right there when I called you, and you talked to Pastor Mitch on the phone. Remember? The pastor asked you if you'd gotten the deposits."

Charles slouched back in his chair, shaking his head. He

started to speak a couple of times but seemed too confused to know what to ask. Emma was determined not to let him slip back into the mental swamp he'd returned to her in. She was almost ready to back down and let him think the money was the reward for superior life coaching. But then Charles took his phone and tapped open his contacts.

"I wonder," he said. "You tell me Andre disappeared right after he heard about my life coaching income?"

"Yes. After he heard it came from the pastor and Bea."

"That's strange. It's almost as if he thought we were colluding with the pastor and Bea on the Paradise project."

"You think, Charles?" He was slow coming to this conclusion, but at least he got there. "So call him and tell him we're not."

"I'll give the damned money back, if that's what he thinks."

"There you go."

Charles let her hear Andre's message. It was different this time. Instead of *The number you are calling is not in service*, it said *The party you are calling is not available*.

"*Not available*," Emma observed. "That means the line is busy, or he's turned his phone off. Anyway, he's still there. Alive somewhere. I guess that's what it means. Ugh, I was so worried."

Charles sipped some beer. "Don't hyperventilate about it, Emma. You'll make me start worrying again."

"He's your friend, too, Charles." She didn't care what he thought. "Call him again."

He handed the phone to her instead. She tapped the number. Same message. She sneaked a look at Charles's face as she handed it back, then pushed her hands up through her hair.

"Come on, now, Baby." Charles used his consoling voice. "No need to get all Crazy Mommy over this. Come here." He pulled her from the hassock onto his lap. "He'll show up."

Emma buried her head into Charles's shoulder. "Anyway,"

she said, "we can't give all the money back. I gave $7,000 to the lawyer."

"Lawyer?"

"For Tran and Thieu. I'm sure you didn't understand what they were talking about." She gave him the details of the Immigration and Customs Enforcement raid while he sat finishing his beer, trying to take everything in.

Charles said, "Well, that much money I know I earned, anyway. Nothing could convince me my coaching was worth any less than $7,000."

Emma giggled. "And the $600 I gave Thieu so she could apply for citizenship, too?"

"Um-hum. Sure. That too. Definitely. I'll show you the plans I made for these clients, helping them face their problems, turn their lives around—if you promise to keep the information confidential, of course."

"No need." She thought about it. "Keep the plans, though, and your invoices, just in case."

"You believe me, don't you? That I earned plenty of money. I don't even know how much we have, but—"

"Sure. And we could keep some money to get your Beetle fixed." She laughed. "It's sort of a company car, I guess you could say. A business expense."

"And your diamond necklace, don't forget. I'm sure I earned enough for a nice one. That's what I was aiming for. Then we'll give the rest of it back."

Charles spent the whole next day trying to get in touch with the New York "client" friends of Bea who'd told him they could find him other clients in Nottingham Estates when he went back home. No luck.

"Did you call Bea?"

"Yeah. She seemed angry. I don't know what I ever did to make her so mad. I asked if she still needs life coaching. She just laughed."

"It's probably me she's angry at."

"She didn't seem to remember she promised to get me clients in Nottingham Estates."

"Um, Hon, there are a couple of newspaper reports you should read. Bea and the pastor are in some trouble lately." She showed him the *Ledger* stories on the methods used by INVOKIM to acquire property along the Piskasanet River for the Riverside Paradise project.

"That's bad." He shook his head. "They should be ashamed. But I don't see the connection with life coaching."

What Emma *wanted* to say: Don't you get it? Life coaching in New York was never more than a scam to get you away from Andre so they could work on him. What she *said*: "The thing is, Bea's got other things to worry about these days."

Charles cupped his chin in his hand. The deep frown on his forehead suggested the truth was dawning on him. He looked down at the floor, mumbling, more to himself than to be heard. "So maybe none of my clients really wanted life coaching."

Trying to soften the blow, she said, "You were casting pearls before swine, Hon. You were giving them the opportunity to learn something, but they were too corrupt to benefit from it."

Charles stared blankly ahead, nodding. Then, without saying a word, he got up and went into the kitchen. Emma followed. He went down to the basement and brought up the step ladder and a putty knife. He spread newspapers on the table and floor and started scraping the ceiling. He was working steadily with an expressionless face and stirring up a good bit of dust.

"I'll help, Charles."

"Would you Google how to patch a hole in a plaster ceiling?"

Emma heard the thump of the *Ledger* on the trunk of her car.

Section A, *News*. Something about a shooting in a parking lot. She'd read that later.

Section B, *Real Estate*. No.

Section C, *Classifieds*. A huge new ad in the *Employment* section by the local community college dwarfed everything else on the page like a skyscraper in a tract of single-story houses.

> With providing learning opportunities as its central mission, Piskasanet Community College (PCC) has responded to the needs of a diverse community for decades by offering high quality, affordable and accessible learning opportunities. Established in 1976, PCC is a fully-accredited, public two-year institution that offers national and regional studies that can lead to a degree or certificate, industry credential, transfer to a four-year institution, or career enhancement, personal enrichment and lifelong learning. The college's nationally recognized and award-winning programs have helped tens of thousands of students annually achieve their academic, professional and personal goals.
>
> Located in Piskasanet County

. . . .

Emma skipped over a couple of inches.

> PCC is committed to support-
> ing and sustaining a diverse and
> inclusive educational and work
> environment. Diversity is not
> merely a goal but a value that is
> embedded throughout the insti-
> tution in multiple areas includ-
> ing (but not limited to): learning,
> teaching, student success, work-
> place effectiveness, and engage-
> ment in partnerships with the lo-
> cal and global community.

Emma skipped down further, looking for the job description.

> . . . should be prepared to
> use technology and learning out-
> comes assessment to enhance job
> performance and show commit-
> ment to innovation, excellence,
> and a focus on learning.

That was all. It didn't say what the job was. Maybe the
word "learning" was a hint. Was it some kind of trainee position? At the very bottom was a person to contact: Prof. Mark
O. Shandule, and an email address.

34

Pounding the pavement

It was summer now, much warmer than when Emma had gone for an interview at Executive Homes, and too hot to wear that charcoal skirt suit. She wanted to impress Professor Shandule, whoever he was, and laughed at herself as she went through her closet and blurted out, "I have nothing to wear." Everything looked too dowdy to her now, probably because she hadn't bought any clothes for herself for years, not since she lost her Envirotech job.

One thing she didn't miss about working was the pressure to look good. It had been a relief at first to realize she could sit around the house in her jeans, go buy groceries in her jeans, and hardly ever think about what she was wearing. Maybe she was being foolish in applying for a job again, especially when she didn't really know what the job was. She should probably just put on her work jeans, go downstairs, and help Charles patch the kitchen ceiling. But if Charles didn't have a job, she needed to get one.

OK. One more purchase from the Bea Paradise account. She didn't have to ask Charles to stay home and watch the boys. He didn't have a car. She slipped out saying, "Be back in a while, guys."

Britney shopped at Logan's. So that's where Emma went. She saw the dress she wanted as soon as she entered the designer section—a draped coral crepe that looked fantastic when she tried it on. It might have been the first time she ever bought something that wasn't on sale. She handed the cashier her credit card, catching her breath when she noticed the price.

When the saleswoman was putting the dress into a box, Emma had a thought. "Wait. I know this is crazy, but would you mind if I wore this now? Put what I'm wearing in the box instead?" This way she could go directly to the interview at Piskasanet Community College without telling Charles and Todd about it and getting them stirred up. If she didn't get a job, she might not even mention the interview.

Professor Shandule's email reply had said she could come to his office in the English Department any day after 3:00. The directory said room 203E, which she found at the end of a long corridor only wide enough for one person to pass through at a time. His door was open, and he was bent forward, staring at his computer. She tapped on the door frame, and he jumped.

"Um, Professor, I'm here to apply for the job." She gave him her name. But then what more could she say? She didn't even know what the job was.

Professor Mark O. Shandule had white hair and a broad smile. He got up, shook her hand, and pointed to a chair. "You're the only applicant so far, Ms. Bovant. I'm surprised we have any at all. Apparently the Human Resources office didn't mention what the job was." He shook his head with an ironic smile.

Emma squirmed nervously. He must have thought it was ridiculous for her to be applying for a job when she didn't know what it was.

"It's a tutoring job," he said, then waited as if to see if she was going to stay for the rest of the interview.

"Oh." Emma perked up. "I've done some tutoring."

"Excellent. It doesn't pay much, I'm afraid. Let me see." He shuffled through some papers on the corner of his desk. "May I ask what degree you have?"

"A Master's in environmental science."

"I see. It's a job tutoring English, but never mind. For a

tutor with a Master's degree, the pay is $14 an hour." He searched her face, waiting for a reaction. Emma felt he had kind eyes. She nodded.

"A few dollars more than minimum wage," he noted.

She nodded again.

"It's part time. A maximum of twenty hours per week."

When she didn't get up from the chair, he went on. "We hope to hire several tutors, but since you're the first applicant, you could choose what hours you want to work. The tutoring center is open from 8 a.m. to 9 p.m. Oh, and on Saturdays from 9 till noon."

Was he offering her the job?

"So, if you're interested, would you just fill out this application and these Immigration forms? Then I'll take you over to the tutoring center and introduce you."

The craziest idea crossed her mind as she drove home. She had wasted money on the new dress. Professor Shandule hadn't even glanced at it. And even if he had, he was obviously very near-sighted and couldn't have appreciated it. Why not return it—maybe say her husband didn't like it? Some women did that. She slowed down. But, no. She was going to keep it.

Charles and Todd and even Juan definitely noticed it. Todd cried out, "Mommy! You look like a model."

"She sure does," Charles agreed. He pulled his phone from his paint-splattered jeans and took her picture.

"Guess what," Emma said. "I got a job. Tutoring at Piskasanet Community College. Just half-time, though. I start on Monday."

Charles took another picture.

"That's enough," she said. "I'll get changed and help you with the painting."

"No. Wait. Here's what I'm thinking. I'll take you and Todd and Juan out to dinner tonight. At Sur le Dessus, how about that?"

"But, Charles, you don't like to eat in restaurants. The food is—"

"Never mind. I feel like showing you off."

"Sur le Dessus is way too expensive. We don't have the money to go to restaurants like that."

Charles grinned. "We don't?"

Todd kept tugging at his shirt collar—she'd made him wear a tie. Juan had slicked his hair down with some kind of pomade and looked really cute but a little comical. Emma knew her dress wasn't an evening dress, but she would never mention that to Charles.

A bleached-blond twenty-something girl stopped them in the shadowy lobby inside the door, looking them over. "Reservations only. Do you have a reservation?"

They did.

"Family area," she called out to an assistant. "Follow the hostess, please."

The family area was towards the back, in a separate alcove. A waiter in a black jacket with his hair slicked down like Juan's held the chair for Emma, then shook open each napkin with a crack and handed one to each of them. He signaled to a young man in a white jacket, who came and swept the two unneeded settings from the table into a plastic bin with such speed it looked like he was worried the guests might find their presence offensive.

Emma asked for wine, Charles for beer, and Todd and Juan for Coke. Emma shot a glance at Charles. He didn't approve of Todd drinking caffeinated beverages. But he made no objection.

"It's kind of dark in here," Todd said. The waiter's assistant rushed over and lit the candles.

"I know this place," Juan told them. "My mother's friend

works in the kitchen. Sous chef, they call her."

The waiter who was handing out the menus stopped. "Ms. Pilar? Yes, an excellent cook."

Emma announced, "I know what I want. *Poulet de Kievsky.*"

Juan ordered ceviche à la Guatemala."

The waiter nodded. "Yes. Ms. Pilar's specialty. Delicious."

Todd studied his menu. "I can't read this. Oh, here. Can I get this?" He pointed to *Remoulade au crabe bleu de Chesapeake.* "Must mean Chesapeake blue crab. Like Andre catches sometimes."

The waiter wrote it down. That left Charles. Emma was worried. He was running his finger down the list as if studying for a test. Finally, he said, "*Thon*—that's tuna, right? OK, I'll have *thon noirci.*"

Emma gave him a look.

"What?" he said.

"Nothing. You once said blackening food causes—"

"I'm not going worry about that tonight."

She could hardly believe her ears. Was he finally getting over his orthorexia nervosa as Andre did years ago? Emma sipped her wine and started to relax.

From another alcove leading off theirs, even farther to the back of the restaurant, there was a loud clattering and clinking going on. Emma saw the assistant waiters setting up a long table with chairs for at least ten people. It must have been a room reserved for private meetings. She could hear them talking, fussing quietly with each other about laying out the table just right.

Suddenly all the waiters in the family alcove went on the alert. A well-dressed but raucous group, mostly men, was being led past the tables in the "family" area towards the more secluded alcove where the assistants had just finished setting up. Along with everybody in the restaurant, Emma looked up. A man with an unusually large head was following the hostess. She saw it was Andrew Mauer, the County Executive.

At the end of the entourage came Britney and Bea, with Derek and Pastor Mitch. Britney walked unsteadily. She bumped into people sitting in chairs and brushed against tablecloths. She took hold of the back of Emma's chair as she tried to squeeze behind it, then noticed Emma.

"Oh, my. Is it you? Emma, dear, you look ravish-, ravishing. And who is this gorgeous young man you're with?" She put her arms on Juan's shoulders from behind and leaned over, sniffing the scent of his pomade.

"I am Juan, Esmeralda's son," he said. "We have met several times."

There was a faraway look in Britney's eyes.

Her husband Derek took her arm. "Hello, Emma, Charles. Sorry I have to tear Britney away. We have kind of a working dinner. Can't keep the partners waiting."

Britney clung to Derek's arm with two hands as he guided her back to their group.

"Who's watching her children now?" Emma wondered aloud.

Juan knew. "She has a new girl, somebody from El Salvador the pastor sent her."

Todd twirled his finger next to his head. "Chip's mom is acting weird these days."

"Yes," Juan said. "Miss Chelsea told my mother something. But I shouldn't repeat."

Now Emma wanted to know. "What?"

"Chelsea has these pills, Adderall, to help her in school. She says her mom steals some of them from her. When her mom takes them, she acts loco."

Charles had been enjoying his blackened tuna too much to say anything so far. But when he heard the word Adderall, he stiffened. "That can be dangerous. Taking Adderall when

246

you don't need it."

A heated discussion was going on in the meeting alcove. They could hear Derek's raised voice. "Calm down, gentlemen. I know how to handle this. We start fresh with a new name. Dissolve, cancel, borrow whatever we need." More grumbling, arguing. Derek raised his voice again: "We'll get the loans. Trust me. It's called asset rental, gentlemen. I'll take care of it."

Emma knew from *realestateventures.com* that "asset rental" was pretending someone else's assets were yours so you could get a bigger loan. She wondered why the INVOKIM investors in Riverside Paradise needed a bigger loan.

"Mommy?"

She turned her attention back to her own table.

"Can we have dessert, Mommy?"

Charles answered for her. "Sure we can. I saw a Smith Island eight-layer cake with chocolate icing on the menu. Anybody interested in that?"

Chocolate. It not only contained unhealthy amounts of sugar but caffeine as well. And plenty of fat and salt. This was a new Charles. She slid her toe up his leg under the table. Charles grinned. He sipped his beer—not designated organic—and she finished her wine and let the sommelier pour her another glass.

A knife clinked against a glass in the meeting alcove, and the talk came to a halt. The clinking had the same effect in the family alcove. Derek stood to make an announcement. "Ladies, gentlemen, now to the other business of the evening. I would like to announce that polls are predicting a landslide victory for our County Executive Andrew Mauer in his coming bid for re-election.

After the applause at the table, Andrew Mauer stood and proposed a toast of his own to the "next chairman of the Piskasanet County Republican Central Committee, Mr. Derek Grosbeck," adding, "At last, a chairman who will support the gun rights we need to keep our citizens safe."

Another round of applause. Then Derek stood and made an announcement. "Ladies and gentlemen, I would like to propose a toast to the candidate I have been assured will be the newest member of the Piskasanet County Board of Education, Ms. Beatrice Doggit."

Everyone raised their glasses. "Hear. Hear."

"Speech, speech," one of the investors called out.

Bea stood up, the open V of her black evening dress plunging down between her full breasts. Her bleached hair was sprayed stiffly in place. She held up her glass, took another sip, put it on the table, and lifted her arms into the air, palms forward, eyes closed. "Jesus," she intoned, "we ask you to bless us as we struggle in your name to build earthly monuments reflecting your glory."

An eerie silence blanketed the family alcove.

"And we ask you especially to shine your love upon our children who are beset in their schools by secular books and instruction claiming to be science even though it contradicts the word of God in the only book that teaches the truth, the holy Bible of the Christian faith."

35

A one-car family

Charles finished scraping the kitchen ceiling. There was still a gaping hole where the plaster had fallen. Emma drove to Shady Park Hardware and bought lots of patching plaster and three gallons of (expensive) paint, enough for the whole downstairs. But she made herself a promise to stop spending the Bea money after this.

While they were waiting for the Beetle to be fixed, the family had to make do with one car.

"Is that a problem?" Juan asked. "There is a bus, no?"

Charles needed the car to drive the boys up to Northbrook and take over tutoring Tran and Thieu. Emma took the bus to Piskasanet Community College—and found out quickly what one aspect of Tran and Esmeralda's life was like. It was only five miles from her house, and by car it would only take ten minutes to get there, but it took more than an hour to get there by bus—walking to the bus stop, waiting, stopping at three different places, then trudging uphill from the bus stop to the Humanities Building. She would never complain about her old Focus again.

Professor Shandule hadn't told her anything about the job except that she was to go to room 015 and take over a class in College Entrance Preparation. Dark haired students stopped tapping their phones and looked up when Emma walked in. They stared in silence as if waiting for a lecture. Emma's chest tightened. "Tutor," Professor Shandule had said. She'd pictured sitting down with a Tran or a Thieu one-on-one, not this. She cleared her throat and gave what might not have been the most scintillating of introductions: "Um."

A pleasant looking older woman whisked into the room extending her hand to Emma. "I'm Mastaneh, Professor Shandule's wife. I know it's your first day. I wonder if I can be of some help."

Emma could have hugged her. Mastaneh knew the names of the students because she sometimes volunteered there. She introduced Emma to each one, and Emma started to relax.

A dark young woman wearing a light blue hejab raised her hand. "Is really possible I pass test and get degree? I look at book and do not think so. I think maybe better I quit."

Mastaneh seemed deeply affected. She sighed, "I thought that sometimes. But may I tell you my story?"

All the cell phones clunked down on the tables, and everybody looked up.

"I got married to an American I met in my country. Didn't know any English when I came here. It was hard at first. But my teachers helped me. I went to this community college for two years. Then I transferred to the university, in the nursing program. And now I am a nurse. I never thought it could happen. But if you work hard enough, you can make it."

There was complete silence in the room, all eyes, even Emma's, focused on Mastaneh. But that was the end of her "story." Finally, a young man with straight black hair hanging past his eyebrows raised his hand.

"Yes?" Mastaneh said.

"I would like to know, can you tell me please, what is the difference between *in* and *on*?"

Several students tittered, and there were *tsk-tsk* sounds from some of the women.

Mastaneh smiled. "Well, that is a question I think we should let Mrs. Bovant answer. She's the expert." She bowed to Emma and made her exit.

After four hours, Emma was exhausted but surprisingly elated. When she walked into the house in her white cotton blouse and black A-line skirt, carrying a textbook, Todd blinked. "Mommy. You look like a teacher."

Charles—paint on his face and hair—kissed her.

She looked around. The dining room was painted—Special Latte Cream Deluxe One-coat. Charles beamed. "Todd and Juan helped. And, see? I patched that hole in the kitchen ceiling. It's not as smooth as it could be, but I don't think it'll fall down."

Charles put pizza on the table for dinner. Should she make a comment about his eating normal things again? Better not. When Todd was learning to ride a bike, every time she said, "You're doing great" he would get self-conscious and fall off.

After dinner, still affected by thoughts of her students, many from Central America, she sat next to Juan and took out her phone. "Let's call you mother, Juan. You've only called her once since she left."

She could hear both sides of the conversation but didn't understand much of it. Juan was doing more listening than talking. She heard Esmeralda tell him, *Dile a Emma gracias por todo.* Then she heard his father say the word *recuperándose*, which she took to mean recuperating. Juan was smiling when he hung up. "Mom says he's doing better."

Emma wanted to give him a kiss, or tousle his hair, still a little stiff-looking from his restaurant coiffure. But he was almost fifteen and as tall as she was. Not exactly a kid. She settled on "Great, Juan. That's great news."

That night, Charles came into the shower with her, something he had never done before. Emma was trembling. He touched her all over until she thought she might faint. They made love there and again in bed. It felt like the first years after their marriage. Afterwards, she lay on her back motionless and drifted off to sleep the minute she closed her eyes.

But soon a husky sigh from Charles brought her back to

consciousness. He turned away onto one side, then flipped back to the other.

"Something wrong, Charles?"

"I don't know. Now things are worse than when I was at Social Services. I don't have a job at all. I mean, I'll paint the rest of the house. Don't worry."

"You'll find something."

He snickered. "That's what I always used to say to you, isn't it?" She raised her eyebrows in an ironic yes, and he said, "The thing is, Baby, you have a job you like now. I can tell you like it. But we can't live on your half-time tutoring money."

"I guess plenty of people live on that much. We're OK, for a while, Hon."

He shrugged noncommittally. Emma thought she knew what he was feeling. He had never worried about money—that wasn't it. He was on edge because he needed to work, to feel like he was doing something useful, something that helped people out. He put his arm under her head. "Maybe I really will advertise as a life coach. I don't know what else to do."

"Sure, Hon. If you want. But maybe you should also go back to Social Services on Monday and talk to LaKisha."

Emma took the bus to the college every day while Charles stayed home with the boys. She took a bologna sandwich and apple in a paper bag and ate it in the cafeteria with the students. In only a few days, she realized the students needed help in more than just learning English.

Kyung— Needed a lawyer. English already good enough to take credit courses but couldn't get visa changed from visitor to student status.

Seo-yeon— Ate crackers from the condiment counter for lunch every day. Her whole family needed Food Stamps.

Akbar— Parents brought him to the States, then immediately divorced. Father returned to Bahrain. Mother living with older son in California. Father sends enough money to rent one-room efficiency apartment. Stays on campus until the last bus in the evening. Needed friends.

Emma understood how Charles used to worry about his "clients."

One day, Priya came to class with a black eye and bruises and scratches on her face. She sat as if nothing was wrong. After class, Emma walked from the room with her. "You OK, Priya?"

"Yes. It is nothing."

"Will you join me for lunch?" It was one of the sentences in an early dialogue lesson in their text.

Priya grimaced when trying to chew a samosa. "What happened?" Emma had to ask.

"I should not say. My husband sometimes gets angry. I study too much. No time for him."

Emma gave her the address of the county Social Services office, the same place where Charles used to work. If Charles still worked there, she could have sent Priya directly to him.

The phone in Emma's backpack rang. Britney. Something about setting up a private school near Nottingham Estates. Evergreen Academy, she would call it.

Emma cut her off. "I can't talk about something like that now, Britney. I'm doing something important."

One day Mastaneh dropped in at lunchtime. She told Emma about her work in the emergency room at the City Hospital. "So many shootings. When we ask them what happened, they always just say, 'Some dude shot me.'" She lifted her deep brown eyes. "So now when they come in, we just ask, 'Some dude shoot you?'"

Emma told her about Priya. Mastaneh said something that sounded like "Okh." The emergency room was full of victims of spousal abuse, she said. "I can sew up the wounds,

but they need much more than that. We hire counselors, but
. . . too many cases. They don't stay long. Doesn't pay a lot,
and it's hard to find people who can deal with one sad case
after another." She said "Okh" again. "And it's not just poor
people in the city. Housewives from the suburbs are coming
in abused. Or addicted to pain killers or shaking from am-
phetamines."

Emma hadn't worked a full week before she had to ask
for Friday off to take the Trans to their citizenship interview.
Emma's whole family wanted to go, but they couldn't all fit
into the little Focus. So Charles stayed with the boys at the
Northbrook lot while Emma crammed Tran, Thieu, Henry,
the baby, and the baby's car seat into her car.
Tran and Thieu were practicing by asking each other questions about the applications.

Tran: "I see you marry. When you did marry?"
Thieu: "I marry one January, two tousand ten."
Tran: "Where your childs did borned?"
Thieu: "They borned in America."
Tran: "You love you husband?"
Thieu: [*A pause.*] "This question not on form, I sink."
Tran: "Ha-ha."
Thieu: "[*Something in Vietnamese.*] Yes, I love very much."

They all passed through a security check and filed into
the huge waiting room. Thieu attracted a lot of attention in
her long white dress as they looked for seats in the rows of
hard chairs. Henry and the baby were not the only children
there. One baby cried almost the whole two and a half hours
they had to wait before Tran, then Thieu were called into the
interview room.
Tran batted his ear with the palm of his hand when he

came out. "Lady talking very loud." Both of them passed the tests. Then there was another three-hour wait until they were called into a paneled room to take the oath. There were chairs so family and friends could watch while the new applicants lined up holding little U.S. flags on thin sticks. Emma was more moved than she'd expected to be.

"Excuse me. Thank you." A short man in a rumpled gray suit too heavy for the season stood in the aisle with a small camera—the lawyer Edward Donnelly. He snapped pictures of Tran and Thieu holding their miniature flags in one hand and holding the other hand over their breasts as they repeated the oath allegiance.

"Excuse me, Mrs. Bovant. If you would." The lawyer handed her his camera and posed for a picture next to Thieu and her family. "Beautiful dress," he said. "A few more pictures, please. If you have any friends who need immigration help, you'll know where to send them."

Donnelly pocketed his camera and took Emma aside. "I've worked it out with Immigration. By leaving voluntarily, your friend Mrs. Morello has been declared eligible for a visitor's visa when she wants to return. I have the paperwork in my office when the time comes."

"Moreno."

"Pardon? Ah, yes. And when she gets here, I may be able to help her get a permanent residence permit to stay with her son. That part will be extra, of course." He gave Emma three of his business cards.

36

The turn of the tide

Saturday morning Charles got up early to paint the living room. The boys wanted to go to the river and swim. Emma packed some ham and cheese sandwiches for lunch, and they crammed into the hot car. Last summer it bothered her that she seemed to be the only person in Shady Park who didn't have central air conditioning in her house or air conditioning in her car. She couldn't be bothered by first-world problems these days.

They rolled down the windows and headed for the river. On Shady Park Lane, huge hydrangeas dripped with white flowers, and along the southern part of the highway the honeysuckle was in bloom, its sweet smell permeating the air.

They went to the same sandy beach where she had taken them before, not far from Andre's pier. The beach was empty now. The water was warmer, and the tide was high. Todd and Juan, already in their bathing suits, splashed in. Juan started showing Todd how to take strokes while turning his head to breathe.

Emma didn't have her bathing suit on, just white shorts and a short-sleeved white blouse. She stood up to her knees in the water, thinking that if this beach belonged to the owner of a Riverside Paradise villa rather than one of the old fishermen, they would never be allowed to swim here. Private property. Keep off.

Out atop the tall buoy in the river, the osprey was sitting in her nest. The river was so calm she could hear her chicks peeping. Thin clouds drifted slowly past the high white sun, casting rippling shadows on the water. Emma looked from the horizon, where the river met the bay, back to where she was standing, and the only boat to be seen was a small wooden skiff drifting along the far shore. She dipped her hands in the water, wet her face, and turned to look the other way. She could see Andre's pier. A motionless figure stood there watching her. Andre.

She ran towards him along the beach. The sand got coarser as she got closer, and her feet hurt by the time she ran out on the pier and threw her arms around him. "Andre. You're back."

Arms folded, he stood as still and expressionless as an Indian sentinel. She stepped back. "What's wrong, Andre? Where have you been?"

He looked away across the river and said, "The drive to acquire, I suppose, has always been a corrupting force in the course of human civilization. Primitive tribes are driven to annihilate neighboring tribes in order to take their land, the Mongol invasions—"

"Andre, stop. You have to believe Charles and I haven't been corrupted by any drive to acquire. We've always been on your side."

He looked at her with his sad blue eyes. "I want to believe that."

"Did you go away because you heard we got money from Bea and the pastor? We did, but—"

His eyes seemed to be looking straight through her as she tried to explain. Finally, he said, "I guess I understand." He looked back out at the river. "I've come to understand some other things, too."

"What? What do you understand? Where were you?"

"I've been experimenting with something."

She tapped him on the chest with both hands. "That's all you'll say? You didn't even tell your mother where you were."

"She sort of knew. My mother helped me pay for it. It

wasn't cheap."

Before she could ask any more questions, she heard Todd calling out. She said, "Make sure your phone is on, Andre. I'll call you." And she ran back to the beach.

The four neighborhood children were there now. Bill, the taller boy, had made a raft out of scrap lumber left at a construction site. It looked like a sheet of plywood with some bigger boards underneath. He held a rope out to her. "Can you hold this while we get on it?"

"All of you?"

"Yeah!" The two girls got on first, then Bill and Alan helped Todd on. The plywood was just barely above the water. Then one more boy after another got on, Juan last, all their legs overlapping and their arms around each other. "Can you hold the line and push us out?" Bill said. "The tide's going out now, and we're scraping the bottom a little."

Emma dug her feet in the squishy sand, bent forward, and pushed with all her might, giggling as she felt her shorts get wet. As soon as the raft was afloat, it drifted out with ease, and she had to tug on the rope to keep the kids from drifting out too far. The raft didn't actually sink, but all their butts were under water. "Woo-hoo!" they yelled.

Beth cried out, "My brother's a boat builder. Look at us."

"Let's sail to Guatemala," Juan shouted.

Alan started rocking the little raft, trying to get the younger girl, Fran, even wetter, or maybe bounce her off. She clung to Todd's shirt, and he took her hand.

Emma was surprised at the strength of the ebb tide. Before she knew it, the raft was about twenty yards out in the river, and she was holding the end of the rope, the raft pulling hard against her. She leaned back and pulled, trying to keep the raft from drifting out any farther. Her heels slipped, and she found herself sitting up to her chest in the water, completely soaked. Of course, all the children on the raft laughed, but

Emma was a little scared. She struggled back up and pulled on the rope. It was all she could do to hold the raft where it was.

Two powerful arms reached around her from behind, steadying her. Andre. His two sun tanned hands took hold of the rope alongside of hers, and he pulled both her and the raft back to the shore.

Soaked and muddy, Emma plopped down on a clump of beach grass. Andre stood grinning at her.

"Mr. Andre, Mr. Andre." Todd and the others came running up to him.

Emma realized her black bra and pants were showing through the wet clothes. She pulled up her knees and folded her arms across her chest.

"This is Juan. He's staying with us," Todd told Andre.

"Did you hear the news about the Graysons?" Beth was excited. "My mother says they're coming back."

Andre sounded confused. "I heard they were living in a trailer in Florida."

"I don't know what happened. My mother says they got money from somewhere. They're going to build a new house on a lot they still own back there." She pointed towards the woods behind Andre's house.

Andre held a finger against his temple, squinting.

Fran added, "And the Trouts are coming back. They got money, too, my grandmother says. They might buy our house from us." She smiled at Todd. "If they do, we're going to move to Shady Park. And I'll go to school in Shady Park in the fall."

Andre sat on the beach, and the children gathered around him. He doodled in the sand with a stick the same way they did. Emma let the kids do the talking. They told Andre how many crabs they'd caught while he was gone. "My dad says he found a reef where there are still some crabs he can catch and sell," Alan told him. Fran said, "You should tell my grand-mother you're back. She canned some tomatoes for you."

The sun was hot, and Emma's clothes were drying. You couldn't see through them very well any more. She knew she looked a mess, but she felt relaxed. It must be wonderful to grow up here. As it was right now, that is. Not if villas full of Beatrices and Britneys lined the shore.

By the time they finished eating their sandwiches, a red-dish glow was reflected on the river, and Emma knew it was getting late. She couldn't make herself worry, though. Andre glanced at her. Her legs were caked with sand, and she knew her hair was straggly from the damp salt air, but none of this seemed to register on him any more than on the children. She closed her eyes and let the sun drive everything from her mind but the bliss of its warmth.

Charles was sitting on the porch drinking a can of beer, waiting for her. She knew from his smile he'd finished paint-ing the living room. She brushed the sand off her legs and shorts and went in. "Beautiful," she told him. "It's gorgeous. What a difference!"

He beamed. "Maybe I'm getting better. What do you think, Juan?"

"Excellent job, Mr. Bovant." Juan looked closely at the edges along the ceiling and nodded before he and Todd went upstairs to shower and change.

Emma met Charles's eyes. "Andre's back. We saw him at the river."

"So. Well. I guess he'll text me."

But he hadn't yet, and he hadn't called, either. She said, "You know, Charles, we have to stop using that Riverside Par-adise money and give the rest back."

"I guess."

"Who actually made the deposits, anyway? Bea? Or was

it the pastor?"

"I assume some by Bea, some by my other clients."

She logged on to their bank account on her iPad and showed it to Charles. After his last electronic paycheck deposit, there were nine or ten cash deposits under $1,000. Then there were four cash deposits, each one for an even $15,000.

"You didn't bill any client for $15,000, did you, Charles?"

He scoffed. "No."

"So that's $60,000 that you didn't really earn."

Charles squirmed. "Well, you say didn't *earn*. I told you, I did do life coaching."

"So, again, what was that worth, Charles? At least $7,000, you say. OK. But we're talking about an extra $60,000. No, we have to give that back. It's bribery money."

Charles's mouth dropped open. "Bribery? I wonder if you could be right."

"There's no doubt about it. I'm giving it back."

Emma's phone rang. Anthony Mansfield. He said he'd had a call from Pastor Mitchell Rainey claiming the Piskasanet River homeowners had been fully paid for the houses they lost. "The pastor told me Beatrice Doggit at Executive Homes could confirm this, and she did."

"What great news! Looks like the tide has turned."

"And I put in calls to two of the families, the Graysons and the Trouts. Waiting for them to get back to me. I'll check the county records on Monday."

"Who paid the owners? INVOKIM?"

"No. Executive Homes itself paid. Pastor Mitchell and Beatrice Doggit both emphasized that. They said Executive Homes had decided to avoid further negative publicity by voluntarily making the payments although it had done nothing wrong. They put the blame on INVOKIM. Said they've severed their relations with them."

"But they *are* INVOKIM. It's their shell corporation to

handle their dirty work."

"We know that, but it's hard to prove. At least the families are getting reimbursed for their property."

There was a faint sound which she recognized as Anthony's eraser tapping on his notepad. He said, "Here's what I'm wondering. It's a lot of cash for a real estate developer to pay out all at once. See, I've talked to our business reporter, and he says developers of projects like Riverside Paradise are usually mortgaged up to their ears."

Emma thought about the meeting at the Sur le Dessus Restaurant. She told Anthony what she remembered. "They were talking about raising money. I heard them mention asset rental."

"Oh, boy. Do you remember anything else?"

"Well . . . ."

"Once again, if you want, I'll keep your name confidential."

"Andrew Mauer was at the meeting."

"I see. This looks bad." There was a pause. "I think I told you, our publisher's a friend of the exec, so I have to be careful. I'd like to keep a lid on this until I find out as much as I can." More pencil tapping. "Did you recognize anybody else there?"

"Um—"

"In strict confidence."

Emma didn't know whether to expose Britney's husband or not. She thought about it, then finally decided honesty is honesty. "Derek Grosbeck," she said. "He seemed to be in charge of the meeting."

As she ended the call, Charles came in with the paper. He tapped on the headline. "Another shooting in the city, Emma." He sank into his chair, engrossed in the article. "Says that's number 175 for the year, and the year's only half over. Gun sales are up. People say they need to protect themselves."

"Any other cheerful news, Charles?"

He flipped through the pages. "Hmm. Look at this."

It was a quarter-page picture of Bea—Bea quite a few years younger than she was now and about fifteen pounds lighter. Under her picture, Emma read: "Executive Homes. *A Realtor You Can Trust*. Contact Beatrice Doggit of Executive Homes to make your dream come true."

37

Payback

As soon as they finished breakfast, Emma said she had important business at the Church of the Invokers of Jesus. Charles furrowed his brow as if sensing danger, and Todd's eyes widened. "Mommy, those people are crazy."

"I'm going to straighten them out."

Hoping the pastor would be in his office before the Sunday service began, she sped up North-South Highway towards the Invokers building.

Nobody was in the worship room yet. The red, white, and blue Andrew Mauer posters were still on the walls of the aisle leading to Pastor Mitch's outreach office. She clicked open the door and walked in.

Pastor Mitch was sitting behind his desk with the chair turned towards a mirror on the wall, spraying something into his throat. He swiveled towards Emma and twitched as she slammed the door behind her. "What do you want? You can't come in here."

Emma sat down in the chair across from him. "I'm in desperate need of pastoral counseling." She folded her hands on his desk.

"I'm preparing for the service." He stood up, pointing to the door.

"Please, Pastor. The devil is tempting me. I need your help."

"Is this some kind of—"

"I have seen sin. I know it is for Jesus alone to wash away a sinner's guilt, but the devil is tempting me to expose this sinner myself." She took out her phone and tapped the screen.

He frowned and sat down.

"I have witnessed in the very parking lot of this holy house of worship a married man in a sinful embrace with a woman who is not his wife. Forgive me, Jesus, but I have taken a picture of this sinful act." She turned the phone so he could see the picture Natalie had emailed her of the pastor kissing Bea. "Help me, Pastor, to resist the temptation to expose these sinners." Immediately, she turned the phone off, jamming it into her purse.

"Is this some kind of threat? Get out."

She stood up. "I understand. Through you, God is telling me to bring the sinners to public shame. For their own good, to shame them. That they may publicly beg Jesus for the healing power of his heavenly grace."

Pastor Mitch clenched his jaw. "No. Sit down. What is it you're after?"

"I want your pastoral help in righting a wrong done to my friend Andre Smyth. I want him exonerated. I want you to call the police office and explain that you lied about him. Or just say you reviewed the video of every minute Andre worked at the youth center and found no evidence of abuse. You can say you showed the video to the 'parent' who made the complaint, and he is convinced he made a mistake."

"And you'll destroy that picture?"

"I'll let you personally delete it from my phone, if you want."

The pastor closed his eyes and took a long, deep breath. He looked devastated. "You win. My wife doesn't deserve to be put through something like this. I can't let that happen."

"But there's something else. A loan to Andre's mother. I want to pay it off and for her to get the title to her house back in her name."

The pastor was leaning forward on the edge of his chair. "What are you saying, exactly?"

"The $60,000 the church loaned to Mrs. Smyth." She

opened her purse, took out a check, and put it on his desk. "This is for half of the loan. I'll give you the other $30,000 when you give me Mrs. Smyth's loan satisfaction document and the deed to her property reissued in her name."

The pastor eyed the phone sticking out of her purse, digging his manicured nails into the padded arms of his chair. "This is outrageous." He looked away for a moment, then back at her. "But I need that picture destroyed. If that's what it takes, we have a deal."

After dinner, Charles slouched in his chair reading the paper while Todd, Juan, and Emma played hearts in the dining room. Charles had fallen asleep and didn't hear the knock on the door, so Emma opened it.

"Andre!" Emma nudged Charles with her knee. "Charles, it's Andre."

Charles shook Andre's hand but didn't give him a hug. Emma tried to remember if they'd ever given each other greeting hugs. She didn't think so.

Andre seemed to be waiting for an invitation to come in. He stood in the hallway in newish-looking long blue jeans rather than his usual short shorts. Emma recalled he'd been wearing long pants and a collared polo shirt at the beach, too. It might be a new, more conventional look for him. He was holding two poles.

"I made these from a willow tree in my yard." Andre grinned. "For Todd. And Juan, if he's still staying with you. So they can fish if you bring them back to the river."

"Andre!" Todd rushed in, followed by Juan. The boys grabbed the poles and started flicking them, practicing their casts.

"Take them outside," Emma chided. "You're going to hurt somebody." She pulled Andre in by the hand. "Yeah, Juan's staying with us until his mother gets back. It's like Todd has an older brother now."

Charles cleared his throat. "So, tell us where you've been, what you've been up to."

A direct answer was too much to be expected from Andre. He said, "Emma tells me you quit your job. Sounds like a good idea. As long as the proletariat allows the one percent to exploit—"

"I'm a life coach now, assuming I can find some new clients."

"Are you still into that?"

Charles changed the subject. "Wherever you've been, good to be back, huh?"

Andre took a breath, and Emma knew it was not going to be a short answer. "They say the desert heat is dry and not as oppressive as the humid heat here on the east coast, but I think that observation could be examined more objectively and . . . ."

And so Emma theorized that he might have been away somewhere in the desert. She knew Andre might talk until midnight and still leave without their knowing where he'd been. There would be hints, but probably also some diversions, wild goose chases. She went to make him some tea. When she sat down on the couch, she interrupted, "So, Andre, where did you say you've been?"

He didn't seem to hear. The fly of her question landed, but it wouldn't bite until he'd finished talking about the sky in Arizona. That was another clue, of course. Maybe he'd been to Arizona.

"You're looking healthy," Charles slipped in as Andre paused a second to take a sip of tea. "Nice tan. Have you put on some weight?"

"Part of the regime requires eating large proportions of red meat. I don't know if I agree with . . . ."

So. Another hint. He'd been somewhere where there'd

been a regime. Emma curled her legs up on the couch and listened. It was something like when she listened to Spanish. She knew lots of the words, and some basic grammar, but the flow of words went by so fast she could only pick out a few key phrases and try to guess the meaning from those.

". . . in the motorcycle position until—"

"Wait a minute," Charles interrupted. He knew even less Spanish than Emma. "Back up. Suddenly you're talking about 'the motorcycle position?' You never explained what that is."

The fly didn't bite. Andre continued with his analysis of something, they didn't know what. Emma thought the analysis was skeptical of whatever "regime" he had been through, but couldn't be sure. She felt a chill run down her spine when Andre referred to "healing touch" and "all-night holding sessions."

Charles interrupted again. "Oh, I think I see what you're talking about. I'm afraid this kind of conversion therapy has been broadly discredited. Dismissed as comical, at best."

"It's a kind of counseling," Andre declared. "I don't see much difference between that and life coaching. They're both basically scams, aren't they?"

Charles took offense. There was a difference, he insisted, but Andre stared over his head, a sad, trance-like expression in his eyes. Emma imagined him brooding over ordeals endured at what she now realized was some sort of de-gaying camp.

When Andre left, they walked him to the door. Emma clapped her hand on his back and quipped, "Andre, sometimes your face reminds me of Eeyore. Just remember, you do have your friends."

That night, Emma could tell that Charles still had questions about her and Andre. She said, "Out with it, Coach. Don't repress any primal possessive instinct you might be feeling. Anything you want to ask me?"

He sighed.

"I did kiss Andre while you were away." She didn't want to hurt him, but she felt she had to get that out.

"It's true, then. I can tell you two are closer now."

"We are, but . . . ."

Charles sent a look of helpless defeat up towards the ceiling.

"We're not lovers, if that's what you imagine."

"And yet you kissed him."

She nodded. "Why, I don't know myself."

His chest heaved, and he breathed out slowly. It was almost a sob. "Well, he's good-looking. Lots of women have been interested in him." He took her face gently in his hands. "But he always ignored them. And you say he's gay."

She nodded again, looking up to meet his gaze. His trusting hazel eyes showed her the man she had fallen in love with years ago, a man who believed in her. She gave him a long kiss.

"Emma, am I vain to believe you find me more attractive than Andre?"

"What a silly question."

"Good."

He was touching her, and she could tell he was aroused.

"I mean, you're not vain."

He forced a laugh.

"You want me now, don't you?" she taunted.

"Yes."

"Then . . . prove it. Call Bea a bitch."

"What?"

"Do it. Let me hear you say it." She turned her back to him. "That's the only way."

He put his arms around her from behind.

"Say it."

"Come on, Emma."

"Say it."

There was a pause, then, "Bea's a bitch!" It came out stronger than she'd anticipated.

38

Chez Shandule

When Emma got home, she found Charles sitting in his chair, head in hands.

"How was lunch with LaKisha?"

He looked up, blinked. "We talked a long time. I should have answered her calls."

"Why didn't you?"

He shrugged. "Don't know. Guess I thought she wouldn't understand me turning from my clients to life coaching."

"Maybe not."

"She wants me to come back. They already replaced me, but the supervisor job is still open. She says I should apply for it." He sighed. "I guess I will."

"You don't sound excited about it."

"Well, I need an income. It pays more than my job as Interventionalist did. Besides, I didn't get a single reply to my life coach ad." He still seemed to find that perplexing.

It depressed Emma to think of Charles taking a job he didn't really want. Sure, she'd pushed him to apply for it before, worried about paying for Todd's swimming lessons, fixing the kitchen ceiling, keeping their cars running—and mainly driven by resentment that they had to struggle just to stay in the middle class where she felt they belonged. That all seemed less important now. She put her hand on his shoulder. "I'd like you to meet a friend of mine from the college. She invited us to dinner with her husband."

As expected, Charles didn't look enthusiastic. That night, he seemed to have lost his recent enthusiasm for making love, as well. He turned on his side, pulled the pillow over his head, and went to sleep.

Emma's mother came to stay with Todd and Juan.

"I don't know what to wear, Mom. I mean, are professors formal?"

"You need that What-to-Wear app, Hon. You take pictures of your whole wardrobe, then each day you plug in the weather and describe the occasion. The app suggests an outfit."

"Seriously, Mom. This is no time to make up silly stuff."

"It exists, Hon. Todd tells me his friend Chelsea uses it every morning. Solved her biggest problem in life."

Emma put her hands on her hips, tilted her head.

Her mother giggled. "But I guess you'd have to own a pretty large wardrobe to need that app."

"I can't even believe you're saying the word 'app,' Mom. Anyway, I'm going to wear the same coral dress I bought for the interview. Something tells me Professor Shandule won't remember."

The Shandules lived on the north side of Shady Park out near the college in an old stone house with a huge chimney on each side. Standing apart from clusters of nearly-identical vinyl houses crammed close to each other, it must have been the original building on a farm now subdivided into a hundred lots.

There were shoes in the hallway. Emma nodded to Charles, and they both removed theirs. The high ceilings of the old house provided a huge amount of wall space, and the walls were completely covered with paintings and drawings. Professor Shandule and Mastaneh led them to a low table in the middle of what must have been the dining room although the only furnishing other than the table was a huge Persian carpet. "We like to sit on cushions when we eat," Mastaneh explained. "Hope you don't mind."

Charles asked the professor if he was an art collector.

"Oh, no. These were all done by Mastaneh. That one there, it's our son Ken. He's a teacher now himself, in Syracuse. The one next to it is our daughter Pari. She graduates from State University next week."

"She's beautiful," Emma trilled. "Looks just like her mother."

Charles examined one painting after another. "They're wonderful, Mrs. Shandule."

Mastaneh put her hand on her heart. "Thank you." She passed him a plate of pistachios. "Actually, when we married, I didn't take my husband's name. My name is still Sufizadeh. Most people here shorten it to Sufi."

As Mastaneh poured them tea, Emma imagined Andre launching into an account of Sufi poetry at this point.

"If you've heard about when the Iranians took over the American embassy in Tehran," Professor Shandule told them, "we left Iran a few years before that happened." He took his wife's hand. "There was a lot of hatred of Iranians here. It was hard at first."

"We managed, though," Mastaneh assured them. "Things gradually settled down."

Charles asked about the current atmosphere of panic over terrorism and fear of anybody from the Middle East. "I hope—"

"That's just some people." Mastaneh shrugged. "Our friends have made us very happy here." She put dish after dish of unidentifiable food on the table. Emma glanced at Charles, who thankfully no longer seemed to be worried about the provenance of what he ate. The new Charles. He ate everything he was served, only commenting to say "delicious." Emma reached under the table cloth and patted him on the leg.

Professor Shandule taught world literature and introduc-

tion to linguistics. "And I do some community work, too."
He took a quick look at Charles and Emma, perhaps reluctant to say more until he knew their politics.

"He is about to lose his position on the Board of Education," Mastaneh complained. "To a woman supported by the County Executive."

"Oh," Emma exclaimed. "I think we know her."

"Of course, I'm prejudiced," Mastaneh admitted, "but I don't see how anybody could be better than my husband."

Emma didn't know the Shandules' politics, either, but she had to say, "It's a woman who believes public schools should defend Christian beliefs and that teachers should be armed."

"Okh," Mastaneh said. "Guns and religion. From what I've seen, that's a bad combination in any country."

Emma wanted to turn the conversation to Mastaneh's work at the hospital. She said, "You told me you treat lots of people with gunshot wounds. That must be terrible."

Mastaneh nodded. "We need counselors to work with these people. Sometimes we fix them up, and then they're back again with another gunshot wound or after a drug overdose."

Emma saw the chance she'd been waiting for. "You should tell Charles what these counselors do. That's kind of his field."

Charles was fascinated to hear Mastaneh tell how the hospital counselors worked with patients after their medical treatment. He asked questions and even surprised Emma with the amount of medical knowledge he had beyond his psychological training. He compared cases he'd had in Social Services to cases Mastaneh described and explained how he'd handled them.

Mastaneh got more and more excited. "I wish we could get somebody like you to come work for us. You're the kind of counselor we need."

"Are there any positions open?" Charles ventured. "I'm

about to apply for a position at Social Services, but I'd like the kind of work you're describing much better."

When they left, Charles had the phone number of a person to call at City Hospital.

That night, he seemed ten years younger. He said, "Emma, we're never going to be in the one percent. But when we grow old—"

"I know what you're thinking. Neither are Professor Shandule and Mastaneh. And they seem happy enough."

39

Good deeds

Charles took the car, first to Social Services to get a letter of recommendation from LaKisha, then to City Hospital—which left Emma with the boys because her mother had a doctor's appointment that morning. She felt guilty calling the college to say she needed yet another day off. But then she shrugged. In her mind, she saw Andre grinning. Bourgeois anxieties.

It turned out to be a busy day at home. First, Esmeralda called. Her husband was better. Emma gave the phone to Juan but couldn't understand much of the Spanish.

"They both want to come back to the States," Juan told her. "One way or another."

Then there was a loud rap on the front door. Pastor Mitch Rainey stepped in, his bushy eyebrows meeting in a frown. He was holding a manila envelope.

"Boys, how about playing outside?" Emma didn't offer the pastor a seat.

"I guess you know what I came for, Ms. Bovant." He took two documents from the envelope and handed them to her.

The first paper was a satisfaction of loan issued to Andre's mother, Mrs. Smyth, by the Church of the Invokers of Jesus. She unfolded the second document to its full legal size. It was the deed to Mrs. Smyth's house recently re-issued in her name.

"And now, your phone, please."

She pulled the picture up and handed him her phone. "Hold your finger down on it until you see the trash can. Then touch the trash can." The picture was whisked away with a satisfying *swoosh*.

"Ah. Can I be sure there was only this one picture?"

She showed him all the pictures on her phone—there weren't many. He flicked through them and nodded. "I see. Well, then." He seemed about to leave.

"Wait a minute." She handed him a check for $30,000.

"Oh, right. Yes." He stuffed it casually into his jacket pocket. At this point, Emma thought, men would probably shake hands. The last thing she wanted was to touch this man, but she forced herself to hold out her hand. Instinctively, perhaps, the pastor took it. It was crazy, but both of them seemed to relax after the shake.

As soon as the pastor left, she called Andre. Of course, she had to leave a message. It wasn't even noon, and Andre would still be asleep. He arrived a few hours later, a box of Tastee Donuts in hand. "I know Todd likes Boston cream. I don't know what Juan likes, so I got a variety."

"Fine. Thanks. There's something I want to tell you before I call the boys in." She spread out the lien satisfaction and deed on the dining room table. Andre wanted to talk, not read legal documents, but she insisted.

"So you're saying my mother took a loan for $60,000? No wonder she could give me the money for my, you know, my retreat."

"Well, she doesn't have to pay it back now. And the house is in her name again."

"I still don't understand. Why do you have these papers?"

She told him the whole story, slowly and simply, almost as if explaining to Eeyore. But she skipped the part about the picture of the pastor and Bea kissing, which came close to being blackmail. Which *was* blackmail, actually.

"So, basically, you're the one who paid off my mother's $60,000 loan. Is that what you're saying?"

"With money we got from the pastor and Bea."

An uncomfortable shadow spread over his face. He parted

his lips several times to say something, but each time fell silent. It was a new experience to find Andre speechless.

"You were right to be angry," she reassured him. "We feel much better after giving it back."

"But it's more like you gave the money to my mother."

"Well, let's not quibble over details." A tiny suppressed laugh slipped out.

Andre put his finger to his temple, the sign that he was thinking. "I wasn't angry. More like confused. Well, maybe a little angry." He folded and re-folded the deed to his mother's house. "I could have accepted you keeping the money." He set his hand on the table, one finger touching hers. Traces of tears were forming in his bright blue eyes. She hoped he wasn't going to cry. He didn't. Instead, he closed his eyes, took a breath, and said, "Karl Marx defined materialism as—"

"Andre! I'm sorry if I seemed materialistic. I don't want to be."

"You're not. You and Charles are practically the only people who understand my ideas." He put the documents in the envelope and asked her to keep them safe for him.

"I'm sorry you wasted some of the money on that, um, retreat."

Andre's face clouded over. "You know how people in pain will try anything, no matter how ridiculous? I was like that, I guess. But the therapy isn't even designed to work."

"No?"

"Beating an effigy of your father to death with a baseball bat? I loved my father. Lying squished together in a mass of male bodies? Sitting on the floor between the spread legs of another man, your back towards him and his arms around you? It didn't take long before I realized what these men are really paying for."

Emma felt her cheeks burning.

Andre's eyes narrowed. He seemed amused at something.

"I did learn one thing from the therapy, though." He gave a wry smile.

"What?"

"That men my own age can find me attractive." He gave a weak chuckle.

Emma cleared her throat. "That's what you got from the so-called therapy?"

He shrugged. "It wasn't the reason I went, but yeah. I never knew it."

"Andre, of course, people your own age are attracted to you. You're handsome, you're . . . ." She stopped herself.

Now it was Andre blushing.

Emma was curious. "You said that wasn't the reason you went. What was the real reason?"

He hurried his eyes away from her face. "It's silly, I know."

She took his hand. "Tell me."

"There were exercises to enhance heterosexual potency." His face turned a deeper red. "Of course, they're a scam."

The crack of a bat hitting a ball came from the back yard. Outside, Todd and Juan were whooping. Emma's mouth was still gaping open when they came in for donuts.

Todd said, "Mr. Andre, did you hear? Juan's mother and father might come back."

"I mean, I hope they can," Juan said. "It won't be easy." Juan knew the complexities of immigration better than Emma. The more he talked, the less hopeful he sounded until finally his eyes were watery.

Andre gave Emma a questioning look. "Aren't there lawyers or something who can take care of these things?"

"Yes. I know one. Legal help isn't cheap, of course."

Finger against temple—Andre was thinking. He turned to Juan. "I'll tell you what. How about using that lawyer Emma knows? You can tell him to send the bill to me."

That evening Charles was too excited to sit down. "Emma, can you believe it? I got the job. Hospital Counselor. I start the day after tomorrow."

His phone beeped. *Message from Andre Smyth.* He frowned. "What's this? You told him about the Beetle?"

"He was here today. He asked where it was."

"This is ridiculous. He says he'll take me to the shop tomorrow and pay for the repair."

It occurred to Emma what Andre was doing. Thanks to her, he had extra money—and he was spending it.

Charles dialed. "I'll tell him there's no need to do that. It's embarrassing."

She could hear Andre's deep voice on the other end. "My mother had an unexpected 'gift' from somewhere. Emma will tell you about it."

Charles couldn't dissuade him. He looked at Emma for help, but she wouldn't take the phone. She heard Andre say something about a party he was going to have at his house. And the call was over.

"I just don't get it," Charles said. "Why would Andre want to pay for our car repair?"

"Well," Emma replied, "I told him it was an expensive restoration job, including a complete repainting." She grinned. "He said he still had some paint left and offered to paint it for you himself, but I told him that was too much trouble."

40

First-world maneuvers

"Emma, I need your help. Physics camp is over. I can't trust the new girl to watch both kids when I'm out getting petitions signed."

"Petitions?"

"We need to expand the mall parking lot. First thing you know, it'll be Christmas season and the mall will be so crowded it'll be impossible to get a parking spot. It's a problem we have year after year."

Emma was getting ready to walk to the bus stop. "Isn't that what Nottingham moms have sport utility vehicles for? So they can drive over the curbs and park on the grass medians to do their Christmas shopping when the lots are full?"

Britney hissed out an exasperated sigh.

"I have to go tutor a class, but my mother will be here," Emma offered. "You can bring the kids over to play."

"Well, all right."

So. Chip could play with Todd, and even with the City urchin Juan, when it was convenient for Britney? Emma was glad, though, because Todd missed playing with him.

When Emma got home from her tutoring, they were all sitting at the dining room table, Todd and Chip with Emma's iPad on one side, and Juan and Chelsea with Chelsea's iPad on the other, playing Minecraft. Emma's mother, watching over Todd's shoulder, was the only one who looked up. "I'm the coach."

The kids were so absorbed in the game, it looked as if you could operate on them without anesthetic. Emma watched for a while, then got nervous and checked the time on her phone. She didn't want Charles to walk in and observe the scene. "Overstimulation from too much screen time." That's what he would call it.

A horn beeped in the driveway.

"The Beetle," Todd shouted. Everybody went out to see Charles's car, now a gleaming dark blue. "Beautiful, Daddy. I love the color."

Andre got out of his car, which he had pulled into the driveway behind Charles.

"Isn't it great, Mr. Andre?" Todd was feeling the smooth finish in a spot that had been all rust before.

"Um-hum. I like a lighter blue myself," Andre replied. "But, yeah."

There was a louder honk. Britney had started to pull into the driveway, but there was no room. Her window silently lowered. "Emma, you've got to be the last person on earth to have a single-lane driveway. Chip, Chelsea, get your things and get in. God knows what that new girl will cook for dinner if I don't watch over her."

As Britney sped away, Andre watched, moving closer to Emma and lowering his voice. "There are times like this when I realize why the whole heterosexual thing would never work out for me."

Then came the car jockeying. Andre had to back his car out of the driveway and park on the street so Charles and Emma's cars could get out.

"What time do you leave for work tomorrow, Charles? Should my car be in front of yours or behind it?"

"In front. I'm leaving at seven." He paused. "No, wait a minute. You'll be taking your mother home soon so she can feed her cat. So I'll pull in front of you. Then when you get back, we'll have to switch them again."

Emma noticed Juan staring in amazement at the maneuvering and discussion. "We don't have these problems in Guatemala," he assured them.

41

It's in the paper

"Charles, look at this."

Realtor Cuts Ties to Investment Corporation, Reimburses Homeowners

Anthony's article quoted Beatrice Doggit of Executive Homes: "The Riverside Paradise project has severed its relationship with INVOKIM, LLC, and is no longer being funded by that corporation." Bea blamed INVOKIM for the seizure of property along the Piskasanet River and said, "Executive Homes has taken upon itself to reimburse the evicted owners for the unfortunate loss of their property." The article stated that INVOKIM had been dissolved and was no longer in existence.

"So," Charles said, "Andre's neighbors get something for their property, but Bea keeps her license and the pastor keeps his church."

"Looks like it. At least there won't be an INVOKIM any more. And the Riverside Paradise project seems dead."

Anthony called. Emma thanked him for his work.

"Sure. Um, one more thing."

"Not about An—"

"Mr. Smyth? No. I followed up with the police, and they said the parent who filed the complaint retracted it. Told them he made a mistake."

"Of course, you realize it wasn't a parent. It was the pastor himself, trying to force Andre to sell."

"If proof of that turns up, I'll publish the story. You can be sure. What I wanted to ask was about your son, Todd. Is he there? I'd like to speak to him."

"What? He's playing baseball at Northbrook with his friends."

"Did he do a school project on cleaning up the bay? One of the school parents is on the Bay Foundation. He thought the clean-up experiment was done by Todd Bovant. I wanted to make sure."

"What's this about?"

"Look in the paper tomorrow."

Bay Foundation to Use Idea from Local Science Fair

"Todd, Charles, look."

"What now?" Charles looked over Emma's shoulder. "Fantastic. Todd, you've got to see this."

"I know." Todd had a sly look. "Mr. Anthony asked me some questions yesterday. When we were playing baseball. What does it say?"

"It quotes Todd Bovant." Charles's eyes widened. "Listen to this: 'Mr. Bovant said it was an idea he got when they studied about oysters in school.' And here: 'Mr. Bovant said the Piskasanet River needs cleaning up to keep all the oysters, fish, and crabs from dying.'"

"*Mister* Bovant. Is that what it says?" This was Todd's chief reaction.

Juan gave Todd a pat on the back. "Good work, Mister Bovant."

"Don't call me that, Daddy."

The house phone rang. Principal Prosterner. He was "excited about this testament to the quality education provided by Shady Park Elementary/Middle School."

Another call. Department of Natural Resources, wanting to put a piece about Todd on their blog.

Another call, to Emma's cell phone. Britney. "Did Chip leave his glove at your house?" Britney didn't read newspapers.

42

Beyond tribal rivalries

"**W**here are the boys?"

Charles looked up from the paper. "Todd's at your mother's. I had to go, um, go see about something." He seemed to be blushing.

"And Juan?"

"Andre came and picked him up."

Emma couldn't help feeling apprehensive.

"He said he needed to talk to Juan about something. Not to wait dinner. They'd eat together."

"Dinner?" Her voice came out squeaky. "Call Andre."

"You don't mean you're worried because Andre is—"

"He likes young men. He told me."

"Young men? You mean Juan?" Charles's mouth opened. He took his phone and dialed Andre. No answer. He headed for the door. "I'll drive to his house. Still, Andre's my friend. Juan's like family. I can't imagine . . . ."

He opened the door to leave, but Emma stopped him. "I guess you're right. Try calling Andre again first. We don't even know if he's at his house."

She stepped out onto the front porch while he called. Twilight. Just dark enough to see the stars, bright and large in the clear sky. Romantic. Andre and Juan having dinner together. Or maybe walking along the river under the stars. She knew she was letting her imagination run wild, but she couldn't help it. Her breath quickened as she pushed her hands over her cheeks and up through her hair.

Charles was in his chair, sending Andre a text. "Hey, Crazy Mommy, come here. Everything's going to be all right."

She slid onto his lap, snuggling against him. "I know. Andre's our friend. We have to trust him."

Charles smoothed her hair, his voice comforting her. She leaned her head against his chest and could feel his heart beating. Memories of other times he'd held her this same way came flooding back. "I don't know what I'd do without you, Charles."

"I just want to hold you like this forever, Baby."

She closed her eyes. "That's all I want, too."

They held each other without speaking. Emma couldn't tell how long it was before the silence was broken by the sound of a car pulling into the driveway. They both hurried to the window. Andre's baby blue car.

Juan rushed in, beaming. "The lawyer says he thinks he can get both my parents visas."

Andre stood holding a pizza box, a pleased smile on his face. "We had dinner at the Grab 'n Go. Very nice man working there. Tran. He recognized Juan from the baseball field at Northbrook. Says he knows your family."

"You took Juan to see the lawyer in Baltimore? He's taking Esmeralda's case?" Emma grabbed his hand, then let go self-consciously.

"Yes. An excellent attorney." Andre lifted his head. Looking off into the air, he began: "The history of immigration restriction can be traced back to rivalries among primitive tribes in—"

Emma tapped him on the shoulder, but Andre continued. ". . . when nationalism came into—"

"Andre!" Emma nearly shouted.

Andre handed her the box. "The pizza's a gift from the Grab 'n Go manager, Mr. Tran. I invited him to the party, but he has to work."

"Tran's the night manager now?"

"He gives you credit for the promotion. It's interesting

how the drive to climb the corporate ladder—"

"Andre. Back to Esmeralda."

Finally, Andre gave some details of what he'd been up to. The lawyer Donnelly had drawn up papers showing that Esmeralda and her husband had financial support in the States.

Emma stopped him there. "Support?"

"From my mother and me. We're sponsoring them. It's interesting that national borders historically developed when—"

This time it was Charles who cut him off. "It must be expensive, Andre. Hiring a lawyer. Offering financial support. How can you afford it? I know what you get in disability benefits."

Andre reddened and glanced at Emma. He only repeated what he'd previously said on the phone. "My mother came into some extra money."

"And what's this about a party?" Charles asked. "You've never had a party in your life."

Andre looked sheepish. "My mother's idea."

Emma and Charles shot each other bemused looks. The idea of Andre throwing a party was inconceivable. Yet there he was, grinning in simple anticipation.

43

Resurrection

As they turned down Piskasanet River Road, the air blasting into the Beetle's windows began to feel more humid. Sunflowers stood above an undergrowth of switch grass, and the catalpa trees were now hung with long, narrow pods that looked like enormous string beans. In the lots bulldozed to make way for Riverside Paradise, however, there were no trees. Muddy puddles from recent rain stood in the bare dirt. Construction had stopped, and the empty lots now seemed abandoned.

Emma thought Bea's villa had a forlorn look. All the curtains were drawn, the grass was high, and mallards were padding up the driveway, probably towards the pool behind the house—feeling free to take it over. No one home.

The paved part of the road in front of the villa ended, and as soon as they were on the crunchy gravel again, the smell of burning wood and children's voices filled the air. They turned down the dirt road between the last bulldozed Paradise lot and Andre's house. Crape myrtle trees blooming pink and white lined the road beside Andre's house and the fishing cottages behind it.

There was Andre, in a yellow bathing suit, putting logs on an open fire. Two boys—she recognized Alan and Bill—were stripping willow branches and holding them out for girls to put marshmallows on.

Todd rushed over. Little Fran handed him a stick. "I remember your name. Todd. Do you remember mine?"

He did.

Music blared from Andre's ancient boom box—a folk

song from the 1960s. A thin old man stood beside Andre, singing along. Charles introduced Mr. Trout. He'd played pinochle with him and Andre in his college days. Mr. Trout's house was next to Andre's on Piskasanet River Road and had been the one most recently demolished.

Emma heard Fran tell Todd, "The Trouts lost their house, but they got some money back, and now they're buying *our* house. My grandma and me, we're moving to somewhere in Shady Park. Where you live, right? My dad's going to come back and live with us. Isn't that great?"

It was Fran's father, Emma remembered, who'd been forced to quit fishing as a living and move "up north" to find a job. Maybe he planned to live on the money from the house sale until he found a job near Shady Park. Emma smiled to think she had something to do with the family's change of luck.

An old couple came up to the fire, the man carrying a guitar slung over his shoulder. "Mr. and Mrs. Grayson," Charles told Emma.

"Folks around here mostly call me Old Man Grayson."

His wife chuckled. "But nobody dares call me Old Lady Grayson."

Emma remembered little Fran saying the Graysons were back. They were living with friends in one of the houses behind Andre's. "While we build another on a lot we still own at the edge of the woods." Old Man Grayson scratched his head. "Money came from Executive Homes. First they take our house, flat out. Nothing we can do about it. Then they come back later with a different story. Say they're paying us for it."

His wife cradled a dish of hot dogs and beans. "We won't have a view of the river any more, but it's better than that trailer we were living in. Plus, we'll have money to live on."

A weathered picnic table was set up near the fire. An old

woman Emma didn't know brought a huge dish of bread pudding. She introduced herself as Fran's grandmother. "My Franny hasn't stopped talking about your Todd since the last time he was here."

Old Man Grayson put a can of Budweiser into Emma's hand. She didn't like beer very much but was about to politely drink it when Andre's mother arrived, sliding a squash casserole and a bottle of plum wine onto the table.

"Why, hello, dear," she said. "Put that nasty beer down and drink some of this." She filled a paper cup. "Isn't it wonderful to have Andre back with us? We're all so happy, especially the children."

A man and woman came down the dirt road behind Andre's house struggling with a bushel basket, each holding one handle.

"Dad! Mom!" Alan ran over to help. "Here they come with the crabs."

His father seemed shy around company. "They're not very big, but I was lucky to catch them. Gets harder every year."

"Who wants to watch me cook them?" Andre called out. The children threw down their marshmallow sticks and ran into the house behind him. Emma wanted to see, too.

"You put some vinegar in the water, some salt, some beer, and Old Bay Seasoning—that's the most important part," Andre explained. "Put a sieve over the water. You steam them. You don't boil them." He opened the basket and the crabs scurried and scraped against each other, holding out their open claws.

Juan stood back from the younger kids, wide-eyed. He'd eaten steamed crabs before, but he'd never seen them cooked.

Bill and his sister Beth, nine and eight years old, held the basket while Andre gingerly picked the crabs out and dropped them into the pot one at a time. "You have to grab them from the back," he told Juan. "So they can't get you with their claws." He reached into the basket again.

"Ouch!" Andre cried out, shaking his hand.

Juan jumped. Emma did, too. The children laughed.

"Just kidding." Andre ducked as Emma reached over to rap him on the head.

They could hear the crabs scratching around in the pot.

Fran stood between Todd and Emma, holding on to their shirts and tiptoeing up to look inside. "Can I put the top on?" She couldn't quite reach, and Todd lifted her up. When he set her back down, Fran took a bracelet of tiny mussel shells from her pocket. "I made this for you."

Todd held it in his palm. The shells were strung together with fishing line. He started to put it on, then stopped. Emma knew what he was thinking.

"Go ahead," Juan told him. "Put it on. Baseball players wear things like that to bring them luck."

They all sat around the fire, some on kitchen chairs and some on top of wire crab traps, Andre's mother keeping Emma's cup full of sweet plum wine and Andre passing around cans of beer, although he drank herb tea himself—with a little honey in it. Charles helped the skinny Mr. Trout carry the kitchen table outside with the crabs piled high on sheets of the *Shady Park Ledger*, and the cracking, crunching, and picking of an East Coast crab feast began.

"I'm surprised you haven't made inquiries about the food," Andre taunted Charles. "There are probably miniscule traces of fertilizer in the river, you know."

Charles slurped some crabmeat out of a claw. "I've been working at the hospital lately. It gives you a new perspective. You don't see many people hospitalized by microscopic traces of fertilizer."

Towards evening, the air under the trees got cooler. The crabs were gone, but most of Andre's guests were still drinking. Old Man Grayson took up his guitar and strummed it softly as the fire turned to glowing red embers. Andre brought out a box of donuts for the children and sat on the kitchen doorstep to watch them eat. Emma heard them giggling as he recited Ogden Nash poems.

She looked around and didn't see Charles. Then she spotted him sitting on a bucket some distance from the dying fire. He'd been celebrating like the others, but now he seemed distracted.

She walked over. "Something wrong, Charles?"

Embarrassed and grinning at the same time, he said, "Uh" and reached into his back pocket. "Maybe I'm foolish. I know you think we can't afford this. I just had to. For your birthday next month. I couldn't wait."

Emma opened the box and her heart stopped. It was a glittering diamond necklace.

"Oh, Charles!"

"It's not from any of the Bea money. I promise."

"I love you, Charles."

Laughter from the group by the fire made them turn. "Hey, you two," Old Man Grayson called out. "There are children present. Come back over here."

"My goodness," Andre's mother said. "What a wonderful day." She lifted her cup of plum wine in a kind of toast. "I'm so happy we can all be here together."

"It's kind of a miracle," Mr. Trout proclaimed, popping open another can of beer.

"I never thought we'd be back," his wife agreed.

"What was it?" Fran's grandmother wondered. "What made Executive Homes have a change of heart and pay us for the houses they took?"

"I know how it happened," Andre's mother announced. "It's that man of God, Pastor Mitchell Rainey, we have to thank for this."

Andre smiled and shrugged. Emma bit her tongue.

It wasn't until the sun had set over the river and the fire had turned to dim patches of red among the gray ashes that anybody thought of going home. Todd had to go to the bathroom, and Andre went to show him where it was. Emma followed along. "So," she said to Andre while they waited for Todd. "It looks like INVOKIM won't be bothering you or these people any more. What a relief."

Andre grinned. "I'm not so sure. Let me show you something that came to me in the mail today." He handed her a large envelope that contained a glossy flyer and a letter. It was a new offer to buy his property. "Look here." Andre pointed to the name of an LLC on the letterhead. RES-RECT.

CPSIA information can be obtained
at www.ICGtesting.com
Printed in the USA
LVHW051514121219
640280LV00002B/249/P

9 780998 380551